MONKSHOOD, TEA, & MURDER

JONI FOLGER

OLIVERHEBERBOOKS

Cover Art by Diane Kreider

Published by Oliver-Heber Books

0 9 8 7 6 5 4 3 2 1

❀ Created with Vellum

ACKNOWLEDGMENTS

As always, thanks to my CP, Liz Lipperman, for her friendship, encouragement, and tough love when I need it. Having you as my critique partner for over a decade has been a lucky break for me. I love you, my friend.

To my fabulous agent GDC—Christine Witthohn, you da best, pal! Not sure I'd still be writing if it wasn't for you. As always, thank you for the support.

A huge shout out goes to my long-time buddy, Natalie Bellissimo, for challenging me, supporting me, and for your enthusiasm no matter what I write. And of course, for your supernatural editing skills.

A very special thanks to Melissa Jenck & Val 'Valine' Braun. Love you guys sooooo much and couldn't do it without you...

1

With the afternoon sun warm on her face, Lydie Charles cruised up the coastal highway toward home, windows down and the radio blasting the local oldies station. It was a fine, late summer day on the coast, and she scanned the sparkling Pacific Ocean to her left as she bopped to the music. There wasn't a cloud in the blue, blue sky, and in the distance, the horizon was clear as far as the eye could see. But that was about to change. They were on the cusp of fall. It couldn't be seen yet, but their lovely summer weather was coming to an end, and they were in for some rain—and a good soaking by the feel of it.

Lydie was a Hedge Witch, a highly individualistic type of witch with close ties to nature and the four elements of this world, as well as the spirit world beyond. She lived by her own code and felt a deep connection with the environment and natural order of things. Sensing weather changes long before they happened was just one of her many gifts.

Fortunately, the coming storm wouldn't hit until late tomorrow evening at the earliest, so that would be welcome news to Vanessa Deerborne, Lydie's business partner and fellow Hedge Witch. Meeting at a mutual friend's dinner party eight years ago, she and Vanessa had hit it off from the start and had worked hard to build Lavender Fields into a business they could both be proud of, a business that was now thriving.

The annual Seal Cove Garden Society Tea and Awards Banquet was scheduled for tomorrow afternoon and would take place in the Garden Society's expansive gardens. Lydie and Vanessa's event side of the business, Enchanted Affairs, was handling the garden party again this year from start to finish. This year's event was Vanessa's baby, and she had the outdoor celebration ruthlessly organized down to the very last detail. To have the party ruined by rain would not do at all.

They were in the final stages of preparation, and Lydie had the box of extra linens she'd borrowed from her grandmother in the back seat of the SUV. She and Vanessa would finish packing up the van this afternoon with all the necessary items: linens for the tables the Society had provided, the little teapots and dessert plates, cutlery, and table centerpieces to be setup by their team first thing in the morning. They'd follow with the pastries and elaborate layer cake that Vanessa was putting together. It would be a well-oiled machine once they got to the venue and a show-stopper once executed.

Turning off the highway onto Calypso Lane, Lydie smiled to herself as she sped down the backroad toward the little slice of heaven where the business headquarters, industrial kitchen, and storefront—as well as her own cozy upstairs apartment—were located. While Vanessa didn't live on the property, she'd chosen a charming little cottage a stone's throw from the ocean. So, these days life was good, and they were just a couple of happy Hedge witches spreading joy and doing no harm.

Flipping on her blinker, Lydie turned through the gates of

Lavender Fields and bumped along the lengthy stretch of gravel drive, pulling up in front of the lovely, old, remodeled farmhouse that now housed the storefront and Enchanted Affairs. For event food preparation, they'd had the industrial kitchen built the year after the farmhouse was remodeled using the same aesthetic, so it all blended perfectly.

In addition to event planning, they grew all of their own herbs for potions and healing, and had several greenhouses behind the building for propagation and wintering their more fragile plants. They did a surprisingly brisk business out of the shop with herbs, charms, and lotions during the fall and winter months, as well as at the farmers' markets in the area during the season.

Climbing out of the vehicle, Lydie retrieved the box of linens from the back seat and turned as Circe, her large Russian Blue feline threaded herself around and through Lydie's legs.

"Hey sweet thing, how's your day?"

Circe blinked her bright green eyes and gave a positive meowed response.

"I'm glad to hear it, darlin'," Lydie said with a chuckle. "Now, where's Vanessa?"

She followed as the cat meowed again and started for the building at a trot, the little bell over the door tinkling their arrival as she and Circe entered the storefront.

"Vanessa, I'm back," she called as she continued around the counter and down the hallway to the workroom at the rear of the building. Then she stopped abruptly and frowned when she found the space empty. A handful of tubs for the garden party were filled and neatly stacked next to the workbench, with several others at varying stages on the table. Vanessa's notebook was lying open next to them, as her partner wrote literally everything down in her notebook for each event Enchanted Affairs handled. "Now where do you suppose she got off to, Circe?"

The cat padded over to the closed door of the casting room, and looking back at Lydie, meowed again.

"In there, is she?" Skirting the work table, Lydie tapped on the casting room door twice before opening it and sticking her head into the room. She found her partner staring into her divination pool with a worried look on her face.

"Vanessa? What's up? I can literally feel your tension from here."

Vanessa gave a distracted wave and motioned her over. "I've had an uneasy feeling all day, so finally decided to check the pool. There's trouble brewing, Lydie. And it ain't good."

"What kind of trouble?"

"Unclear." Vanessa turned and skewered her with a cornflower blue-eyed stare. "You haven't had any of your weird dreams, have you?"

"For the thousandth time, my dreams are not weird. They're foretelling. And no, I haven't had any prophetic dreams, weird or otherwise in the last couple of weeks." Lydie made a face. "But thanks for bursting my bubble. I was just beginning to think that the universe was on an even keel at the moment."

Vanessa shook her head, her sandy brown ponytail swishing from side to side as she turned back to study the pool. "No such luck, pal, if this is any indication."

"So, how do you know that it's trouble?"

"The divination pool started out cloudy, which isn't a real positive sign, but then it went very dark. See for yourself. That's not good... not good at all."

"Well, there is a storm brewing," Lydie quickly put up a hand when her partner whipped back around. "But no worries, it won't get here until late tomorrow evening at the earliest, so the garden party is in the clear. We'll be long finished by the time the rain hits. Could that be what you're seeing in the pool?"

"No, I don't think so." Vanessa shook her head again. "This

isn't weather related, or even related to the four elements, that I can see. This has a darker energy. I'm telling you, I think something bad may be coming. I just can't see exactly what it is."

"You think it has to do with us somehow?"

"Again, it's unclear, but I'm gonna consult my runes in a bit to be sure. Maybe they can give me more detail. In the meantime, we should put together a couple of protection pouches to carry with us for the next few days, just to be on the safe side."

"Good thinking. Better safe than sorry, although not knowing what kind of dark energy we're talking about is worrisome. Is it physical, spiritual, emotional...?"

"I know. How to prepare, right?"

"Yeah." Lydie frowned and crossed to the apothecary cabinet to begin pulling the herbs needed. "How strong do you think we need to go with the protection spell?"

"Hmm. Sage and thyme for starters."

"Yep. Some dried rose petals... definitely lavender."

"Absolutely. And don't forget the Jet stones for clearing negative energies. We'll need one for each pouch."

"That should make a good, strong defensive mixture."

But just as Lydie was setting everything up on the casting table to begin the process, the workroom buzzer sounded, indicating someone had pulled into the parking lot. With a sigh, Lydie closed the apothecary cabinet doors and nodded toward the table. "You get started on the pouches. I'll go up front and help whoever's on their way into the shop."

As she headed out of the room and down the hall, she heard the tinkle of the bell over the shop's front door, and found Winnie Douglas, the Garden Society contact for the annual awards banquet, glancing around the store with curiosity. Winnie was sweet as she could be and had a good heart, but having her stop by the afternoon before the garden party was not a good sign. Neither was the monstrous binder the woman was carrying or the apologetic look on her freckled face as she turned.

"Hey, Winnie. Ready for the garden party tomorrow?" Lydie asked as she stepped behind the counter. "We're just doing some final packing in the back, and I can assure you it's gonna be a fabulous event."

"Afternoon, Lydie. I'm glad to hear the preparation is under control, but the party is actually why I've popped by."

Uh-huh. Of course, it is.

Since Lavender Fields was twelve miles outside of town, nobody just *popped* by. This visit had 'I have some last-minute changes' written all over it.

Lydie hopped up onto the stool behind the counter. She figured it would be best to be sitting down for whatever was surely coming. "Okay. So, what's up?"

Winnie laid her big binder on the counter and fidgeted with the edges. "Well, I know the event is tomorrow, and this is a little 'eleventh hour-ish', but Henrietta insisted I come by."

Oh, goodie. And there it is, folks. Henrietta Stone has more suggestions.

"And?" Lydie prodded when Winnie shoved back a lock of bright red hair and continued to stare at her with wide green eyes. "What does Henrietta want now, Winnie?"

The woman nervously cleared her throat. "Um... well... she was hoping that it wasn't too late to add umbrellas for the tables... or maybe those big event canopies? Like I said, I know this is last minute, but she's afraid it's going to rain. And this *is* our main event every year," she finished in a rush.

Winnie was obviously under tremendous strain, which considering her muddled aura, wasn't healthy. But then this was all coming from Henrietta Stone, President of the Garden Society, so Lydie took a cleansing, mental breath before responding in a calm, rational tone. "I'm sorry, Winnie, but there's not much room for changes at this point."

When the woman's shoulders visibly sank, Lydie reached out and took her hand. "But not to worry. We've considered every angle, and I guarantee tomorrow's event is covered. Besides, it isn't going to rain until late tomorrow night, so all will be well."

"But—"

"I promise, Winnie. The garden party will go off without a hitch, and the weather will be beautiful, just like it is today. There is a storm coming, but it definitely won't arrive until well after midnight."

Winnie frowned. "How can you be so sure about that? The weatherman said late afternoon."

Lydie chuckled. "And I'm certain that he's very well-meaning, but he's wrong. And I can be sure because weather changes are one of my magical gifts." She gave the woman's hand a squeeze before letting go. "Seriously. Trust me. In the last three years, has Enchanted Affairs ever let you down?"

"Well, no. It's just that... you know... it is Henrietta," Winnie's voice ended in a whisper, as if Henrietta might hear.

"I totally understand. You can have her call me, if need be, and I'll see what I can do to put her mind at ease, but don't stress about it. Really. We've got this." Slipping off her stool, Lydie came around the counter and chose a packet from one of the shelves. Turning, she placed it in Winnie's hand. "Here. A healing gift. Take this and boil the contents in a sauce pan on your stove when you get home."

Winnie looked at the small packet warily. "Um... what is it?"

"Don't look so worried. It's only sage, but it has very strong magical properties." Lydie gave the woman a knowing smile. "And sage is not only wise but protective and the bringer of good luck. It will cleanse your energy and soothe and strengthen you emotionally, which is something that I sense you need right now."

The woman laughed out loud. "Oh, Lydie, you have no idea. How much do I owe you? If it will do all of that, I will gladly pay you whatever you ask."

"You don't owe me a thing. As I said, it's a gift."

"Thank you, Lydie. That's very kind of you."

"No problem." Turning Winnie toward the door, Lydie put an arm around the woman's shoulder and spoke in a soothing tone. "Now, go home and please don't worry. Tomorrow will be fabulous. You'll see."

After watching Winnie's car disappear down the drive, Lydie hurried back to the casting room where Vanessa was just finishing the protection spell for their pouches.

"Who was that?" Vanessa asked as she tied the bow on the second bag. "You weren't gone long."

"Winnie Douglas."

Vanessa looked up at that and groaned. "Oh geez! What now? We're less than twenty-four hours out. The Society event is tomorrow, for goodness' sake."

"And when, pray tell, has that ever stopped Henrietta Stone from wanting the sun and the moon and the stars?" Lydie asked with a chuckle. "And all of that right now."

"Henrietta Sto—" Vanessa huffed. "For the love of... So, what did she want this time?"

Picking up one of the finished pouches, Lydie put it to her nose, and inhaling the lovely scent, felt her spirits lift immeasurably. "Oh, you know, nothing much. Just 'hey, I know this is last minute and all, but can we have umbrellas or canopies for all the tables. 'Cause the weatherman said it's gonna rain.'" She smiled at her partner. "That's all."

"*What?* Well, I hope you set her straight," Vanessa grumbled.

"I did, as gently as possible, of course, because it's not

Winnie's fault. She's just the messenger, and you know Henrietta bullied her into it. Lordy, you should have seen the woman's aura. She's stressed to the max and was so embarrassed to have to come out here last minute like that." Lydie sighed. "I felt so sorry for her that I gave her a packet of sage and told her to go home and boil it to cleanse her energy. She needs all the help she can get."

"I just don't understand that woman."

"Who? Winnie?"

Vanessa frowned at her over the pouch in her hands. "No, not Winnie. Henrietta Stone."

"Yeah, well, join the club. But be advised, we'll probably get an earful from her tomorrow when we show up without umbrellas for every single table or ginormous canopies to hold off the impending rain. I feel for Winnie having to tell Henrietta the bad news this afternoon. I told her we'd take the heat, so I wouldn't be surprised if Henrietta calls out here before the end of the day."

"Let her." Vanessa jabbed a finger in Lydie's direction. "I do not like that woman. And I won't have a problem putting her in her place. She's just awful."

Lydie burst out laughing. "You'll get no argument from me, that's for su—"

She felt the change begin even before she'd finished her sentence. Her smile faded, and her hearing filled with white noise so quickly that she could barely hear Vanessa's voice asking her what was wrong over the roar of it. Then the room began to dissolve before her eyes. Lydie had prophetic dreams at night all the time, but it had been ages since she'd had a waking dream. Breathing in deeply, she let the vision take her, felt herself slide into it.

Flowers, the scent of them sweet and fragrant filling her nostrils—sunshine warm on her face. Laughter and joy danced on the air. It was a party and a thoroughly charming setting. Yes, a garden party was in progress. Lydie could see the tables, the ladies in their finery. She smiled through the haze of the image. Winnie Douglas's face came into view then, and the woman looked decidedly distraught. She was saying something, and it seemed a bit frantic, but Lydie couldn't quite make it out. Something... about death?

No, that can't be right, can it? It's a party...

In the next instant, dark clouds began to cover the beautiful blue sky blotting out the warmth of the sun. But these weren't rain clouds. No, these were something else entirely.

"Yes, a portent of things to come," Lydie murmured. "The shadow of something dreadful and malevolent hovers near."

Then, as quickly as it had come over her, the waking dream began to melt away, leaving Lydie breathless and shaken.

"Lydie!" At Vanessa's concerned voice, the remnants of the vision broke apart completely. "Lydie, talk to me. What portents?"

Sinking to the floor, Lydie closed her eyes and waited for the sensation of vertigo to pass. "Give me a minute, wouldja?"

Vanessa knelt down next to her. "Are you okay? You just... went away right in the middle of a sentence. Your eyes glazed over, and your mouth was moving but no words were coming out. Scared the crap out of me. I haven't seen you with a waking dream in a very long time."

Lydie took another deep, cleansing breath. "Wow. That's because waking dreams—especially ones that come on that abruptly—are pretty rare. Normally my visions come in dreams at night while I'm sleeping."

"Toward the end you were murmuring about omens and something dreadful hovering close by. Do you remember what you were seeing?"

"It was a garden party. Everything was lovely at first, but then there was Winnie Douglas looking terrified. She was rattling on...

something about death, but I couldn't make it all out. Then dark clouds covered the sky, and all I could think of was that something terrible was coming." Lydie looked over at her friend. "Unfortunately, the vision dissolved before I could figure out what it was, but it looks like your divination pool was spot on. And I'm afraid the garden party may be involved."

2

"Move your buns, Vanessa," Lydie urged as she hurried toward the van. "We need to be at the venue in twenty minutes if we want to stay on schedule, and it's gonna be close as it is."

Vanessa prayed for patience before turning to stare at her friend over the box she was carrying. She didn't know what was up with Lydie today, but she'd been scattered and edgy all morning, and there was an agitated look of concern in her partner's turquoise eyes that Vanessa didn't like. "I'm fully aware of the time factor, Lydie. However, if I drop this layer cake because I'm hurrying, we won't have the *pièce de résistance*, now will we? And though it's a fabulous work of art, if I do say so myself, this monster was a bitch to put together. To lose it before we get to the garden party would break my heart and leave us without a centerpiece for the buffet table. Plus, I used the last of my special harmony spice for the batter, so there's that."

"Sorry. You're right." Lydie stopped, took in a breath, and let it out slowly before shaking her head. "I'm obviously a little more keyed up than I realized."

"If you'd have finished the calming herbal tea that I made for you when I got here this morning, it would have centered you and steadied your nerves."

"Maybe, but after my dark waking dream from yesterday afternoon, and then the ominous follow-up I had late last night, I'm not sure how much the tea would've helped."

"What? You had another visionary dream? So that's what your anxious mood is all about?" Vanessa stopped and blinked several times. "Why didn't you tell me that straight away?"

Lydie shrugged. "I don't know. You've had a lot on your plate taking lead with this Garden Society gig, and we're down to the wire here. I guess I didn't want to distract you with anything new until after we'd gotten the party set up." She made a face. "This new dream was a little more disturbing than the last, but I still don't have a clear picture of what we might be up against."

As Lydie opened the van's back doors, Vanessa eased the large box holding the elaborate layer cake into the open space on the bottom shelf. "Well, I'd rather know what was brewing in the ether, no matter how vague, than to go into this event unaware. Forearmed is forewarned." She stopped and narrowed her eyes at Lydie. "You said more disturbing. What was it this time? Additional omens or something worse?"

"Similar but this time with a few disquieting embellishments added. Although, it still seemed pretty chaotic and didn't make much more sense than the last one. My visions are like that in the beginning." Lydie sighed. "But it somehow *felt* worse, you know? Along with the dark, garden party theme, Winnie Douglas was a prominent figure again, so I'm a little worried for her."

"Great. Possible mayhem involving our most lucrative gig of the year," Vanessa muttered. "We should've given Grandma Charles a call the minute you had the waking dream yesterday. I don't have anything but my divination books to guide me where my runes and scrying pool are concerned. But you and your grandmother have the same gift of dream prophecy. She probably could've helped you decipher your vision a little better than our random guessing games."

Lydie was a third generation Hedge witch and had learned just about everything she knew from her grandmother. Vanessa hadn't felt a calling to the craft until her early twenties and was the only Hedge witch in her lineage, as far as she knew. Where Lydie had family members to guide her, Vanessa had no one and often got flack for her lifestyle from some in her family. And though Hedge witches were often solitary individuals, Vanessa was grateful that Lydie and her family had welcomed her into their fold.

"You're right," Lydie said. "We should've called Gram, especially if whatever's coming is tied to the garden party, which seems likely, since both of my visions have been centered there. But that's a missed opportunity and too late to do anything about now. We'll just have to stay on our toes this afternoon and see what happens."

Vanessa nodded. "You did remember your protection pouch, didn't you? With darkness hovering in my divination pool and rearing its ugly head in your visions, we can't afford to be unprepared."

"Yep. Got my pouch right here in my pocket."

"Good. Keep it close, but on the other hand, let's try not to worry too much about it. We've handled this Garden Society gig for the last three years, and I've got everything wired right down to the napkins. I spoke with Darcy an hour ago. She and the team are already there and have the twinkle lights up and the tables in place and dressed. All we need to do is show up with the cake and the rest of the spread. Sug and Carrie will fill the little teapots, and we're golden. So at least we won't have to worry about the banquet."

"Right. It's just the darkness that may or may not develop during the affair that we need to watch out for."

Since they'd started Lavender Fields and the event arm of Enchanted Affairs literally out of the old farmhouse and Lydie's home office seven years ago, they'd remodeled the old girl. They'd added the storefront and workspace within the first year and a half they'd been in business. And these days they had more clients than they knew what to do with, not that Vanessa was complaining. She and Lydie both loved planning, creating, and executing spectacular events of all shapes and sizes.

And they were damn good at it, Vanessa thought with a smile. But sometimes she worried they might lose their touch, that their success up to this point had only been a fluke.

"The Garden Society has been very good to us," Lydie said as she secured the cargo doors and went around to the driver's side. Climbing in, she fired up the van and then turned to Vanessa. "We've gotten so much word-of-mouth business from them. I want to make sure that everything is perfect again this year. And with the trouble in the air possibly centered on the Garden Society, that's all we need. You know what they say. You're always just a few bad reviews away from ruin. Now, add nebulous cosmic misfortune to that scenario and see what you get."

"Geez, Lydie, that's the most negative thing I've heard you say in quite a while. I think your chakras may be out of balance or something. I mean, of course we want to give our customers the best product we can, but nothing in life is perfect, right? And we can't always predict or change what the universe has in store."

"That's true. But we don't know what kind of trouble you've seen in the divination pool, do we? And your runes didn't clear it up, either. Then, with me having not one but two visions of darkness, you'll excuse me if I'm a bit on edge."

"Okay, okay. So, we don't know what's coming... exactly. All we can do is prepare, which we've done the best we can. And we're really good at rolling with positive energy no matter what happens, so I think we can handle whatever comes at us today.

Besides, after having to deal with Henrietta Stone for the last three years, we should probably be put forward for sainthood, don't you think?"

Lydie laughed out loud and carefully guided the van down the long gravel driveway to Calypso Lane. "You got that right, pal. Henrietta is a piece of work, for sure. I don't know why she feels the need to be so harsh with just about everyone she meets, or to be so demanding. I have a feeling we'll have to do some pacifying there before the party begins. Talk about out-of-sync chakras."

"Yeah, I think it's more than a chakra issue there, don't you?"

Vanessa was still baffled by Henrietta's re-election as Garden Society president. The woman was a nightmare to deal with, making change after change in the party's agenda and setup. And usually, like yesterday's canopy request, at the last possible moment. But a paying gig was a paying gig. And the Garden Society usually went all out for their end of summer garden party extravaganza.

"I still don't understand what the group was thinking re-electing that woman," Lydie said as if reading Vanessa's mind. "She's a terrible choice."

Vanessa giggled. "Glenda Beaumont said that she was sure that the vote was somehow rigged. That it was the only explanation for the outcome because nobody has a good thing to say about the woman, and she doesn't know of anyone who voted for her."

"Glenda's a master gardener, right?"

"Uh-huh." Vanessa nodded. "She really knows her stuff, too. I've actually run a few planting and propagation questions by her in the past."

"So, why didn't she run for president against Henrietta? She probably would've won hands down. Everyone likes Glenda."

Vanessa made a rude sound. "Come on, Lydie. Glenda hates being responsible for anything whatsoever, let alone the entire

Garden Society. She mostly just wants to putter in her own garden and be left alone. The only reason she's a Society member in the first place is that her sister Margot pitched such a fit." She rolled her eyes. "You know Margot."

Lydie laughed again. "Yeah, she doesn't like to do anything on her own, poor thing."

"Poor thing?" Vanessa gaped at her friend. "Poor thing, my butt! I think she acts that way for effect."

"Margot does like to be the center of attention."

"Anyway, I heard that Glenda about had a cow when Winnie Douglas suggested she run for president at the nomination meeting."

Lydie grinned. "Man, I would've *loved* to have been a fly on the wall for that meeting."

"Me, too." Vanessa could just imagine the bedlam that would have ensued.

"On the other hand, I'm just grateful that their Garden Society squabbles are none of our concern," Lydie said with a smirk as she switched on her blinker to turn onto the coastal highway. "I just want to get in, get out, and get paid."

Vanessa nodded again. "Amen to that, sista!"

Fifteen minutes later, they were pulling up at the service entrance for the Garden Society's headquarters. Vanessa checked her watch—straight up noon—and climbed from the vehicle as Lydie shut down the engine. "Hate to say I told you so, but we're right on time."

"Yep. We have two hours to get everything set and ready to go. Piece of cake."

Vanessa grinned. "Easy as pie. Let's get to it."

They spent another fifteen minutes organizing the long table in the pavilion that held several forty-five cup coffee urns and all the little teapots. Just as they'd moved on to the buffet table on the lawn outside the pavilion and started unloading the pastries that would surround the layer cake, Vanessa looked up to find Henrietta Stone barreling toward them, a perpetually sour look on her face.

"Heads up, Lydie," she warned her partner under her breath. "First sign of trouble at two o'clock and closing fast."

"Ms. Charles, Ms. Deerborne, a word please," the Society president called as she neared.

"Good afternoon, Henrietta," Lydie greeted her with a smile. "A lovely day for a garden party, isn't it?"

The woman glowered at them in return. "It's decent weather at the moment, but I'm assuming you have a contingency plan should the rain start before the event is finished. I'd hate to give Enchanted Affairs low marks in my review, after three years of adequate service."

"*Adequate Ser*—" Vanessa began in an outraged tone but Lydie put a hand on her arm.

"Not to worry, Henrietta. The rain won't be coming in until late tonight, as I told Winnie yesterday."

"So, she said." Henrietta made a disgruntled sound. "Silly, gullible woman will believe anything she's told. Did you at least take my advice and bring canopies with you in case you're wrong?"

Lydie patted Vanessa's arm when she opened her mouth to give the woman a piece of her mind and answered for them both in a patient tone. "We do have everything under control. But there's not a cloud on the horizon, Henrietta, so don't concern yourself over the weather. It's going to be another beautiful party this year. You have my word."

"Your word?" The woman harrumphed. "That remains to be seen, doesn't it?" she muttered as she turned and stalked toward the main building.

"Of all the nerve!" Vanessa sputtered. "Adequate service? Did you hear that?"

Lydie sighed as she gathered the tubs and headed back into the pavilion. "Yes. She's unpleasant, there's no doubt about that. But don't let her get to you. She's had her swipe at us, now she's off to swipe at someone else. Let's just make sure our part of the deal is spectacular so that she can't gripe about it later."

Vanessa rolled her eyes. "That's very generous, considering that I'm not sure this shindig can be a big enough hit for her *not* to complain about something." She put up a hand and took a deep breath, trying to release the negative energy Henrietta had imparted with her exhale. "But you're right. We can't let her ruin it for us. We do exceptional work, and everybody knows it."

"That's the spirit. Now, let's get the teapots ready to fill."

They continued with the setup, organizing and fidgeting with details alongside the team for the next hour and a half before Vanessa stood back and surveyed the final result. The twinkle lights they'd put in the small fruit trees bordering the outdoor pavilion sparkled merrily and added a festive feel. With the tables dressed in white linen, the pink floral centerpieces coupled with the gold-trimmed dessert plates made an elegant statement and complemented the buffet table perfectly. When they added the little floral teapots and cups for each place setting, the effect would be complete.

She smiled to herself. *Take that, Henrietta Stone!*

Before they knew it, Society members began to trickle in. She and Lydie split up to greet the members as they arrived, helping them find their assigned places and exchanging pleasantries.

"Oh, Vanessa, this is just charming," Doris Mayfield gushed as she glanced around the grounds. "I absolutely *love* garden parties, and it looks like you and Lydie have outdone yourselves yet again."

"Thanks, Doris. We aim to please."

In her mid-thirties, Doris wasn't gorgeous but attractive in her own way with highlighted brown hair and big blue eyes. She was friendly and gregarious with a perky personality and ready smile. Vanessa liked her.

"I thought last year's event was spectacular," Barbara Drake chimed in as she approached. "But Doris is right, this is elegant and magical. A party fit for a princess, which I most certainly am," she finished with a musical laugh.

"That's very nice of you to say, Barbara. We were going for elegant and magical, so I guess we hit the mark."

"Oh, Vanessa, I'm never nice, as Doris here will confirm. I just call 'em like I see 'em," Barbara said with a smirk as she sat down next to Doris and hung her purse over the back of her chair.

A former beauty queen who'd married extremely well, and divorced even better, Barbara was the very definition of high-maintenance. Now in her mid-forties, the woman was tall, svelte, with not a platinum blonde hair out of place or a line on her face. Vanessa thought Barbara probably could've still given a pageant field a run for their money. However, behind the carefully applied makeup and glossy smile, there was also a sharp wit and a volatile nature. And if even a few of the stories she'd heard were true, Vanessa was certain she never wanted to find herself on the wrong side of Barbara Drake.

"This is really lovely, as it has been every year," Barbara continued. "So, don't let our completely unworthy, cheating, and incompetent blowhard of a president tell you any different."

"Barbara! What a horrible thing to say," Doris exclaimed with a couple *tsks* thrown in for good measure. "Don't be so unkind."

"Please. Like you and half the membership haven't been thinking the same damned thing. You ran against her for president, Doris. You would've won, too, if Henrietta had run a clean race. But as you found out the hard way, she prefers to sling muck whenever possible and cheat at every turn. But she'll get hers in the end."

Doris turned bright red and looked away, and Barbara focused on Vanessa with a cunning twinkle in her eye. "Oh, don't look so shocked, Vanessa dear. I keep my ear to the ground, and trust me, I hear everything."

I'll just bet you do.

"Well, you ladies enjoy the party, and if you need anything, just give a wave," Vanessa replied with a frozen smile. "Excuse me. I need to see how things are going in the pavilion."

Before either woman could reply, she made a quick exit and found her partner in the pavilion checking on the tea and helping the team prepare the little teapots. Pulling Lydie aside, she quietly told her about the conversation she'd witnessed between Barbara and Doris.

"I tell you, that Barbara Drake is a nasty piece of work wrapped up in expensive polish. She's not someone I'd like to get too close to, if you know what I mean."

"Yes. I do. But that whole conversation actually makes some sense," Lydie replied.

"Really?"

"Not the conversation itself, but the feel of it. Remember I told you that my dream last night was pretty disturbing and had more details? Well, I just didn't tell you what those details were." Lydie frowned. "But even with this new information, I don't quite know what to make of it all."

"What do you mean?" Though Vanessa wasn't sure she wanted to know the answer, she asked the question anyway. "What did you see, Lydie?"

The look in her partner's eyes sent a shiver down Vanessa's spine.

"Death, Vanessa. I saw death. And a terrified Winnie Douglas pointing toward a group of women—Barbara Drake among them —and repeating one phrase."

"Good Lord!" Vanessa gasped. "What was she repeating?"

"She said, 'Death is coming... beware!'"

3

"*Death!* You saw death in your dream? Why in God's name didn't you tell me that before we left the shop?" Vanessa hissed. "What are we going to do now, Lydie?"

"I don't know what we can do." Lydie shook her head. "I didn't say anything earlier because last night's dream was still so vague and jumbled. There was a huge group of women standing behind Winnie in the vision. We have no way of knowing which woman, or for that matter, how many of them she was pointing to when she warned that death was coming."

Vanessa narrowed her eyes. "Nice. Thanks for putting the possibility of multiple deaths in my head. Now I'm going to be freaked out for the rest of the afternoon."

"Look, we can't panic."

"But what if something happens during the garden party? Or worse, what if that something happens after we're gone?"

Lydie put up a hand. "Again, we don't know if whatever Winnie was showing me in the vision is gonna happen today. She might not have been referring to this garden party at all."

"Oh, right," Vanessa said in a dry tone. "Because this particular group of women has more than one garden party that they'll all be attending en masse in the coming weeks."

"Okay, don't get snarky. That's not what I meant." Lydie looked around and pulled Vanessa closer. "Look, my dream could just signify that death is hovering for someone in this *group*. And that could be today, tomorrow, or it could be next month, for all we know. That's how these things work."

"Alright, alright." Vanessa waved a hand in the air. "I just wish we could warn whoever may be in peril, that's all."

"Without knowing who that is or what's waiting for them, we'll just have to keep our eyes peeled for anything abnormal and be ready to act if something does happen here today. Seriously, with so little to go on, I don't see any other way." Lydie scanned the pavilion and saw Doris Mayfield enter, crossing to where Sug and Carrie were loading the prepared teapots onto large serving trays marked for each table in the garden. "Besides, if the universe has a heart attack or car accident planned for someone's future, there's not much we can do about that. And I don't know that warning them would be a help, in any case."

Vanessa frowned. "True. But after what I've seen in my runes and scrying pool, it feels like something more, something darker than just your average universe tapping some random person on the shoulder. And I think you've felt the same thing with your visions."

"Yes, I know what you mean." Lydie sighed. "But the tea service is starting, so we need to stay focused on the event. Let's just get out there and mingle. If you see or hear something that alarms you, give me a heads up and we'll go from there. Agreed?"

"Agreed."

They started for the door at the same time that Doris was returning to her table, and Lydie called after her. "Did you need something, Doris?"

The woman turned and gave a nervous laugh. "Oh, no, thank

you, Lydie. I have certain allergies and just need to be careful about what I ingest. It's all good."

"Ah. Well, give me a shout if you need anything else."

Lydie winked at Vanessa as they followed the woman out of the pavilion. There they split up, heading to opposite ends of the garden where they moved from table to table mingling with the Society participants as they arrived and were seated. The Garden Society boasted fifty-four members, most of whom made a point of attending the annual garden party, so the twelve tables with five place settings each were close to full as the event commenced. The tables were large enough to accommodate additional settings if needed, but by the looks of things that wouldn't be necessary.

"Hey, Lydie," Margot Beaumont called as Lydie approached the table where she was seated next to her sister, Glenda. "Fabulous setup. Very nice. Isn't that right, Glen?"

Glenda Beaumont made a face, looking less than pleased to find herself amid the festivities. "Yes, yes, and I've told you so several times. I don't know why you feel the need to keep carrying on about it." The woman shook her head and looked up at Lydie. "No offense, Lydie. Enchanted Affairs always does a great job, and I'm sure this time will be no exception. I'm just not in the garden party mood today. I've had a headache and a bit of indigestion all morning." She hooked a thumb toward her sister. "This one insisted I come with her even though I didn't feel like it."

"Well, why didn't you say something earlier?" Margot complained with a sour look for her sister.

"What are you talking about?" Glenda asked with an incredulous expression. "I did. Several times, as I recall. But as usual you heard what you wanted to hear. You meant to attend, so obviously I would need to accompany you, right?"

Margot's mouth formed a hard line and she frowned. "Well, excuse me for wanting to get you out of that garden of yours and into the world for a few hours."

Glenda's booming laughter filled the air. "Oh, Margie, don't pretend to have my interests at heart. We both know that it had less to do with me and more to do with what you wanted. I tell you, if you weren't my sister..." She suddenly seemed to realize where they were, and after looking at the uncomfortable faces around the table, she sighed. "My apologies, ladies. To you as well, Lydie. Please forgive my outburst. Again, I'm not myself today."

Lydie studied Glenda's aura. Nothing really out of the ordinary there, so it was doubtful Glenda was the one her dream had been about. A little pale in the face, a bit of agitation, perhaps still suffering from the remnants of a tension headache, but Lydie had a feeling that Glenda's foul mood had more to do with wanting to be left alone than it did with the headache. And she'd chosen a public moment to give her sister grief about it.

"No need to apologize, Glenda. Nothing to forgive," Lydie said. "It looks as if you may still have a bit of a headache, though. I have a remedy for that in my bag and can fix you right up, if you'd like. Just let me know."

Glenda grinned, and Lydie could see that her original thoughts were very close to the mark. "Thanks, Lydie. But I'm good for now." There was a twinkle in the woman's eyes as she lifted her teacup to her lips.

"Alright, then you ladies enjoy the afternoon and let me know if you need anything."

Lydie kept moving, chatting with the ladies at each table and keeping an eye peeled for anything out of the ordinary. Soon she began to relax into the routine, and the afternoon spun out in a satisfying manner, with everyone seeming to enjoy the event, the lovely weather, and good company. Even Lydie was having a great time of it.

That is, until she got to Henrietta Stone's table.

The odious president was holding court, or more like dominating the women at her table. Lydie had been putting it off, but taking a deep breath, she pasted a smile on her face and approached the group.

Kathryn Wilks-Raymond, the Society's Treasurer, was seated to Henrietta's right, gazing off into space as the woman rambled on about the importance of maintaining the 'right' kind of leadership for the Garden Society. Winnie Douglas and two other ladies who Lydie didn't know filled out the table and looked to be completely ignoring Henrietta, though she certainly didn't seem to notice.

"Good afternoon, ladies," Lydie said as she stepped up to the table. There was an audible sigh of relief at the interruption. "I just wanted to make sure you've visited the dessert table. It's been replenished, so if you haven't already, please indulge in some of the tasty pastries and scones that we've provided to go along with your tea."

The two unknown women practically leapt from their seats and headed off in the direction of the buffet table without a word or a backward glance.

Winnie looked up and smiled. "Everything looks so awesome, Lydie. And it seems you were right about the weather."

"Like I told you yesterday, it's one of my gifts. Just make sure you batten down all your hatches before midnight. We're in for quite the deluge around the witching hour."

Henrietta made a scoffing noise and looked away, and Winnie laughed nervously.

"Oh, and I wanted to thank you again for the little gift packet you gave me yesterday," Winnie continued with a sidelong glance at Henrietta. "I'll admit that I was skeptical at first, but it worked wonders just like you said it would."

Lydie grinned. "I'm glad to hear it. If you need more cleansing herbs, you know where we are. Everything else okay?"

"Oh, yes! The grounds are magical, and I especially love the twinkle lights in the fruit trees. The pastries on the buffet table look wonderful, and this tea is delicious. Do you carry this blend in the shop as well?"

"We do indeed. It's the special Enchanted Affairs house blend."

"It's great," Kathryn added. "I've already finished off one pot and am working on another. I might have to come out and pick up some for myself."

Henrietta snorted and finally spoke up. "I don't know what the two of you are prattling on about. While the service is adequate again this year, I could barely suffer through one cup of that nasty concoction in *my* teapot. And it was anything but delicious, believe me. More like a flowery, bitter mess."

"Bitter? Oh, dear, I'm terribly sorry, Henrietta," Lydie said. "Here, let me go get you a fresh pot."

"I should say that's the least you could do."

Lydie picked up the woman's teapot and cup. "I'll bring you a clean cup as well. Again, I apologize. Be right back."

Hurrying into the pavilion, she set the half-full pot and empty cup down on the counter and threw a towel over them both. Of all people to get a bad pot of tea at their premiere event. Lydie was certain they would never hear the end of it. Whether there was anything wrong with her tea or not, Henrietta would be sure to milk it for years to come.

Quickly gathering a fresh place setting out of the tub of extras, along with a clean teapot, she added two scoops of the tea blend and filled the pot with hot water from one of the urns, then tossed a tea cozy over it as she waited for it to steep.

"What are you doing, Lydie?" Vanessa asked as she came into the pavilion. "I saw you hurry in here. Is everything okay?"

"Oh, everything was going along perfectly, and then Henrietta complained about her tea. I told her that I'd get her a fresh pot and cup. I swear that woman is a nightmare, and this is just another thing for her to grumble about."

"You'll get no disagreement from me." Vanessa frowned. "Anyone else have an issue?"

"No. Actually, both Winnie and Kathryn made a point to say how delicious our house blend is." She made a face. "Unfortunately, it'll give Henrietta more ammunition for next year. You see anything out of the ordinary yet?"

"Not a thing. All's quiet and running smoothly on my end of the garden. Everyone seems to be having a great time. You?"

Lydie shook her head. "Glenda Beaumont was complaining of a headache and indigestion, but that started before she arrived. And to be honest, I think it was mostly just that she really didn't want to be here at all today."

Vanessa laughed out loud. "Let me guess. Margot nagged her into coming."

"You got it. And Glenda let the whole table know it as well." Lydie chuckled. "I can tell you, Margot was *not* happy."

"Ha! I bet. So, then no issue with Glenda?"

"No. I don't think she has anything to do with what may be coming. She was a little pale, but the only thing I could detect was the telltale signs of the headache she'd been talking about."

"That's good then. Maybe you were right. Maybe whatever we both saw has nothing to do with this event."

"From your mouth to God's ears." Picking up Henrietta's new cup and fresh pot of tea, Lydie turned and started toward the door. "Keep an eye out all the same," she called over her shoulder.

When she got back to Henrietta's table, everyone was seated and enjoying their pastries, but the president was nowhere to be seen, which may have been the reason the ladies at the table were all smiling. Henrietta had a way of throwing a wet blanket on any festivity.

"I've got Henrietta's fresh tea, Winnie. Where is she?"

"Um... she's gone to the ladies' room," Winnie replied, looking toward the public restrooms. "She said she was feeling a bit queasy and wasn't looking well at all."

"What? Oh no! I hope she's okay." Lydie set the cup and teapot down at Henrietta's place. "I'd hate to think our tea made her sick."

"I don't think that's it, Lydie," Kathryn said with a shake of her head. "At least, I can't think why it would be. I mean, we all had the same tea, right? And mine was delightful."

Winnie and the other two women all nodded in agreement.

"She said her throat was tingly, and her tongue felt a little numb," Winnie added. "And she was kind of... sweaty-looking. That's when she said she was queasy and headed to the restroom. Maybe she was having an allergic reaction or something."

Lydie was getting a bad feeling. Perhaps she and Vanessa had relaxed their guard too soon, and their optimism was premature. Could Henrietta be the one from her visions, the one in trouble?

"Which ladies' room did she go to? Maybe someone should check on her to make sure she's okay."

"No need," Kathryn said, pointing toward the main building. "Here she comes."

Lydie studied the woman as she made her way back to the table. She did indeed look slightly unwell. She was definitely perspiring, and her color was a little off.

"Are you all right, Henrietta?" Winnie asked as the woman dropped down into her chair.

Henrietta glared at her. "I'm fine," she growled, and then turned her ire on Lydie. "No thanks to you and your nasty tea. After just the one cup, it made me sick to my stomach."

"I'm so sorry, Henrietta. But I don't understand how that could be."

"Yes, we all had the same tea, Henrietta," Kathryn said. "So, it must have been something else. Maybe you're getting some kind of flu bug."

"Maybe," Henrietta replied. "But doubtful. Other than my blood pressure issues, I'm never ill."

"Do you want one of us to give out the awards?" Winnie asked. "Any one of the leadership team would be happy to do it for you."

Henrietta became indignant at that. "Oh, I just bet you'd like that, wouldn't you, Winnie Douglas? Well, you can just put that thought right out of your empty little head. I was elected as Society president fair and square, and nobody's going to take over for me, do you understand?"

Winnie turned as red as a poppy, and her eyes went wide with shock. "Henrietta, no one is trying to take over for you. I just thought... well, you don't look good. I was only trying to help."

"You want to help me? Go get the honors tub and the wireless microphone so I can get started on handing out the awards," Henrietta replied with annoyance as she poured herself a glass of water from the carafe in the middle of the table and guzzled down three quarters of it in one breath.

"Of course. I'll do it right away."

As Lydie stepped back and watched Winnie hurry toward the main building, Kathryn tried to smooth things over. "Henrietta, there was no reason to snap at Winnie that way. She's just concerned about you, as we all are. You really do look ill. Are you sure you're okay?"

Henrietta turned to Kathryn with a steely look. "I said I'm fine, didn't I?"

With a sigh, Kathryn nodded and looked away.

Fortunately, Winnie was back in record time with the wireless mic and a small, plastic tub holding the awards. Snatching the mic from her, Henrietta got unsteadily to her feet and tapped the top of it with her finger. Taking another sip of water, she cleared her throat. "Alright, ladies. It's time to hand out the accolades for this year, so settle down and let's get started."

After a short speech, the first few awards were handed out without incident, but as the minutes passed, Lydie could see that Henrietta was having more and more difficulty. Continually dabbing at her face with a handkerchief and breathing rapidly, the woman actually sounded giddy when after the fifth award she put a hand to her chest and turned to Kathryn.

"I'm unable to read the award cards, and I'm having chest pain, Kathryn," she whispered in a frightened tone. "I can't seem to catch my breath."

"Should I fetch Dr. Landon, Henrietta? You don't look well," Winnie murmured.

"I... think... that would be... good," the woman said, her voice barely a whisper now.

Almost as soon as the words were out of her mouth, Henrietta cried out and doubled over. Winnie and Kathryn got up and hurried to her side, and Lydie ran toward them just as the woman dropped to the grass, writhing in pain.

Pandemonium ensued when everyone rushed to help, and Lydie had to grab Kathryn's wrist to get her attention. "Call 911. Right now! And Winnie, go get Dr. Landon. She's at table eight."

As Winnie sprinted away from the table, Kathryn nodded and got up to dig in her purse for her cell phone while Lydie shouted for the other women to move back. "Give her some air, ladies. Please! Henrietta? Can you hear me?"

"It hurts. God, it hurts," the woman moaned. The next minute she went into convulsions, and Lydie worried that she would bite her tongue during the seizures.

Vanessa shoved her way through the crowd and dropped down next to her. "I called EMS. It shouldn't be long."

Lydie nodded. "I think Kathryn called, too. Winnie went to get Dr. Landon. Where is she?"

"She went to the ladies' room. Winnie will bring her straight away," Vanessa said. "Do you think Henrietta's gonna be okay, Lydie?"

Lydie could hear the fear in her partner's voice, feel it pouring from her. "I don't know, but it doesn't look good."

Lydie looked down at Henrietta and watched the woman's eyes go glassy, heard her slow exhale of breath. Then there was nothing. Reaching down, she checked for a pulse. Finding none, Lydie began CPR.

4

D r. Kelli Landon came running from the ladies' room and took over CPR on poor Henrietta within minutes of Winnie finding her. Relieved to have a medical professional take over for her, Lydie began coordinating efforts to make sure everyone stayed calm and seated at their tables before joining Vanessa on the periphery of the emergency. Slipping an arm through hers for support, together they watched the doctor work on Henrietta. Though Lydie was holding out hope, she was pretty sure she already knew what the outcome would be. And by the look on her partner's face, so did Vanessa.

"Lydie... " Vanessa whispered.

"I know. But there was nothing we could do."

Henrietta had obviously been the victim their forewarnings had predicted.

"Let's just hope that Kelli can work some magic of her own."

Dr. Landon, the Durham County Medical Examiner, and a forty-two-year-old doctor of internal medicine, was a master gardener and long-time member of the Garden Society. Lydie knew Kelli also had a degree in toxicology and handled all sorts of situations like this county-wide, so she prayed that her vision had been wrong or that she'd misread it, and that this would end without tragedy.

On the heels of that thought, she could hear the ambulance siren getting louder as it got closer—like an omen of things to come—arriving on the scene moments later. The EMS team took over for the doctor in a flurry of activity before loading Henrietta into the ambulance, and they were on their way to the hospital in less than ten minutes.

"Vanessa, why don't you go and see if Carrie and Sug are ready to start the breakdown. I think they went to the van. I'll stick to Kelli like glue and see what I can find out."

Vanessa ran a hand over her face. "Better you than me, pal. I'll find you in a bit."

Lydie watched her go, and then followed Dr. Landon to Henrietta's table.

"Is Henrietta going to be okay?" Winnie asked as they approached.

"She's in good hands, Winnie," the doctor replied. "In the meantime, I need some help piecing together what happened. Can y'all help me with that?"

When Winnie, Kathryn, and the two other women at the table all nodded, the doctor continued. "Was Henrietta having any issues before she collapsed?"

"Yes," Winnie replied in a trembling voice. "She complained that her throat was kinda tingly, and her tongue was sort of numb."

One of the other women at the table who Lydie didn't know spoke up then. "Yes, and that was right before she said she was feeling queasy and headed to the ladies' room."

"And she was sweating like a pi—" Kathryn began, then paused, and obviously re-thinking her words, licked her lips and continued. "I mean, she was obviously perspiring profusely. She also complained about her tea being bad." She gave Lydie a sheepish look. "Sorry, Lydie."

"Nothing to be sorry about, Kathryn."

"What was wrong with her tea?" Dr. Landon asked.

"She said it tasted floral and bitter," Lydie replied. "But all the teapots were filled with the same Enchanted Affairs house blend. Everyone had the same thing, but she was the only one with the complaint. There's nothing in our house blend that would cause such a reaction, or taste in that specific way."

"And you replaced her pot? With the pot here on the table?"

"That's correct. Right away. I also brought her a clean cup with the fresh pot."

"And where is the first pot and cup? Did you dump the contents?"

"Uh, no. Henrietta can be pretty challenging, and I wanted to get her a new set quickly, so I left the pot and cup on the side table in the pavilion. I threw a towel over them for clean up later. I can get them for you, if you like."

"Please do." Dr. Landon said, and then put up a hand. "On second thought, I'll go with you in just a minute." Looking around at the strained faces, she continued. "Is there anything else any of you can think of that would be pertinent?"

Kathryn frowned. "Henrietta turned to me right before she dropped to the ground and said she was having trouble reading the award cards, which I thought was odd. She also said that she couldn't catch her breath."

"Yes. I noticed that she was having trouble, too," Lydie added. "And I don't know if this makes any sense, but at one point she almost sounded giddy."

The doctor looked thoughtful. "All right. Thank you, ladies. Lydie, let's go get that teapot."

Together, they crossed to the pavilion to the table where

Henrietta's original teapot and cup were still sitting under the towel Lydie had tossed over them earlier.

"If Henrietta had an allergic reaction to something in our tea blend, I'll be just heartbroken, and quite frankly, stunned," Lydie murmured as she watched the doctor don latex gloves and load the teapot and cup into the small box that Lydie had provided. "We use this house blend for all events like this. We have for years and have never had a problem. We used it last year for this very occasion."

"Let's not jump to conclusions, Lydie. Without more information and testing, we can't be sure Henrietta's symptoms are consistent with an allergic reaction."

"What do you mean?"

"I'd rather not elaborate, and it would be irresponsible of me to speculate. So, let's just wait to see what the test results tell us."

"Would you like a sample of our house blend as well?"

"Sure. We'll test that to be thorough. I'll go get my kit from the car and take samples of the tea from my pot for comparison, as well as samples from the dessert table if necessary."

"Your kit? Do you get this kind of situation often, Kelli?"

"Not frequently, but from time to time. In my role as Medical Examiner, I've just found that it pays to be prepared for every circumstance possible." The doctor turned and smiled. "Don't worry, Lydie. I'm only taking samples to see if we can narrow down what caused Henrietta's symptoms. I'll run them down to our lab for analysis. It will help us to know how to treat Henrietta and get her back on her feet."

Dr. Landon may have not wanted to elaborate, and she obviously didn't want to cause a panic, but Lydie could clearly read the doctor's aura and sense exactly what she had left unsaid. However, she simply nodded and followed the doctor out of the pavilion with her thoughts running wild in her head. If what the doctor said was true, and Henrietta's symptoms weren't consistent with an allergic reaction, then what was happening here? The scenario that entered her mind was too horrible to imagine. Yet, after the distressing visionary dreams she'd had over the last couple of days, and the foreboding turn of Vanessa's runes and scrying pool during that same time period, that thought was the most likely conclusion.

Henrietta may have been deliberately poisoned.

But by whom, and how would they have done it without being seen. And for what reason? Sure, the woman was not the most pleasant human being on the planet, but still... What could she have done that would have deserved this kind of retribution? And that Enchanted Affairs tea blend could have been the vehicle of that retribution was a heinous thought, indeed. Nevertheless, Lydie promptly reminded herself that Kelli was correct. It would be foolish to jump to conclusions before all the facts were in. Still, she was having a really hard time setting the dark thoughts aside.

Lydie had a sample baggie of Enchanted Affairs house blend tea ready for Kelli when she returned from her vehicle with her kit.

"Thank you, Lydie," the doctor said as she took the baggie and dropped it into her kit. "I'd like to take a sample from my pot and then a few from pots around the event, just to have a good range for comparison, if you'll assist me. Then we'll go to the dessert table."

"No problem. Darcy's manned the table for the event, so when you went to get your kit, I told her to stay put and wait for us. She'll also be able to tell you if Henrietta took anything from the table and what that may have been."

"Excellent. Looks like a lot of ladies have already left, so let's get this done."

They took tea samples from five vacant tables—with the doctor meticulously labeling each—and then headed over to the dessert table where Darcy was waiting.

"Hey, Darcy," Dr. Landon began. "Can I ask you a few questions?"

The young woman nodded, her blonde ponytail bobbing up and down with the movement. "Sure. Lydie told me you had questions."

"Great. First, can you tell me if Henrietta came by the dessert table at any point during the event today?"

"Oh, she came by alright. Right off the bat, just as the members were starting to arrive." Darcy wrinkled her nose. "Had her clipboard and pen ready. She walked the full length of the table, lookin' over everything with a frown on her face. Then she marks down something on the clipboard sheet, looks over at me, and gives me a nasty look. Then she just stomps off."

"Did she take anything off the table? Any of the finger sandwiches or desserts?"

"Nope. Not a thing. I offered, but that's when she went to writing on her clipboard like we'd failed some kind of test that only she knew about." Darcy shook her head. "This table and the entire event were put together so beautifully, yet she complained about everything. I just don't get why some people have to be so negative."

"Did she return after that? At any time during the event?"

"No ma'am. That was the last I saw of her, and I was here at this table from the start to this very minute."

Dr. Landon nodded. "Okay. I think that's it then. Thank you."

"You can start packing up now, Darcy," Lydie said. "You and the team can just drop everything off at the store and then head home. We'll debrief and unpack tomorrow afternoon. I'll text you."

"You got it, boss."

"I'm going to pack these samples in with Henrietta's original pot of tea and drop it all off at the lab on my way home, Lydie. Thanks for your help," Dr. Landon said. "This was a terrible way to end such a lovely party. With the exception of Henrietta's ailment, the event was really first rate—yet again—I might add. Enchanted Affairs did a great job."

"Thanks, Kelli. Will you let me know how the tests turn out? I'm really hoping our tea wasn't the culprit."

"Of course. Try not to worry about it. I'll come out to the shop and we'll talk soon."

As Lydie watched the doctor cross the lawn, she couldn't help thinking that it would be sooner than the doctor thought.

"Lydie, what's going on?" Vanessa asked as she came up beside her. "It looked like Kelli was taking samples."

"Yes. She's going to test and compare them."

"But why? Has there been a suggestion of foul play?" Vanessa blurted.

Lydie took her arm and turned them away from the attendees still lingering at a few of the tables. "Keep your voice down, pal. We don't want to cause a panic or start any unfounded rumors."

"Oh, my gosh! She *does* think there's been foul play," Vanessa replied in a frantic whisper.

Lydie sighed. "I don't know that for certain, and Kelli didn't say as much, only that Henrietta's symptoms may not fit an allergic reaction. But that doesn't mean that there was foul play. She's just being thorough. However, with her expertise in toxicology, I worry that she's thinking along the lines of a poisoning. Now, again, whether that involves foul play or just some kind of accidental thing, I don't know for sure."

Vanessa narrowed her eyes. "But you think it's foul play, don't you?"

After a moment, Lydie nodded. "Given the dark portents you've seen in your runes and your divination pool, as well as the path of my recent visions, I'm inclined to lean in that direction. It's all just a little too dark and ominous for me. And regardless of her placating words, I got a very unsettling vibe from Kelli. But again, I don't have any evidence, just a feeling. I gave her Henrietta's original teapot and cup, as well as a sample of our house blend of tea to go with the other samples she collected."

"Lydie! Why would you do that?"

"Why? Because out of the fifty-plus women at this event who all received the same tea in their pots, Henrietta was the only one to complain about the taste. She explicitly told me that it tasted *floral and bitter*. Does that sound like our house blend?"

"No. No, of course not, but if someone put poison in Henrietta's tea, it could very well implicate us. We brought the tea and the pots, not to mention the food. I don't want to get Enchanted Affairs caught up in a poisoning investigation, and you shouldn't either. And what if Henrietta doesn't make it? I don't want to be callous or anything, but being implicated in a death like that could crush our business."

Lydie shook her head. "Vanessa, if that's what this turns out to be, we're already involved for those very reasons. Giving Kelli the tea, pot, and cup was the right thing to do, and transparency is important. Darcy said that Henrietta didn't take anything off the dessert table, so Dr. Landon didn't take any food samples. At least we don't need to worry about that." Lydie put a hand on Vanessa's shoulder. "Look, we need to get to the truth no matter where that leads. If someone put something in Henrietta's tea that made her so ill, we need to know that."

"And if we get blamed for it? If she dies?"

"Then we'll deal with what comes, but better to volunteer the information now so that if this all goes sideways, we won't look like we tried to hide pertinent evidence."

"So, you're thinking it will probably go that way?"

Lydie blew out a breath. "Oh, yeah. I've remembered a few bits and pieces from my latest waking dream. So, yes, I think this is very likely to *go that way*, but I haven't had any visions that included jail time, have you?"

Vanessa made a face. "Don't be a smart-ass. And don't put that out into the Universe. It has a very snarky sense of humor, you know. And you need to bring me up to speed on what you've remembered. I need all the facts, too."

"Fair enough." Lydie smiled at her tone. "Van, no matter what my Spidey-senses tell me, we just have to be patient and not jump to conclusions. I know it's hard not to speculate, but like Dr. Landon said to me, we need to wait for the test results and go from there."

Taking a deep, cleansing breath, she waved a hand in the air. "Anyway, come on. Let's go pack up. We should get back to the shop so you can give your scrying pool another look. We're gonna need to stay sharp and ahead of what's coming, if we can."

If that's even possible, she added silently as they went to help with breaking down the tables and chairs.

By the time they got everything packed up and hauled back to the shop, Lydie's head was pounding like a bass drum, and she just wanted to take some aspirin and curl up in a dark room. But there was still more to do, so she settled for aspirin and dove in.

"Lydie, I can see that you have a headache," Vanessa commented when she brought in the last load of linens from the van. "We can do the rest of this tomorrow."

"I suppose. I just want to get the linens in their tubs and ready for the cleaners. I'd like to get them dropped off tomorrow or Tuesday at the latest."

Vanessa frowned. "Again, we can do it tomorrow. You aren't doing yourself any favors by trying to muscle through with your head pounding."

"I know, I know, it's just with everyth—" The vision came on so quickly and with such a meanness that Lydie cried out and dropped the load of linens she was carrying. Sinking to the floor among them, the white noise began in her head in earnest, and the smell of death filled her nostrils.

Henrietta, with pale white skin and eyes black as coal, stood surrounded by the same group of women as before. Winnie stood off to one side shrieking and pointing toward the group.

"What are you saying, Winnie? I can't understand you," Lydie murmured. "Oh. Oh, yes, I see. More death is coming. Must be vigilant, to be sure. You're right. Third time is the charm..."

Like all of her waking dreams, this one came and went in a flurry, and Lydie could hear Vanessa calling her name as if from a distance.

"Lydie! Come on, breathe. That's right. Take it slow. Let go of it, let it fade."

Taking a last deep, cleansing breath, Lydie felt the vision finally ebb away, leaving her feeling washed out and shaken. "Well, that was more brutal than it really needed to be."

"I'm making you some lavender tea for that headache. It will calm and help settle you. Then you can tell me about your vision when you feel up to it," Vanessa said as she helped Lydie into one of the over-stuffed armchairs in the casting room. "You sit right here, and I'll be back in flash."

True to her word, Vanessa wasn't gone but five or six minutes and returned with a fragrant cup of the lavender tea. Lydie took her time, letting the vapors do their thing. And after a bit, her headache began to recede, and she started to feel more like herself.

"So?" Vanessa began. "Do you feel up to talking about it? You said more death is coming, and something about the third time being the charm. What does that mean, Lydie?"

Lydie leaned her head back against the chair and closed her eyes. "It means that you need to check your runes and the divination pool, because we're in for a bumpy ride, my friend. And we're going to have to be on our game. Henrietta is just the beginning."

5

Though Monday dawned with partly cloudy skies and cooler temps, the air was fragrant and fresh after being washed clean by the overnight deluge just as Lydie had predicted. Her headache had evaporated as well, thanks to Vanessa's lavender tea and a good night's sleep. The simple combination seemed to have done the trick, and her mood was lighter as she headed downstairs just before ten.

Putting on the kettle, she went to open the shop for the day, and had just moved to the workroom to get started on packing the linen tubs when she heard Vanessa's car. Moments later, the tinkle of the bell above the shop door signaled her partner's arrival.

"Lydie?" Vanessa hollered from the storefront. "You didn't turn on the 'open' sign."

Vanessa entered the workroom and stood with her fists on her hips, annoyance clear in her baby-blue eyes. "We paid good money for that sign. A sign that you rarely use, I might add."

Lydie gave her a bland look. "Please. Don't make it sound like I don't use it. Besides, it's not like customers are beating down the door this morning. I'm just a bit off today and got sidetracked is all."

"Define a bit off. Do you still have that headache?"

"No, no, it's gone. Thanks to your tea, I slept well. In between the dreams, that is," Lydie replied and made a face.

"Oh, my." There was a touch of concern in Vanessa's eyes. "Let me get a cup of tea, and you can tell me all about it while we get the linens handled."

She disappeared down the hall, and Lydie went back to packing while she waited.

A few minutes later, Vanessa came back in, cup in hand, and hopped up onto one of the stools at the work table. "Okay. Spill it. What were your dreams about? Any new clues about yesterday's event?"

Lydie put the lid on the tub she'd just filled and stuck a label for the cleaners on the top. Straightening, she pulled her chestnut brown hair up into a ponytail with a scrunchy she fished out of her pocket before giving Vanessa a sober look. "Not so much clues... more like a conclusion."

"What does that mean?"

"It means that Henrietta has crossed over."

"*What?*" Vanessa shot up off the stool with a look of dismay on her face before slowly sitting back down and blowing out a breath. "I was hoping we'd been wrong, but... you're sure? You couldn't have misread the signs?"

"Uh, no. She was really very clear." Lydie frowned. "And I'm here to tell you, she was pretty ticked off about it, too."

Vanessa's mouth dropped open. "You actually spoke with her? In your dream?"

Lydie laughed out loud at that. "I wouldn't call it speaking *with* her. Turns out, Henrietta is just as unpleasant in death as she was in life, and she was very vocal about her displeasure."

"But has that happened before? Actual interaction with the dead?"

"It's rare but has happened a time or two. It's really disturbing."

"I bet. So, did she give you any clues about what caused her death?"

"No. But I got the distinct impression that all of the previous signs were spot on. This was no accident. That's really all I know for sure. I imagine we'll be hearing more from the living as soon as Kelli gets the test results. Maybe sooner if they confirm foul play before then."

"Oh, goodie. Now, *there's* something to look forward to," Vanessa said in a tone dripping with sarcasm. "Which means this whole thing will get worse before it's all said and done."

"Probably." Lydie ran a hand over her face and shook her head. "In the meantime, we need to get ahead of the storm."

"How do we do that?"

"We need to look at what we know—the information we got from my dreams and visions, as well as what your runes and divination pool have told you."

Vanessa sighed. "Yes, but we really don't know what they've told us, do we? I mean, other than most of it being unclear. All we've really known for sure is that death was coming, right?"

"Oh, we've been told much more than that, my friend. We just need to look at it all in context."

"You mean, like putting together a timeline and all the information—no matter how unimportant it may seem—into some kind of form?" Vanessa's eyes lit up. "Like they do on murder mysteries. A murder book or board or something."

Lydie jabbed a finger at Vanessa. "Exactly like that."

"Then I think we should get started. We may not have much time before we get those unwanted visitors."

They spent the next hour laying out and examining everything Vanessa had seen in her runes or divination pool, and everything Lydie could remember from the few prophetic dreams she'd had over the last week.

"So basically, all we still know is that death was coming for someone, and that someone turned out to be Henrietta," Vanessa said with a sigh.

"Nope. We know that Henrietta is just the *first*. Remember my waking vision from yesterday afternoon?"

"The third one with Winnie?" Vanessa frowned "Or was it the fourth?"

"It was the third. The poor woman was screaming and pointing to the same group of women from the first two visions. She said that more death was coming and that we should be vigilant. Then she said that *the third time is the charm*, remember?"

"So, you think that means two more deaths? From that same group?"

Lydie nodded. "That's exactly what I think she meant. Trouble is, we don't know who the unlucky ones are, or why, so we need to do some digging, ask some discreet questions. Maybe we can unearth some answers or at least a trail to follow."

Before Lydie could elaborate, they heard the sound of a car pulling into the driveway. They walked down the hall to the shop and looked out the store windows. It did not ease Lydie's anxiety over the situation when she saw who had just shown up at Lavender Fields. No, it didn't ease her anxiety, yet after her dreams, their visit wasn't unexpected. Lydie had wondered how long it would be before Vanessa's cousin, Detective Nick Sutton, along with his partner, Detective Andy Gilmor would show up.

"Well, that was faster than I'd hoped," Vanessa muttered as they watched Nick and Andy get out of the car. "That's all my day needs. My cousin poking around, asking questions, and looking down his nose at us."

"Vanessa, I know most of your family gives you grief about

our lifestyle, about the craft, but you know that Nick is definitely one of the most tolerant." Lydie put up her hand when Vanessa opened her mouth to argue. "Before you start, I am aware that he's not always above the occasional dig, which tends to strain your relationship from time to time, but you know he just wants you to be happy."

"The occasional dig... and calling our craft *witchy hoo-doo*."

"Now be fair. He only did that once. And he apologized."

Lydie liked Nick, and truth be told, had secretly crushed on him for several years. She found him extremely attractive, with his sandy-brown hair and sharp, green eyes, but she'd often had to play referee during clashes with his cousin, which didn't exactly lend itself to any kind of romantic hook-up. So, although she admired his good looks and snarky sense of humor, she'd left it at that.

Vanessa narrowed her eyes. "You're just taking his side because you've had the hots for him for years," she said, echoing Lydie's thoughts.

"That's not true." At Vanessa's raised eyebrow, Lydie huffed out a breath. "Okay, not *entirely* true. So, what if I find him attractive? Nick's a good-looking guy, and I'm not dead."

At that, Circe, who'd followed them into the shop, meowed dubiously. Glancing down at the cat, Vanessa burst out laughing. "You are so right, Circe. Me thinks she doth protest too much, as well." When Lydie shook her head, Vanessa smiled. "Okay, okay, have it your own way. I'm just saying that Nick and Andy showing up here can't be good and just reinforces the bad omens I've seen in the runes."

"And *I'm* just saying that after what *I* saw in my dream last night, Henrietta has crossed over. And the police showing up here was totally expected. Nick and Andy are here to do their job."

"Yeah, well, I don't have to like it. And Nicholas just better keep to pertinent questions without any snarky comments."

Lydie and Vanessa turned in tandem to the jingling of the bell as the two men entered the shop.

"Well, well. To what do we owe the pleasure of a visit from Durham County's finest?" Vanessa purred. "You boys looking for flowers from the garden? Herbal remedies? We have it all." She turned to her cousin. "Maybe a potion to bring out your nonexistent personality, cuz?"

There was mischief in those bright, green eyes, but Nick only smiled. "Wow, is that really how you're gonna greet your favorite relative, *cuz*?"

Vanessa laughed. "Oh, you think you're my favorite? That's so cute, isn't it, Lydie?"

Nick glanced at Lydie, and she felt the brief flutter in her belly that she experienced every time Nick was around. But she just took a breath and settled herself. "Just adorable, Vanessa. So, are you going to tell us the reason for your visit? Or are we going to continue this goofy conversation?"

Detective Gilmor jumped in. "We need to take statements from both of you."

"Statements?" Vanessa asked with a straight face. "Statements for what?"

"Please." Nick shook his head. "I'm gonna go out on a limb here and say that you both probably know exactly for what."

"Henrietta's illness at the garden party yesterday," Lydie murmured.

"For starters," Andy replied with a grim look. "Unfortunately, Ms. Stone was pronounced dead on arrival at the hospital."

"But you already knew that, didn't you, Lydie?" Nick asked. "It's written all over your very expressive face."

"Yes, I had my suspicions that's how it would end. I was the one to start CPR when she stopped breathing. I sent Winnie Douglas to fetch Dr. Landon, and she took over a few minutes later."

"Well, we need to get a statement from each of you."

"I don't know what *I* can tell you," Vanessa blurted. "I wasn't anywhere near Henrietta's table when it happened."

Nick smirked. "Then I guess your statement will be relatively short, won't it?"

"Ooo, it really annoys me when you take that condescending tone," Vanessa snapped with a frown.

Lydie reached over and put a hand on her partner's arm, giving it a warning squeeze. "Nick's just doing his job, Vanessa. I'm sure he didn't mean to annoy you. Right, Nick?"

With a twinkle in his eye, Nick smiled at her and had those belly flutters starting all over again. "Right, Lydie. Unfortunately, I usually do whether I mean to or not. That said, Andy will be taking your short statement, Van. I'll be taking Lydie's."

With a disparaging huff, Vanessa stomped away down the hall toward the workroom without another word and with Andy scurrying behind her to catch up. Then Nick gave the store a once over before turning to Lydie. "Is there somewhere we can go sit down for this?"

"Sure. We can go into the office."

They followed Vanessa and Andy down the back hallway and veered into the office. Once there, Lydie closed the door behind them and moved to sit behind the big, cherrywood desk, smiling as Nick took a seat on the other side. She glanced out the side window to the flower beds with their riotous colors. The bright yellow of the daffodils, the lovely pinks and deep reds of the tulips, the dark burgundy of the tall hollyhocks standing stately behind them. It reminded her of the festive trappings of yesterday's garden party, and looking back now, that day suddenly felt like a tragedy wrapped up with an elegant, celebratory bow.

"Lydie?"

Nick's deep voice cut into her thoughts, and she looked up into his compassionate gaze.

"I'm sorry, Nick. This is all just so sad. Yesterday was supposed to be a day of lighthearted celebration."

"I know." Nick took out his little notebook and pen and leaned forward. "You want to walk me through what you saw?" he asked quietly.

"I don't know what more I can tell you other than what I told Kelli Landon yesterday, with whom I figure you've already spoken, since she's the M.E. Is there something specific you want to know?"

Nick frowned. "No. I just need to hear about your movements from the time you and Vanessa got to the venue and any interactions you had with Henrietta before the incident."

"I see. Then my visions are spot on, and this wasn't accidental. You're here investigating a suspicious death."

"Dare I ask what visions you're talking about?" Nick gave her a skeptical look.

Lydie raised her eyebrows. "Are you sure you want the answer to that question? Because I've been having waking dreams for the last couple of days that something dark was coming, and yesterday's event played a prominent role. Also, Kelli was putting off some really potent vibes after the ambulance had transported Henrietta, even as she was saying nothing about what she was thinking." She smiled at him again. "Then there was my dream last night that Henrietta was no longer with us on this plane. I've been expecting you all day."

Nick sighed. "Dreams and visions? Vibes? Lydie..."

"I know, I know. You don't want to talk about that. Look, I'm just trying to understand how this all figures into what I've seen, to make sense of it in my mind. But I don't want to make you uncomfortable, so we'll stick to what I witnessed leading up to me having to start CPR."

"I'd appreciate that. Just start at the beginning. What time did you and Van get to the venue?"

"We pulled in at precisely noon, but Darcy Callen and the rest of the team had already been there for a couple of hours to start the set up. Tables, chairs, urns for coffee and tea, dessert table, that sort of thing. We came later with the floral arrangements, linens, tableware, and desserts to finish it all off."

So Lydie started at the beginning, telling Nick about her visions for context—though as she'd said, he really didn't want to know—and how she and Vanessa had felt something coming but could do nothing more than keep a keen eye. When she got to Henrietta's complaint about the tea, he stopped her.

"So, no one else had this same complaint?"

Lydie shook her head vigorously. "Absolutely not. We had nothing but compliments on it. The tea we used is our house blend. We use it almost exclusively for similar parties and events, have for several years. It's nothing new. The fact that Henrietta said it tasted 'floral and bitter' tells me that something extra was added to her cup or original pot, which is why I gave them both to Kelli. If she hasn't gotten the tests back yet, I think you will find that whatever was added is what killed Henrietta."

"Lydie, you do realize that's jumping to an incredible conclusion, right? But if that's true, if this was intentional, it could put Enchanted Affairs and your team square on the suspect list."

She gave him a sad look. "Nick, I would imagine that we already are, but I'm really not worried about that. We haven't done anything wrong and have nothing to hide. And not one of us has any kind of motive to cause Henrietta harm in any way." She narrowed her eyes and raised a finger. "And for that matter, if I was involved, I could've simply dumped the contents of Henrietta's original pot, washed it out along with the cup, and put it back into the service box. No one would have been the wiser."

Nick pinched the bridge of his nose and then gave her a wry smile. "Geez, Lydie, did you forget that you're talking to a law enforcement officer?"

She laughed out loud. "Again, I have nothing to hide, officer. I'm innocent, I tell ya."

"Okay, okay. Very funny." Nick said, chuckling along with her. "But that admission could be taken in the wrong way, perhaps even as a blueprint."

"What? A dastardly plan? My fingerprints aren't even on the pot or cup because the entire team wore food service gloves for the event."

"That makes no difference, nor does it make any of you more innocent. If anything—unless there are clear prints other than Henrietta's on either the pot or the cup—your movements will probably get more scrutiny."

"Yeah, well, bring it." Lydie frowned. "Look, I didn't have to volunteer to give those items along with a sample of our tea blend to Kelli, you know."

Nick sighed and put up a hand in surrender. "Alright. So, after Henrietta's complaint, what happened next?"

"Well, she wasn't at the table when I came back with her fresh pot, but she returned from the ladies' room shortly thereafter. She said the tea had made her sick to her stomach, but Kathryn pointed out that everyone had the same tea so that maybe she was getting the flu or something. But I gotta say, she had some really weird symptoms, so that seems just as unlikely."

Turning a page in his notebook, Nick looked up. "Where were you when Henrietta started the award ceremony?"

"I was standing just off to the side. Vanessa and I were keeping an eye out for anything that might fit with the bad omens we'd seen. And I was watching Henrietta closely because she didn't look good when she came back from the ladies' room. Winnie Douglas offered to handle the awards ceremony, but that just made Henrietta angry, and she yelled at Winnie to go get the honors tub."

"And what happened next?"

"Well, Henrietta took the mic Winnie handed her and began to give out the awards,-even though her condition seemed to be getting worse. Perspiration was pouring from her, and she kept dabbing at her face and neck with a handkerchief. She was also breathing hard and seemed a bit giddy. Then she told Kathryn that she was having trouble reading the awards cards." Lydie shook her head. "Winnie asked if she should get Dr. Landon, and Henrietta was gasping and nodded. Just as I started toward her to see if I could help, the woman cried out and dropped like a bag of cement."

Nick was scribbling a few more things in his notebook, but his head snapped up at that. "Is that when she stopped breathing?"

"No. That's when she went into some kind of convulsions, and I was afraid she was going to bite her tongue. I told Winnie to go get Kelli, and Kathryn to call 911." Lydie closed her eyes briefly, seeing the whole episode clearly in her mind. "Her eyes rolled back in her head, and *that's* when she stopped breathing and I started CPR."

"Uh-huh. Is that it?" Nick asked when Lydie stopped and took a breath.

"Well, about Henrietta, yes." She went on then to tell him about all the steps that she and Dr. Landon had taken once the ambulance had transported Henrietta, the samples the doctor had taken for comparison, the conversations they'd had. "Now that's it."

Nick looked thoughtful for a moment before he closed his notebook and stood. "Well, then I think that's probably all for now, Lydie."

Glancing up at him, she smiled. "Is this the part where you tell me to stay available and not to leave town?"

"Come on, Lydie. Don't even joke about something like that."

"Oh, lighten up, for goodness' sake," she replied and rose to precede him out of the room. "It's all gonna work out, Nick. You'll see."

"Yeah, not so much for Ms. Stone." He gave her a sad look. "But I just hope you're right for all our sakes."

"I am. You'll get to the bottom of this. I have faith in you, Detective."

Nick looked as if he would say something more, but then just shook his head as they headed back to the storefront where Andy and Vanessa were waiting.

As the girls watched Nick and Andy leave the shop, neither said a word until the men had climbed into the non-descript cruiser and headed down the lane.

"So? What did you tell my jerk of a cousin?" Vanessa asked.

"I'll remind you that Nick isn't the bad guy here," Lydie said as they went back to the workroom. Once there, she sat down and sighed. "And I told him the truth. At least everything that I could remember. I also told him about my visions and your issues with your runes and scrying pool."

"Yeah, I can just imagine his contempt for that whole part of your statement. Bet it went over reeeaaally well."

Lydie laughed. "Well, sure, it was obvious that he didn't want to hear it, but he wrote it all down in his notes and was quite decent about it."

Vanessa frowned. "Are we talking about the same Nicholas Sutton? You *have* met him, right?"

"Come on. He's not that bad. What did you tell Andy?"

"What *could* I tell him?" Vanessa asked with a shrug. "I was on the other side of the lawn when it all went down. And besides, unlike you, I didn't feel the need to volunteer any extra information."

"Well, I think you were correct when you thought this would probably get worse before it was all said and done, so we need to step up our game."

"Agreed. If Henrietta was the first of three, we're gonna have to do some more digging."

Lydie nodded. "And start asking some very pertinent questions of our own... discreetly, of course."

"Well, it will have to be with extreme discretion because Nicky doesn't take interference into his investigations well." She grinned at Lydie. "So, where are we gonna start?"

6

By Wednesday morning, as Vanessa and Lydie had expected, Dr. Kelli Landon had finally come by Lavender Fields, as promised, to give them an update on what the samples she had tested disclosed. Vanessa was up front in the shop by herself while Lydie was in the office finishing up the paperwork for the garden party when Kelli arrived.

Vanessa greeted the doctor with a smile as she came into the shop. "Good morning, Kelli."

"Good morning, Vanessa." Dr. Landon smiled weakly in return as she approached the counter, but there was a melancholy look in her chocolate-brown eyes as she glanced around the storefront. "I just love your shop. It always smells so good in here. I may have to pick up a few items before I leave today."

"Well, you know that you're always welcome here at Lavender Fields," Vanessa replied, studying the woman's aura carefully. "And we've got a variety of potions and remedies for tension and worry. We'll find something to fix you right up before you go."

Kelli chuckled. "That obvious, am I?"

"Well, I can see a bit of fatigue and stress in your aura, is all. I doubt anyone else besides Lydie would even notice."

"It has been a very stressful couple of days, hasn't it? And the ER has been crazy-wild."

Yeah, Vanessa could sense there was some difficult news coming. It was written all over the doctor's face as she struggled with how to begin.

Vanessa helped her along. "It has been exhausting, right? So how about we get this terrible business out of the way first, and then we can deal with your stress relief." Vanessa tilted her head and gave the doctor a knowing look. "Lydie and I have been expecting you. Figured you'd probably gotten the results back on the samples from the garden party by now."

"Yes. That is why I'm here."

"Such a sad turn of events. Looks like you may have some disturbing news for us in the wake of Henrietta's death."

"Unfortunately, I do, Vanessa. But it sounds like you already know that."

"Like I said, we've been expecting you. Lydie is in the back office going over paperwork, so why don't we grab a cup of tea and join her there? You can give us both the lowdown at the same time. Come on back."

Vanessa led the doctor down the hall to the little kitchen off the workroom and brewed them both a cup of lavender tea while they made an attempt at small talk. She figured they would need the tea's calming effect for the conversation to come. Lydie had mentioned earlier that after doing a bit of research, and having yet another foretelling dream, she'd developed a theory about what may have killed Henrietta. After doing some research of her own, Vanessa thought she might know what had done the deed, as well, but wanted to wait for the lab tests.

Guess we're about to get the final verdict, she thought as they crossed to the office. Giving the door a couple of raps, Vanessa opened it and entered with the doctor right behind her. "Kelli's here, Lydie. She's got the results of the tests on the samples she took."

"Hey, Kelli," Lydie greeted the doctor. "Good to see you again. Just wish it was under better circumstances."

"I know what you mean." The doctor sighed as she took a seat opposite the desk. "Turns out, this is quite the nasty business."

Lydie nodded. "We figured as much, but like you'd said on Sunday, we wanted to wait for the official results."

The doctor took a sip of her tea. "Well, I guess I'll just get to it then. It turns out that you were right. All the peripheral samples of the tea, as well as the sample baggie of your house blend were exactly the same. And it's a really lovely blend, I might add. Unfortunately, Henrietta's original pot was a different story."

Vanessa nodded. "We've come to the same conclusion. If Henrietta's condition was from an external source, it almost had to have been from that original teapot and something added to it after it was poured."

"Especially when Henrietta complained of the 'flowery, bitter' taste," Lydie added. "That is so not our house blend, and no one else had the same complaint. I'm just angry with myself that I didn't snap to it earlier. Henrietta might have been saved."

Kelli shook her head. "You had no way of knowing what was coming, Lydie."

"Actually, that's not entirely true, Kelli," Vanessa interrupted. "Lydie and I had both seen dark portents of something coming and were actually keeping an eye out for trouble that day."

"What do you mean *dark portents*?"

Lydie spoke up. "I'd had several prophetic dreams and two disturbing waking dreams that alerted me to something dark coming. I just couldn't see what it was."

"Yes, and my runes and divination pool both had reflected the same, that something ominous was on the horizon," Vanessa added leaving out any specifics.

The doctor looked a bit skeptical but nodded. "I see. Well, I can't really speak to any of that, but I will say that you would've been correct. Henrietta's teapot did have a little something extra added to her mix, an ingredient that wasn't in your house blend. I conducted the autopsy yesterday afternoon, and Henrietta had a few health problems that would have hastened the onset of symptoms, but the added ingredient was definitely what killed her."

Vanessa frowned. "And that was?"

"An extract of Aconitum napellus."

"Monkshood," Lydie murmured. "I thought that might be the case."

"Also known as wolfsbane," Vanessa added. "We were on the same page there, Lydie, because I thought so as well. It's such a beautiful perennial herb, and has actually been used for the pain of sciatica, arthritis, and rheumatism."

"Yes, and also some chronic skin problems," Lydie added. "We have a few of the plants out in the south flower garden. But we're very careful with it because every part of that plant contains toxins."

Kelli nodded. "It's also used as a narcotic and a topical anesthetic ointment in Chinese and homeopathic medicine. But why would you have it in your garden? Do you use the herb?"

"Oh, Lord, no." Lydie said. "As you probably know, the process to make it safe to use is very difficult, so like foxglove or hydrangea, we have it in the flower garden for its beauty only."

"In any case, Henrietta's symptoms fit perfectly with monkshood poisoning," Vanessa said.

Lydie nodded. "It's most noted as a heart poison, but from my research, it's also a nerve poison as well, which like you said, matches with Henrietta's symptoms at the garden party just before she went down."

"Correct on all counts. Aconitine is a neurotoxin and the principal alkaloid in most subspecies of monkshood. I've seen aconitine poisonings before, some ending in death, and some patients recovering after a time. But it's very fast-acting and never pleasant."

"And that's what killed her? For sure?" Vanessa asked. "I mean, we don't want to get you in trouble for telling us confidential information or anything."

Kelli smiled. "I've already shared my findings with law enforcement, and Detective Sutton, who is handling the case, knows I was coming out here today. I can't speak to an ongoing investigation, but I can say that there was a high concentration of aconitine in Henrietta's teapot. Even a few swallows could have done the trick, and from what you told me, Lydie, she drank the better part of a cup, which was reflected in her tox report."

"That would mean whoever added it to Henrietta's tea knew exactly what they were doing," Vanessa said. "And considering we were at a Garden Society event, there were any number of women there who would have the expertise to do this."

"Yeah, but why?" Lydie asked quietly.

"Well, not to speak ill of the dead, but Henrietta wasn't the most well-liked member of the Society, right?" Vanessa shook her head. "You know full well that she was incredibly hard to deal with and pretty mean-spirited and petty most of the time."

Lydie frowned. "Sure. But I can't see how that would have been enough to want her dead. And besides, that could describe several women who attended the event."

"I don't know. Some people are just plain crazy. I'd like to think that anyone who I'm acquainted with would not be capable of doing something so heinous as poisoning someone, but then again, do we ever really know what each of us are capable of? And I did talk to a couple of ladies on Sunday who weren't shy about how much Henrietta was disliked. Barbara Drake for one, and she was pretty vicious about it."

Kelli nodded. "I know. Doris Mayfield ran against Henrietta for the presidency and there was talk going around that Henrietta didn't exactly play fair during their respective campaigns. Doris has said some really terrible things about Henrietta if the idle gossip is to be believed. I can't see that as a motive for murder, though, but I've seen some disturbing things in the ER over the last several months... and it doesn't seem to be getting much better."

"But craziness aside, what I'd like to know is how the poison got into Henrietta's teapot," Lydie said. "I mean, the pots were in the pavilion on trays marked for the specific tables, but no one could have known which pot would end up with which woman."

Vanessa pointed a finger at her partner. "That's true. Which means that the deed was either random and whoever did it didn't care who was poisoned, which would indicate some sort of a serial killer scenario. To my mind that's both doubtful and ludicrous. Or it would have had to have been done at the table after the pots were set out, when it was obvious where Henrietta was sitting and which teapot was hers."

"That makes sense," Kelli replied. "But in that scenario, it would have taken some major stones to spike Henrietta's pot with so many people milling around. I'd think the chance of being seen would've been really high."

Lydie laughed. "You would think, right? But sometimes in plain sight is the best cover. Anyway, I appreciate you coming out here to tell us what you found. We've already had a visit from Durham County's finest, so I imagine we'll get another visit, especially since we deal in all sorts of herbs here at Lavender Fields, including the few innocent monkshood plants in our garden."

Vanessa snorted. "Let 'em come. My cousin better have his ducks in a row if they come back out here."

"Oh, my gosh. Nick Sutton is your cousin," Kelli blurted. "I'd totally forgotten that. Now that you mention it, he did say that he would be stopping by."

"And as we've established previously, Vanessa, Nick is just doing his job. So, we will continue to cooperate as much as we can, won't we?" Lydie asked with a cheesy smile.

"Whatever."

"At least we know that Henrietta was poisoned, with what, and how it was administered. Now we just need to figure out who did it, when, and why."

Kelli frowned. "Isn't that a job for the police... like you just said?"

Vanessa cleared her throat and gave Lydie a meaningful look. "You are absolutely correct. I'm sure that's what Lydie meant, right, pal?"

"Of course. Don't be silly. It was just a figure of speech."

"Anyhoo. Why don't we go out to the shop and find you that stress relief potion we talked about, Kelli? I think I know just the thing."

Vanessa rolled her eyes at Lydie as she followed Kelli out of the office. They were going to have to be much more discreet so as not to raise any red flags if they were going to do more digging in the days to come. Nick would pop a vein if he found out they were investigating right under his nose. Although, the thought did make Vanessa smile.

Twenty minutes later, after seeing Kelli off, Vanessa went back to the office to debrief with Lydie.

"So? Thoughts?" she asked as she plopped down into the chair that Kelli had vacated.

Lydie closed her laptop and sighed. "Well, Kelli's information was not unexpected to either one of us, right? I think we were both contemplating monkshood as the poison before she got the results back."

"Correct. It all lined up, and combined with your visions and my runes, it seemed to make the most sense."

"And we're both in agreement that this was intentional?"

"Absolutely. No way this was an accident."

"Good, but here's my issue. I keep coming back to the logistics."

"I know. I've been thinking about that, too. We'd both been given a heads-up on something dark coming, but without knowing what it would look like, we were concentrating on anything that caught our attention—anything obvious. I never thought to be on the lookout for something small and inconspicuous, which spiking Henrietta's pot would have had to have been."

"Agreed." Lydie looked thoughtful. "You know, the only thing I noticed that's been tickling the back of my mind is that we saw Doris Mayfield go into the pavilion and was right there where the pots were sitting just prior to distribution."

"Yes." Vanessa nodded. "And as I recall, she was quite jumpy when you asked her if she needed anything. Said something about having allergies and checking on ingredients." She waved a hand in the air. "Which would be a perfectly plausible explanation on any other occasion, but looking back, now seems a little suspicious in combination with her nervous demeanor. Though I'll admit, that could just be my suspicious mind conjuring details."

Vanessa thought for a moment. "Also, another thing that bothers me is that the buffet table was already set up at that point. There wasn't much food left in the pavilion with the exception of replenishment portions. And why not seek one of us out if she had those kinds of questions? If she wanted to know anything about ingredients, we would have been the ones to ask."

"All true. But there again, if she was the one to poison the tea, how would she have known which pot was Henrietta's even if she could have spiked it without Carrie or Sug noticing? And that would've taken some stealth. After all, they were both right there as well."

Vanessa put up a finger. "So... here's another terrible thought. What if it wasn't Henrietta that was being targeted?"

"What do you mean?"

"The teapots were loaded on trays marked for the individual tables, right?"

"Go on."

"Well, there were at least five women per table and five pots. What if the intended victim wasn't Henrietta but one of the other women at that specific table?"

Lydie blanched. "That is a terrible thought."

"Think about your visions, Lydie. There was always a group of the same women in each one, right?"

"Yes. But there were two women at Henrietta's table that I didn't even know and that weren't in any of my visions. So, other than Henrietta, that only leaves Kathryn Wilks-Raymond and Winnie Douglas, both of whom *were* in my visions."

"Okay. And you said initially that you were worried about Winnie. Plus, she played a major role each time, didn't she?"

"Yes, but she was the one indicating that danger was coming. She was pointing at the group of women in the background." Lydie shook her head. "And there's still the issue of knowing which pot was for which woman, regardless of who the intended victim was going to be."

Vanessa sighed. "I guess that brings us back to square one."

Silence reigned for a few moments as they both pondered what they'd learned. Then Lydie looked up and shook her head. "No, my gut tells me that our initial conclusion is the correct one.

I think Henrietta was the intended victim, and the poison had to be added to her pot at the table."

"So, you think one of the other women at the table did the deed? Kathryn or Winnie? Or maybe one of the two women you didn't know?"

Lydie scrubbed her hands over her face in frustration. "I don't know what to think at this point. Again, Winnie was the one in my visions who told me death was coming, so I'm not inclined to think she would be the one responsible. And besides, if it was one of the other women at the table, they had to have known that they would be the first ones on the suspect list the minute Henrietta's death was made public."

"True, but with so many women arriving, all of them moving around and socializing at the beginning of the event, they'd have had to be stealthy, but literally, anyone could have spiked that teapot once it was on the table in Henrietta's place."

"There is one other thing we need to take into account."

"What's that?"

"That Henrietta was only the first."

Vanessa sat forward at that. "Oh, geez! I'd forgotten about your vision where Winnie was saying 'third time is the charm.' Cripes, just what we need. More death to worry about." She narrowed her eyes. "You have any bright ideas about who could be next? Anything you remember in those visions that could be an indicator?"

"Unfortunately, no. I told you everything I could remember at the time."

Vanessa grabbed a pen and pad from the desk as an idea came to her. "All right. How about this? Close your eyes and think back. Tell me exactly which women were in the group that Winnie was pointing to in your visions. Maybe that will give us at least a possible starting point."

Lydie raised an eyebrow. "Really?"

Vanessa mirrored her look. "You have a better idea?"

They stared at each other for a few moments before, with a resigned sigh, Lydie took a deep breath and did as she was told. After a moment, she began. "Okay, in both visions, Winnie was standing a bit off to the side and gesturing toward the group. Henrietta was in the center in both visions with the others standing around her."

"Who were the others, Lydie? Give me their names."

Lydie's eyes moved back and forth beneath her lids as if she was perusing the group of women in her vision. "Barbara Drake and Kathryn Wilks-Raymond were on one side of Henrietta with Betty Morgan, and Glenda Beaumont standing just behind them."

"Betty wasn't even at the event on Sunday. Glenda's sister Margot is her neighbor and told me that Betty's been in the hospital for a couple of weeks recovering from surgery, so it seems like she would be out of harm's way. But we'll leave her on the list for now. Keep going."

"On the other side of Henrietta... Doris Mayfield, Letitia Edwards... and Margot."

"Interesting. Anyone else in the frame?"

"Um... no... wait... yes. Anna Ingram was standing just behind Margot." Opening her eyes, Lydie blew out a breath. "That's it. Those were the women in both visions."

Vanessa gave her a grim look. "Okay, then. If your visions are correct, and we should expect two more murders, then two of these women are next on the hit list. So, how do we go about figuring out which two?"

Lydie frowned. "I have no earthly idea, pal. But we better get a handle on it quick, because I have a strong feeling that time is running out for someone."

7

Despite the restless night and more snippets of ominous dreams, the next morning dawned bright and clear with glorious rays of sunshine streaming through the plate glass windows of the storefront as Lydie set about opening shop. Vanessa had a doctor's appointment down the coast, so she wouldn't be in until the early afternoon. In the meantime, Lydie had plans to get some of their more popular herb packets and potions started for replenishing the shelves of the shop. Her favorite UPS driver arrived about ten-thirty with some much-needed supplies, including the new book she'd ordered on herbal remedies, and a fresh collection of crystals that they'd been awaiting.

She'd just finished putting the supplies away and was about to check out her new book when she heard a car pulling into the parking lot. Expecting the much-anticipated visit from Nick and Andy for additional grilling over Henrietta's death, she was surprised to see Winnie Douglas getting out of her car when she went out to the shop.

Lydie greeted her as she came through the door. "Well, good morning to you, Winnie. Lovely day to be out and about."

"Hey, Lydie. I'm sorry for dropping in unannounced, but I wanted to get the check to you for the garden party on Sunday." Winnie rummaged around in her humongous bag, supposedly for said check, looking as if she wanted to be anywhere but there.

Lydie shook her head. "No need for apologies, Winnie. The check could have waited, but that being said, you are always welcome here."

Winnie looked nervously around the shop. "Yes, well, that's very kind of you. The garden party was really first rate. Everyone said so. You, Vanessa, and your team did a wonderful job." She stopped fidgeting long enough to give Lydie a tortured look, then suddenly blurted, "Oh, Lydie, I just feel so badly about the horrible way the party ended on Sunday. I can't seem to put it out of my mind."

"Yes, Henrietta's death was a tragedy on such a beautiful Sunday meant for fellowship and fun." With a sigh, she came around the counter and took the woman's trembling hand. "I can see that you're quite upset about it all... and geez, Winnie, your hand is cold as stone. Why don't you come on back to the workroom with me, and I'll make you a nice cup of lavender tea. It'll calm you and warm you up a bit. Then you can tell me what's on your mind, because I can see there's something really bothering you."

Winnie took a deep breath and let it out slowly. "Yes, a cup of your tea would be lovely. Thank you, Lydie. This week has been very stressful in light of Henrietta's death. I-I'm afraid I don't cope well with stress these days."

Lydie wasn't sure if Winnie Douglas had ever coped well with stress, given her anxious disposition, but she just nodded as she led the way back to the workroom.

"Now, you just sit down right there, and I'll be back in a jiffy with your tea," Lydie said, gesturing to one of the overstuffed armchairs in the small reading area in the corner.

It didn't take Lydie long, as she'd recently heated the pot, and Winnie seemed a bit calmer when she came back with the tea. "Here we are," Lydie said as she handed the woman the cup and sat down in the matching chair with a cup of her own. "Now, why don't you tell me exactly what has you so upset—besides Henrietta's passing, that is?"

Winnie took a sip of her tea and then nodded. "I don't know. Like I said, I haven't been able to think about anything else, since the garden party. And then... well, I've just come from Margot Beaumont's house and heard some very disturbing news."

Knowing Margot, I'm sure you did, Lydie thought, but said, "Now, Winnie, not to be disrespectful, but you know how Margot tends to embellish a story. Why would you let her upset you this way?"

"Oh, I know. She likes to spread rumors, and she sometimes exaggerates, but she does keep an ear to the ground, Lydie."

More like an ear out for unfounded gossip.

"Well, what did she tell you that troubled you so much?"

Winnie set her cup on the small table between the chairs and leaned forward. "She said that Anna Ingram told her that Letitia Edwards had heard that the police are treating Henrietta's death as suspicious."

Bad news sure does travel like lightning.

Lydie could just well imagine the gossip chain that had spread that line of thought and wondered what other little tidbits Winnie had heard.

With another sigh, Lydie nodded. "I can tell you that they are indeed investigating Henrietta's death as suspicious, so in that regard, Margot, or should I say Letitia, is correct."

And I can't believe I just said that sentence out loud.

With a devastated look, Winnie put a hand to her chest and added in almost a whisper as if someone might overhear, "She also said someone may have actually poisoned Henrietta... intentionally."

And I wonder where Letitia heard that...

"Well, there is definitely that possibility, but I wouldn't speculate just yet on what suspicious activity may be afoot. I think waiting until the medical examiner has made her final conclusion is probably the best thing, don't you?" she asked, not wanting to add to Winnie's distress just yet with facts they already knew. Those would be made public soon enough. "I mean, I know Henrietta could be a bit overbearing, but who on earth would've wanted to poison her? And what could Henrietta have done that was so bad that someone thought she deserved a death by poisoning?"

"Well, you know I don't like to repeat gossip but..."

When Winnie sat back and didn't finish her thought, Lydie prompted, "Yes?"

The woman screwed up her face. "Oh, I really shouldn't."

Lydie tried not to let her impatience show. Nonchalantly, she picked up her own cup. "Winnie, if you don't feel like you can say, I completely understand. I wouldn't want for you to feel pressured to tell me anything that would make you uncomfortable or that was told to you in confidence."

Taking a slow sip of her tea, Lydie just waited. She could feel Winnie's conflicted emotions pouring out of her. There was something there that she knew, something that possibly pertained to Henrietta's death, Lydie was sure of it. And the woman was worried.

After a moment, Winnie did indeed cave. "Oh, well, it's nothing confidential, you understand. Just a few things that I've heard or ran across in recent months. I suppose it would help to get it off my chest, right?"

Lydie gave her a sympathetic look. "Well, I know it always helps me to run things by Vanessa when I'm troubled."

Winnie brightened a bit. "That's exactly it, isn't it?"

With a smile that hid her mounting frustration, Lydie made a noncommittal sound.

"So, there are a couple of things I know of that were hanging over Henrietta's head that only a few select people knew. Things that would cause quite an uproar if they were made public knowledge. One of which was the lengths Henrietta went to during this last Society election cycle."

"Oh? Is that so?"

"Yes. Poor Doris Mayfield." Winnie shook her head solemnly. "By rights, she should've won that election, Lydie. Some people have guessed there may have been impropriety there, but I know for a fact that it was out and out election tampering by Henrietta and perhaps others working on her behalf."

"How do you know that? And what was done?"

"Oh... I'd rather not say or go into any details. It's all just a bit sordid. Anyway, let's just leave it at Henrietta wasn't going to let anyone take the presidency away from her, and she took concrete and unethical steps to make sure that didn't happen."

"That's really awful, Winnie. But look, while I do feel bad for Doris, I can't imagine it would be enough for her or someone else to want Henrietta dead over it?"

"Oh, I'm not saying that was what happened. Though with Henrietta's death, Doris will now probably be voted into the position in a special election vote anyway. I'm just saying that maybe someone should speak with her about it, and also Barbara Drake, for that matter."

"Why Barbara, Winnie?"

"Well, you know Barbara. She doesn't pull any punches, and she was just furious with the outcome of the election. Even though she didn't have any proof, she knew something hinky had taken place and was quite outspoken about it."

"You know, now that you say that, I do recall something

Vanessa told me that Barbara said at the start of the event. She said something to the effect that Doris would've won if Henrietta hadn't cheated, but Henrietta would get hers in the end. Whatever that meant."

"That sounds like Barbara. She can be quite... uncharitable, if you know what I mean. Anyway, it's just one of the things that keeps circling in my mind." Picking up her cup, Winnie took another sip of her tea and stared off into space for a moment with a frown on her face. "Then there was the financial issue," she added, almost under her breath.

"I'm sorry? Did you say a financial issue?" Lydie sat forward. "What financial issue?"

Winnie seemed to come back to herself, and realizing what she'd said, hesitated again. "Oh, well... there was... an audit discrepancy of a little over fifteen thousand dollars from the Garden Society's money market fund about eight months ago. I only found out about it a while ago myself and quite by accident." She looked pained. "See, I dropped by the Society office one day a few months back to give Kathryn some paperwork, and overheard her and Henrietta arguing about it when they thought they were alone. It was just bad timing on my part. I wasn't eavesdropping. I really wasn't."

Lydie nodded. "I know how those things can happen."

"I didn't hear the entire conversation, and I slipped out before they knew I was there, but I did hear Kathryn say that Henrietta had to make it right."

"Make it right? You mean, by paying back the money? Was Kathryn insinuating that Henrietta was responsible for the discrepancy?"

Winnie gave a small shrug. "I guess."

"That would be embezzlement, Winnie."

The woman's head bobbed up and down quickly. "I know. That was what was so disturbing to me."

"What was Henrietta's response?"

"She said that Kathryn should be very careful—should keep her mouth shut if she knew what was good for her."

Lydie set her cup down. "That is a much more substantial problem than election tampering, and with Kathryn being treasurer, maybe for both of them. But I still don't see why anyone would want to kill Henrietta over fifteen thousand dollars of Society money. I mean, prosecution maybe, but murder seems like a stretch."

"I know. Doesn't make any sense, does it? I just hope the police will get to the bottom of it. But I really think they need to talk to both Doris and Kathryn, don't you?"

Lydie nodded. "It definitely sounds that way, and perhaps, Barbara as well. Of course, it may all be unrelated."

"I hate to say it, but I also think that maybe they should talk to Anna about the Society finances, too."

"Anna? You mean, Anna Ingram?"

Winnie nodded. "Anna was the treasurer for the Society when Henrietta was first elected president. From what I understand, they didn't have a very good working relationship." The woman took a final sip from her cup and sighed. "Evidently, Anna didn't care for some of Henrietta's finance choices and what she saw as questionable donations. Henrietta replaced her with Kathryn when her term was up. She was definitely not happy about the whole thing."

Lydie shook her head. "Wow. Sounds like there is a lot of information to be had by interviewing some of these women. But again, these issues may all be unrelated, and the police are just calling Henrietta's death suspicious. So, it doesn't necessarily mean that her death was intentional for any of these reasons. We should probably wait for the police to complete their investigation and not speculate."

With that, Winnie set her cup down on the table and stood.

"You are absolutely right, Lydie. And thank you for listening to me ramble." She collected her bag and smiled. "It did help my anxiety to get my worries out. I feel much better, like you said, just running it all by someone."

"You're very welcome," Lydie replied as she stood and walked the woman out to the shop. "Winnie... have you told anyone else what you know?"

"Oh, no."

"Margot, maybe?"

"No, no, like I said, I don't like to spread gossip. I've only told you as you're not involved in the Society—an outside party—and I figured you wouldn't tell anyone else, right?"

"Who would I tell?" Lydie smiled. "No, Winnie, I won't tell anyone what you've told me. But in light of Henrietta's death being classified as suspicious, until the police investigation gets to the bottom of things, I think you should be careful who you tell. Just to be on the safe side."

Winnie's brows drew together. "You know, I never thought about that," she murmured slowly. "I suppose that's pretty good advice. Thank you, Lydie. I will be careful. And thanks again for the tea and an ear for my neurotic ramblings."

Lydie laughed. "You bet. Glad I could help. And if you feel the need for more rambling, you just come by any time."

Winnie was about to leave when she stopped and slapped a hand to her forehead. "Where is my brain today?" She sat her bag on the counter and began to rummage again. "I came out here to give you your check and then forgot all about it." She pulled out an envelope and handed it to Lydie. "The Society appreciates the excellent services Enchanted Affairs always provides. It was splendid, really."

"It was our pleasure."

Thinking about all the things she'd just learned, Lydie watched the woman walk to her car and then slowly drive away.

She didn't know how much of what Winnie had told her—if any of it—had played into Henrietta's death, but these new issues she'd raised definitely could use some follow-up. And Lydie would run it all by Vanessa when she got back later this afternoon. With those thoughts swirling in her head, she went to get started on the potions and herb packets for the storefront.

It was going on one o'clock when Lydie finished up with the packets and was just contemplating brewing up some of the potions, when she heard another vehicle pull into the lot. She was hoping it was Vanessa, but this time, it was Durham County's finest, at last. Lydie had thought Vanessa would be back before they arrived. She wasn't keen on meeting with Nick and Andy on her own, but she was certain that Vanessa would be glad she'd missed the visit.

"Hey, Lydie," Nick greeted her as they came into the shop. "Got a minute for a few more questions?"

"Of course, Nick. Kelli dropped by yesterday, as I'm sure you know, so we've been expecting you. Unfortunately, I'm on my own this afternoon. Vanessa had a doctor's appointment down the coast."

"No worries. We've just got a couple of follow-up questions in light of how Ms. Stone died."

"Well, we better go back to the office then."

Lydie led the way, and when they were all seated, she gave Nick a wry look. "So, what kind of follow up questions did you have?"

Nick pulled out his little notebook and thumbed through it to a specific page. "Well, I'm sure Dr. Landon explained that aconitine poisoning was the cause of death, and that it was also found in Ms. Stone's teapot, which was how she was poisoned."

"Yes, Kelli told us that yesterday during her visit."

"Do you know where aconitine comes from?" Andy asked.

Lydie gave him a tolerant smiled. "Yes, Andy. I do know where aconitine comes from. Aconitum napellus, or more commonly known as monkshood or wolfsbane. It's a flowering plant."

"You deal with all sorts of flowering plants here, herbs and stuff, don't you? Is this monkshood something you'd stock for your customers?"

"Good Lord, no," Lydie replied heatedly. "It's extremely poisonous."

"But it does have medicinal qualities, right?"

"It does, yes. It's been popular in homeopathic and traditional Chinese medicine for literally thousands of years. It's used to treat all sorts of issues like migraines, arthritis, asthma, even common infections, but it mostly stopped being used here in the U.S. in the twentieth century." Lydie frowned. "Why?"

Andy tilted his head and gave her a thoughtful look. "Do you have any of these plants on the property?"

Lydie sighed. "Yes, we have a couple out in the south flower garden. Again, why do you ask?"

"But you don't use them as herbs?"

"No, Andy. Like I said, aconitum is extremely toxic. And to be able to use it medicinally requires a lengthy process. The only few monkshood plants we have are in our *flower garden*."

"Lydie, why would you have monkshood in your flower garden if it's so poisonous and you don't use it in your herb remedies?" Nick asked. "Seems like that would be a concern."

"It's in our flower garden because it's a beautiful flowering plant, Nick." Lydie shook her head. "And I'll give you another tidbit. That's not the only poisonous flowering plant out there. Geez, do you have any idea how many really common flowers are actually toxic or poisonous to humans?"

"Common flowers?" Andy asked, scratching his head. "You mean, like normal flowers?"

Lydie laughed out loud without humor. "Yes, Andy. Like normal flowers. Like daffodils and bleeding hearts. Like irises and lily of the valley. Certain lilies, tulips, rhodies, azaleas, wisteria—they all have some degree of toxicity. Several are quite dangerous to humans. Then there's the really nasty flowers like angel's trumpet that smell so good but will kill you dead. There's belladonna—deadly nightshade. For the love of God, as kids, we used foxglove spears as swords, completely oblivious to the fact that every part of the plant is toxic to humans."

"Okay, okay, I get it." Andy put up his hands in surrender and sat back with a grin. "Just askin'."

Lydie took a deep breath and blew it out slowly. "Look, if aconitine was found in Henrietta's teapot, I don't know how it would have gotten there. But it didn't come from Lavender Fields."

"Was there an opportunity that you can see for someone to have added it to Ms. Stone's pot before it was brought to the table?" Nick asked.

"Vanessa and I have talked about that. I don't see how." Lydie ran a hand through her hair as she glanced out the window at the beautiful day beyond. "All the teapots were the same, Nick, and loaded onto trays marked for each table. If someone wanted to doctor Henrietta's pot, there would have been no way to know which pot would be hers until they were placed on the table. Plus, both Carrie and Sug were right there the whole time. They were the ones that took the teapots to the tables. They would've seen it happen if adding the poison took place in the pavilion." Looking back at Nick, she shook her head. "If this was a deliberate act, and Vanessa and I think it was, it had to have been done once the pots were at the tables."

Andy leaned forward. "But with so many women around, somebody surely would have seen it happen."

Nick narrowed his eyes as he glanced at Lydie. "Sometimes in plain sight is the safest bet," he murmured.

"Exactly what I said to Vanessa yesterday," she replied.

With a quick nod, Nick stood. "Okay, I think that's it for now. But before we go, can we just take a quick look at the south flower bed and your poisonous flowers growing there?" He ended the question with a flash of a grin.

Shaking her head and giving him a reluctant smile in return, she grumbled, "Come on then. If it's something you feel strongly about, and it will get you out of my hair, let's get this over with."

"Has he lost his ever-lovin' *mind*?" Vanessa shouted when she finally got back to the shop, and Lydie related the events of the afternoon, specifically the account of Nick and Andy's visit. "Nicholas made you traipse out to the flower garden for what? See if we've been snipping pieces off the monkshood plants in order to poison random people? How completely idiotic!"

Lydie snickered as she watched her partner pace around the workroom and rant.

"And Andy, the bonehead. *Like normal flowers?*" she made a face as she mimicked him. "Seriously? What is wrong with men?"

"It was a bit amusing. You should have seen Andy's face when I started to name those *normal flowers* that are totally poisonous. If I wasn't so annoyed, it would have been funny."

"Well, I'm not amused in the least. Insinuating that we might have had something to do with Henrietta's death. It's just insulting."

"It did seem to satisfy them both for the moment, though. So, that's a good thing." Lydie stabbed a finger in Vanessa's direction. "But Winnie's visit was highly informative."

"Yeah. Seems like we have several promising victims... or suspects. Hard to tell at this point. And I'd completely forgotten what Barbara had said to me at the start of the garden party about Henrietta getting hers in the end." Vanessa frowned. "But

I'm with you. I just don't see any of it leading to murder by poisoning."

"Agreed. So, I think we need to check into everything Winnie told me. And speak to Barbara, Kathryn, Doris, and maybe Anna. They all were in my visions."

Vanessa nodded. "And it seems that they all may have had something against Henrietta. But we'll need to watch our step. We don't know who was involved in this. If one of them poisoned Henrietta, we don't want to become victims ourselves."

"Good point. I say we start with Doris tomorrow. See what she has to say for herself and then go from there. Because someone at that garden party murdered Henrietta Stone, and right under our noses."

8

Nick arrived at the station an hour early on Friday morning, intent on getting his notes organized and case board updated with the information they'd received. He had a specific way of working and never deviated. It was definitely a cliché—something you'd see in a bunch of different television shows on the tube—but his case board helped him see the big picture at any point during an investigation. His notes also helped to hone all the data on the board down to the most important facts.

It was difficult to have family and friends involved so closely in one of his murder investigations this way, but in a small town like Seal Cove, it proved almost impossible to avoid. And every instinct Nick had told him that this was indeed a murder. Someone had intentionally spiked Henrietta Stone's tea with a good dose of aconitine. And at a Garden Society party, the suspect pool of those who'd have the knowledge to do so was pretty broad. As the chief investigator on the case, he would need to be extra careful so as not to look biased in any way toward those he was close to. It was the reason he'd had Andy interview his cousin the first time they'd been out to Lavender

Fields, and why he'd let him take the lead with Lydie the day before.

Nick smiled to himself as he thought about the stellar way Lydie had handled the tough questions during their Thursday interview. She'd been angry, that much was obvious, but had shot down every notion of involvement quite handily.

Glancing up at the board, he studied the list of suspects. Enchanted Affairs wasn't off his list... yet. But his gut said the company and those working there had nothing to do with the murder other than their tea being used as the vehicle for the poison. Nevertheless, until he had more concrete proof to exclude them, they would all stay on the list.

By the time Nick had updated his case board and consolidated his notes, Andy came hustling through the door. "Okay, seriously? It's only five to nine. I'm five minutes early for shift. How long have you been here?" Andy asked as he set down his bag. "Please tell me that you actually went home last night and didn't sleep here."

"Very funny." Nick made a face. "Yes, I went home last night... around nine. I've only been here for a little over an hour. I just wanted to get the board updated and organize my thoughts before we got started."

"Just checking. I know how you get with these kinds of intense investigations."

Nick narrowed his eyes. "What's that supposed to mean?"

"Obsessive, my friend. Very obsessive." Andy pulled his own notebook out of his bag and thumbed through it absently before looking up with a grin. "It's okay, buddy. I know you can't help yourself. It's what makes you a great detective."

"Yeah, yeah, whatever." Nick gave Andy a thoughtful look. "So, we're on the same page here, right? Not accidental or just suspicious but definitely homicide."

"Absolutely. No way Henrietta Stone's death was accidental,

not with hers being the only teapot at the event that was poisoned. That's targeted, man." Andy shook his head. "I just can't see how we're gonna figure out how it was done, who did it, and why."

Nick laughed at Andy's befuddled look. "That's why it's called an investigation, pal. We investigate until we find those answers, and then somebody goes to jail."

Andy smirked. "Yeah, now who's being funny?"

Nick considered for a moment. "You know you're not wrong about how hard this is gonna be. I mean, the logistics alone are pretty daunting, especially with what Lydie told us yesterday."

"About the way the teapots were filled?"

"Exactly. The pots were on trays marked for the tables but not for the individual women. It would have been impossible to know which teapot was Henrietta's while the trays were still in the pavilion. And like she said, both Carrie and Sug were right there the whole time. No, the poison would have had to have been added to her pot at the table."

"Unless Carrie and Sug were in on it together to deviously poison Henrietta's pot before they brought it to the table," Andy suggested, tongue-in-cheek.

Nick chuckled. "An interesting, if implausible, theory."

"I still say with so many women wandering around the event, someone had to have seen something."

"Maybe, but not necessarily. It's true. Someone could have seen something odd but not really registered what they were seeing or how important it was." Nick shook his head and looked at his notes. "Granted, there was a small window before Henrietta and the others sat down at the table, but there was time. Someone could have breezed by, dumped the poison into the pot, and kept moving."

"Man, they would have had to be pretty stealthy and have friggin' balls of steel, right?"

"Indeed. Although, under certain circumstances, maybe just a bit of diversion—a slight misdirection—would be all it would take to get the job done."

"I just don't even know where to start with this. I mean, so many choices."

"I know." Turning, Nick looked up at his, as yet, sparsely populated board. "And if the lab tells us that Henrietta's prints were the only ones on the cup and teapot, we'll have a deeper hole to climb out of." He shook his head. "Okay, speaking of holes, let's do some digging."

"Starting with some background on our victim?"

"Yes. Where did she live? Are there relatives in the area that we can interview? Friends? We'll also look at financials, bank records, etc. Was this personal? A grudge, maybe? Or possibly about money? We need to pinpoint what Ms. Stone could have done that was bad enough to make her a target for murder."

Andy flipped back through his notebook again. "Well, from what I've heard, she was really disliked by almost everyone who knew her. And I mean, *really* disliked. So, finding friends may be a stretch." The detective leaned a hip on his desk. "You know, my mom knows a handful of Garden Society members. And yesterday, she told me that nobody she knows or has spoken to had even one good thing to say about Henrietta Stone. That they were all confused as to how the woman was re-elected as Society president, for a third term, I might add. Mom said, and I quote, 'No one knows anyone who actually voted for the woman.'"

"Alright, possible election tampering at a gardener's club. So what? Is that really enough to want her dead?"

Laughing out loud, Andy ran a hand through his hair. "Buddy, these gardeners take their *club* very seriously." He looked back at his notes. "Mom said that Doris Mayfield is well liked by just about everyone and was the favorite to win. Everyone was stunned—her words, not mine—when she lost to

Stone. Evidently, she was pretty steamed about it, too. Also, a Barbara Drake was very vocal about possible election fraud on Stone's part, yammering on about it to anyone who would listen."

"Okay, I guess that's as good a place as any to start. Let's get a hold of both women. We'll start with those interviews this morning, then come back and do some financial digging later or first thing tomorrow."

As it turned out, Andy only got through to Doris Mayfield's voicemail, so he'd left a message that they wanted to meet. However, Barbara Drake was all too happy to have a chat.

"Thanks for making the time to talk with us, Ms. Drake," Nick began as they sat down with the woman in her elegant living room. "We'll try not to take up too much of your time."

"Oh, that's no problem, Detective. And please, call me Barbara," she purred with a seductive smile.

Nick smiled back at her. "Alright, Barbara, what can you tell us about Henrietta Stone?"

Barbara laughed out loud. "Are you sure you want to hear all I can tell you about that intolerable woman?"

"So, you didn't think much of Ms. Stone?" Andy asked.

"That's putting it mildly, Detective, but no, I didn't *think much* of her. Why? Does that make me a suspect?"

"A suspect?"

"Well, come on. I'm not dimwitted. I've heard that you're investigating her untimely demise as a 'suspicious death.' Are you looking around for anyone who may have wanted to do her in?" Barbara grinned. "If so, you're going to have a really long list."

"And that list? Would it include you?"

"Ha! Absolutely," she replied with an amused look.

Nick leaned forward in his chair, eager to get the woman back on track. "What we actually wanted to talk to you about was the Garden Society election."

"Ah, yes. The sham."

"You were pretty vocal about the possibility of election tampering."

"There was nothing so trifling as tampering going on, Detective. The election was out and out rigged—and by Henrietta Stone."

"How do you know that, Barbara? Do you have concrete evidence?"

"No. I haven't got proof, but I challenge you to find one member of the Society who voted for that corrupt witch," she replied in a terse tone. She crossed her slim legs and smoothed a hand over her sleek, blonde chignon. "I'm positive if you go through the Society records you'll find all the evidence you need that Doris Mayfield was the rightful winner. That is, if Henrietta didn't destroy the actual election records as well, which I definitely wouldn't put past her."

"And Doris Mayfield?" Andy asked. "How did she take the results?"

The woman laughed out loud again. "Oh, Doris was furious. She even confronted Henrietta, and I know they had a rip-roaring argument about it at the Society office a few days after the election. Doris demanded a recount."

"And how did that turn out?"

"Well, Henrietta denied everything, didn't she? Big surprise. And without the required twenty-five Society member's signatures, she dismissed Doris' request for a recount out of hand. Said Doris was just a sore loser, that it would be a sad day when someone like Doris could beat her in an election. Blah, blah, blah. God, she was such a heinous cow."

When Andy looked surprised at her answer, Barbara chuckled. "Oh, don't look so shocked, Detective. I have no guilt over speaking ill of this particular dead woman. I would be a complete hypocrite not to say exactly what I thought of her, wouldn't I? After all, I've always made my feelings about Henrietta Stone perfectly clear." She waved a hand in the air. "Anyway, if you're looking for the real skinny on all of Henrietta's various bits of malfeasance, you should talk to her bestie, Kathryn Wilks-Raymond. They were thick as the thieves they are. I dare say, Kathryn will have quite the bag of dirt to fuel your investigation and give you a much clearer picture of your victim."

Nick noted Kathryn's name, and then pocketed his pen and notepad. "Well, I think that's all for now, Barbara. But one last question. Do you know where aconitine comes from?"

A slow smile spread across the former beauty queen's face. "Ooo, is that how the rotten woman died? Aconitine poisoning? How very delicious... and completely apropos."

"So, you do know where it comes from?"

"Of course, Detective. Aconitine comes from the monkshood plant." She gave them both a quick, sugary smile, but then sobered just as quickly. And there was a hard glint in her eyes. "I know it's hard to believe by looking at me—people always underestimate you when you're a beauty queen and look like I do—but I am a master gardener. Of course, I have landscapers on my payroll to do all my heavy lifting around the property here, but I'm very capable in the garden, believe me."

She gave Nick a crafty look. "Now, does that mean I killed Henrietta Stone? No, not necessarily. But could I have? Absolutely. Along with just about every other master gardener in the Society, of which there are about thirty-five of us out of the fifty-plus membership. So, I'd say that you have your work cut out for you, *n'est-ce pas juste*?"

"Yes, well, thank you for your time, Barbara. We'll be in touch if we have any further questions."

"You're welcome, Detective," Barbara murmured as she walked them out. "Do come back any time."

Once they were in the cruiser, Nick sat back and stared out the window. Something Barbara had said was niggling at him.

"What's going on, partner?" Andy asked. "You've got that look."

Nick turned to him. "What look?"

Andy grinned. "The look that says you have something tickling your gray cells. Something maybe just out of reach? Or was it something Ms. Drake said?"

Nick looked out of the windshield again, letting his thoughts percolate. "Various bits of malfeasance... " he murmured.

"What?"

"That's what Barbara said. If we wanted the skinny on *all of Henrietta's various bits of malfeasance* we should talk to Kathryn Wilks-Raymond."

"So?"

"Well, we were discussing the possible election fraud. But with that phrase, she insinuated that there was more wrongdoing on Henrietta's part than just the election tampering."

"Yeah, you're right. She also said that Kathryn and Henrietta were—how did she put it? Thick as the thieves they are? Which says to me that these various bits could have very well been criminal."

"Speculation." Nick glanced over at Andy. "But exactly what I was thinking. We'll talk to Kathryn and see what she has to say. But first, we need to see about a warrant for the Society offices as well as Henrietta's residence and her financials."

"That'll be fun," Andy said with a sigh. "But then, we wanted a place to start, so I think we've gotten our wish."

"Guess so. It's almost noon. Let's grab lunch and then head back to the office and dive in."

They reviewed all they'd learned over a lunch of Chinese

cuisine. And when they got back into the office, the first thing they noticed was the small non-descript package sitting on Nick's desk and addressed to him in big block letters.

"Hey, what's this?" Andy asked. "Who's sending you presents?"

"Don't know. My name's in generic block lettering with no return address. Nothing suspicious about that, right?"

"No, sir." Andy laughed. "Nothing at all."

And because it did have his suspicion antennae humming, Nick donned a pair of latex gloves before taking a letter opener to one end of the package. Inside, he found a sheaf of printed papers. Pulling out the contents, Nick began to skim the first couple of pages and then frowned. "What the...?"

"What is it?" Andy asked, coming closer.

"It looks like someone wanted us to know what Doris Mayfield was up to over the last couple of months."

"And what was she up to?"

Nick looked up at his partner. "If this is correct, it seems like Ms. Mayfield was having affairs—plural—with several different men... and all at the same time."

"So? Last time I looked, having an affair—or several at once—was not against the law, right?"

Spreading the first few printed sheets out on the desk, Nick shook his head. "No, not illegal to have an affair—or even multiple affairs. But this could be a motive for blackmail."

"What do you mean?" Andy started reading the first page, then got to the second page with a list of names. "Oh, well, I see what you mean. It says the names listed here are all husbands of different Garden Society members." He looked up at Nick. "So, Doris Mayfield was having multiple affairs at the same time over a period of months with other Society members' husbands?"

"If this is legit, so it would seem."

"Okay. Maybe a possible motive for blackmail, but we don't

know that for certain." Andy looked perplexed. "And what would this have to do with Henrietta Stone's murder?"

Nick shrugged. "Maybe nothing. But someone connected with the Garden Society wanted us to know about it." He thought for a moment. "How about this? What if Henrietta knew about Doris' affairs and threatened to go public? I mean, Doris was making a squawk about the election. Could be that's how Henrietta shut her down. You keep yammering about a stolen election and several women are going to hear about what you're doing with their husbands."

Andy nodded slowly. "And that could be a motive for murder. Shut Henrietta up before she can tattle, and the place and circumstances of her death are the icing on the cake. At said Garden Society party for all to see."

"And once Henrietta's out of the way, Doris gets the presidency post anyway," Nick added.

"In a weird way, that plays."

"Yeah. We need to talk to Doris Mayfield, like now."

Andy looked at his watch and sat down at his desk. "It's just a little past two. I left a message this morning before we left the office. I'll try again. Maybe we can catch her this afternoon."

As Andy tried contacting Doris Mayfield again, Nick skimmed through the pages one more time. He was struck by how very detailed they were with times, dates, and places, along with the names provided. Someone had gone to a lot of trouble to document all of the meetings.

"Got her voicemail again," Andy said as he hung up the phone. "You think we should just head over there? Maybe we can catch her at home. She could be screening her calls."

"True. She just lives across town. Let me go through the rest of these pages and then we'll take a ride. We might get lucky."

"Anything more jump out at you yet?"

"No," Nick answered absently, then frowned. "It just seems so detailed. Like someone was following Doris everywhere she went over the past couple of months, documenting everything. This reads like a report."

"Like maybe someone hired a P.I.?"

Nick looked up as his desk phone began to ring. "Yeah, that's just what I was thinking."

"Great minds, my friend."

With a grin, Nick answered his phone. "Detective Sutton. Yes. We were— What?" He sighed. "Yes, yes, we'll be right there. Thanks, Kelli."

"What was that about?" Andy asked when Nick hung up the phone.

"That was Dr. Landon. She was calling about another suspicious death. Guess there's a reason we couldn't reach Doris Mayfield. She's dead."

9

After the medical examiner had suggested that Doris' death may not have been accidental, they were delayed another fifteen minutes while Andy put in a call to the CSI team to meet them at the scene. Nick quickly made a few updates to his notes and a couple of calls to check on warrants and lab results. By the time they got on the road and arrived at the Mayfield residence, they were just minutes ahead of the sweepers.

Nick and Andy got out of the cruiser and were met by Kelli at the front door. The M.E. had a grim look on her face as she waved them into the house. They took a moment on the front porch to glove up and cover their shoes with booties so as not to contaminate the scene any further than it had been by emergency services.

"Where's the body?" Andy asked when they followed Kelli into the house.

"She died in the kitchen," Kelli replied as she led them from the foyer and down the hallway.

"We were just about to take a ride out here when you called," Nick told her as they entered the kitchen where Doris Mayfield's body was sprawled on the floor next to the table. "We'd been trying to contact her all morning but kept getting her voicemail. Can you give us a TOD?"

The M.E. nodded. "She hasn't been dead long. I'd put time of death between eleven thirty and one o'clock."

Andy whistled through his teeth as he glanced at his watch. "It's just going on three now."

"Like I said, not long."

"And cause of death?" Nick asked.

"You know better than to ask me that, Nick. I won't know for certain until I get her back to the morgue."

"But you have an idea, right? You wouldn't have given me a heads up, if you didn't."

Kelli blew out a breath. "All right, I'll give you this much. In my personal opinion, the cause is the stitchy part. It looks like anaphylaxis."

"She died of anaphylaxis?" Andy blurted. "What the hell is—"

"I said it *looks* like anaphylaxis, Detective," Kelli snapped with a stern glance. "And hear me, that's not conclusive. It's only an observation from my physical examination of her body *in situ*. Like I said, I'll know more when I get her back to my table. When I know the official COD, you'll know, too."

Nick frowned. "Okay," he said slowly. "But anaphylaxis— that's allergy related, right?"

"Very definitely. And I happen to know that Doris had an extreme peanut allergy, had lived with it for years."

"Extreme?" Andy asked. "So could that allergy have brought on anaphylaxis?"

"You bet. With a peanut allergy, the immune system mistakes peanut proteins as a harmful intrusion. With an *extreme* peanut allergy, direct or indirect contact causes the immune system to release symptom-causing chemicals into the bloodstream. It can happen within minutes."

"And what would be the symptoms?"

"Well, with an allergic response it could be as benign as skin issues like hives or swelling, tingling in or around the mouth or throat, tightening of the throat or shortness of breath. But anaphylaxis is a bit different and much worse. With that you could have constriction of the airway with the throat swelling, making it difficult to breathe. A victim could experience a severe drop in blood pressure, a rapid pulse, and dizziness or loss of consciousness."

"But wait, you said this was a suspicious death on the phone," Nick said. "If anaphylaxis turns out to be the official COD, what would be suspicious about that, especially with her specific allergy?"

Kelli walked over to the counter next to the range and picked up the evidence bag she'd already sealed. "This is what makes it suspicious, Detective," she said as she handed the bag to Nick.

"Peanut oil?"

"*Unrefined* peanut oil," Kelli clarified. "That would make it much more dangerous to someone with a peanut allergy. I found it in the trash can under the sink. The stew in the pot on the stove and in the bowl on the table both smell of it as well. I've also taken samples of the stew for analysis."

"So, why would she put peanut oil in her stew if she was allergic?" Andy murmured with a knowing look. "And why would she even have peanut oil in the house, for that matter?"

"Yes, those would be the correct questions. And the answer to both would be... she wouldn't. Because of the severity of her allergy, I know for certain that Doris was very careful about what she ate or drank."

"But if this was something that Doris had been living with for some time, even if she accidentally ingested peanut oil, wouldn't she have had one of those pens with epinephrine?"

"She definitely should have, but I can't speak to that. That's something you should have your sweepers look for, though."

"And why wouldn't she have called 911 when she started to have symptoms? That doesn't make any sense."

"Therein lies the rub. There actually was a call, which is why I'm here in the first place. The EMS team called it in when they got here and found her deceased."

Andy frowned. "So, who called 911?"

"Unknown. No name, just a whispered 'help me' and then an open line. They traced the address via that open phone line, but there's no phone in here. The open line was in the living room."

"So, Doris didn't make the call."

"Couldn't have. 911 time stamped the incoming call at one forty-five."

"And by your estimate, Doris would've already been dead by then," Nick murmured.

The M.E. sighed and nodded. "Correct. Between the peanut oil and the incongruity of the call, hence my misgivings that this was accidental. And I seriously doubt that bottle of peanut oil was Doris'."

Andy shook his head. "So what? Someone comes in, brings a bottle of peanut oil with them to spike her stew, waits around for her to eat it, and then calls 911 after she's dead?"

"There are so many implausibilities surrounding that statement," Nick said with a chuckle.

"Yeah, seems like a stretch to me, too," Andy replied with a grin.

"As my dear husband is so often fond of saying, 'not my circus, not my monkeys.'" Kelli smiled. "I can only give you the puzzle pieces of her death as I know them at this time. Putting it all together to see the big picture and who's responsible... well, that would be up to you."

"Gee, thanks, Doc," Andy replied.

"You're welcome." Kelli laughed out loud. "Isn't that what you two do?"

"Yeah, well, let's get the sweepers in here to do what they do, and then have some officers run a canvass of the neighborhood," Nick said. "Maybe we'll get lucky and someone saw a car or a visitor who would have been here with Doris." He looked down at the body. "Are you done with her, Kelli?"

The M.E. nodded. "Yes, I can have her transported if that's good with you."

"Yep."

"I'll have more for you once I get her back to the morgue and do a more conclusive examination, run some tests. I'll let you know when I'm done."

"Thanks, Doc." Nick looked around the kitchen then back at Andy. "Okay, partner. Let's get this party started."

"Alrighty then. Where do you want to begin?"

"I'll get the sweepers started. Why don't you get a couple of officers on the canvassing," Nick replied as Kelli's team came into the kitchen to ready Doris' body for transport.

"On it," Andy said before heading down the hall.

Nick followed him out but made a detour into the living room. It looked like the open line was still open, which was good. He'd have the sweepers tag the phone and take it in with the rest of the evidence. Maybe they'd get lucky there as well and find prints other than Doris' to give them another avenue of investigation, or at least another person to interview. However, he wasn't holding his breath. Just because they'd been sloppy in leaving the peanut oil in the trash, it didn't mean that they'd left prints on the bottle or on the phone. Only time and testing would tell.

It took the better part of three hours for the sweepers to process the scene. It gave Nick a bit more to go on, though there were still tests to be run, and he'd have to wait on that data to add it to the mix and see what they'd learn. The canvassing was mostly a bust. Primarily because it was Friday afternoon, and Doris' closest neighbors with the best views of her house weren't home. They would have to check back, but so far, the possibility of a witness to any visitors was remote. More than likely, they were all at work.

However, he did have a better sense of how Doris' death probably went down. Of course, there were still gaping holes to fill before they could sketch out a timeline, but they went over what they knew when they got back to the office.

"Okay, so it seems whoever was with Doris was someone she knew and felt comfortable with, and though there were no signs of struggle, was likely her killer and the one to call 911," Andy summarized. "It would have to be someone who would know enough about Doris to be aware of her peanut allergy."

Nick nodded. "If anaphylaxis turns out to be COD—and I'm betting it will—then yeah. Someone who'd bring the peanut oil with them. Maybe they'd just been waiting for an opportunity, but then they get there and find that Doris already had the perfect vehicle for it with the stew she's got cooking on the stove."

"So, someone who she was comfortable enough with to let into the house and who knew enough about her extreme allergy to bring the peanut oil with them? That's more than an acquaintance. And to watch and wait? That's pretty cold, man."

"Uh-huh, really cold and premeditated."

"Alright. But how would they have gotten the oil into the stew? And how would they get her to eat the stew once it had been laced with the oil? I mean, even if she didn't know it had been added, I'm pretty sure that she could've smelled it or tasted it, you know?"

"One would think." Nick replied slowly. He took Doris' photo over to the case board but turned back as a thought hit him.

"Maybe she was somehow coerced. Forced to eat it while the killer watched and waited."

"But there were no signs of that, of a struggle."

"Maybe Doris snaps to the fact that this person, this very familiar person has added the peanut oil to the stew—"

"Or she catches them doing it," Andy added.

"And now they *have* to make her eat it... somehow."

"But there were no other place settings on the table. Only Doris'," Andy said with a frown. "Not even another coffee cup or water glass. And again, no signs of that struggle."

"They could have planned for that scenario and brought a weapon with them to threaten her with, then cleaned up once Doris was dead."

"Could be." Andy scrubbed his hands over his face. "The whole thing with the Epipen still bothers me."

"Yeah, me too." Nick nodded. "With Doris' extreme allergy and the sweepers doing a very thorough search, the fact that not one pen was found in the house sends up another red flag for me. Obviously, somebody wanted this to look like an accidental death by allergic reaction, and although they took the time to bring the peanut oil to do the deed, it's sloppy and not well thought out."

"Yeah. They force her to eat the stew, watch her die a terrible death to which they deny her life-saving meds, and then stage the scene—but poorly. Like, with the peanut oil just buried in the trash." Andy shook his head. "Really dumb. Should've taken it with them."

"As they no doubt did with Doris' EpiPens. I think we'll find that she had a prescription for them and probably had a couple on hand. We'll dig into that to confirm if we can. Also, there's the 911 call. They waited way too long to make that call, which tells me they were doing some cleanup. And it would have been better to call from Doris' cell phone and leave it with her on the floor instead of calling from the living room phone."

"Exactly. If they wanted this to look accidental, calling it in from a land line in another room was just stupidity. No cell phone was found, but Kelli had a mobile number for Doris so we know she had one." Andy frowned. "You think the killer took it with them? Why would they take that and her life-saving meds but throw something as incriminating as the peanut oil in the trash— leaving it for us to find?"

"I pushed the lab to look at that first. There were no prints on that bottle, not one. So, they probably wiped it thinking they were in the clear, but that just makes it even more suspicious, given Doris' allergy situation. On the surface, the whole thing doesn't make much sense, does it?" Nick shook his head. "Like I said, some parts seem thought out, but all in all, incredibly sloppy."

"Yeah, like someone was imitating one of those badly written crime shows on TV and doing a terrible job of it."

"Or murder is new to them, and they were handling the whole thing scattershot."

After a few moments, Andy asked the question that had been hovering in the back of Nick's mind. "So, you think this is connected to Henrietta Stone's death?"

"I was just thinking about that, buddy." Nick stared up at the case board where he'd just put Doris' photo next to the Garden Society Presidents' and shook his head. "I think it may be a bit too soon to make that particular leap, but it is a hellava coincidence. And you know how I feel about coincidences."

"Oh, yeah. No such thing, right?"

"Correct."

Andy narrowed his eyes. "Both women were killed in much the same way, though Henrietta Stone was poisoned."

"Well, it may not have been actual poison that killed Doris, but with her extreme peanut allergy, it might as well have been. And I think the killer—or killers—knew it." Nick went over to his desk to check his files, and then ticked off his points with his fingers. "Okay, so one, we've got two women who were both members of the same Garden Society. Two, both women were killed with poisons of a sort. Three, Doris ran against Henrietta for Society president and lost, but from what Barbara said, Doris was really steamed about perceived election tampering and made a squawk about it."

"And then there was the packet of dirt someone just sent you about Doris' numerous alleged affairs with other members' husbands. If what's in the packet is true—and we'll have to run those allegations down—that could have easily played into her death somehow. You know, the scorned wife?"

"True, and yes, we'll have to do some digging there. However, both women could have been targeted for very different reasons." Nick looked back at the board again. "We just don't have enough data yet."

"If that's the case, though, are we looking at one killer or two?"

"Excellent question, my friend. But again, too early to tell. There's no evidence to verify that one way or the other. So, at this point, it's just conjecture. But there are way too many connecting points for my liking, and my gut is telling me that their deaths are somehow linked. I just can't see how yet." Nick scratched his head. "Now, does that mean one killer? Or more than one? No clue. But for my money, the Garden Society is the place we begin."

"Well, Henrietta Stone wasn't married and had no children, but she did have a sister in Seattle, a Deanna Martin. Evidently, Mrs. Martin was Stone's emergency contact. I'm sure she's been contacted about her sister's death, but we could reach out for a bit more info there." Andy flipped though his notebook. "I'll start working on Mayfield's background on Monday. We should prob-ably re-check some previously established alibis, too."

"Good point. I'm going to push on those search warrants for

the Society offices, as well as Stone's residence. I've already got a call in for financials."

Andy nodded. "Along with that, I'll see about getting Kathryn Wilks-Raymond in for an interview. She's the current treasurer for the Society, so like Barbara Drake said, she should have some crucial information and insight into what's been going on at the Society over the last few months that we should know about." Andy flipped to the next page in his notepad. "I also found out that an Anna Ingram was the previous treasurer and was ousted by Henrietta when she took over as president. Mom said she'd heard that there was some bad blood there. I'll see if I can get a hold of her as well. She's still a Society member."

Nick crossed his arms and stared at the board for a moment, and then went over and added both names under the suspect list. "I think I want to have another chat with Barbara Drake as well. I got the feeling that she knows more than she was telling us."

"Yeah, she was definitely holding something back." Andy stretched and leaning a hip on his desk, made a show of looking at his watch. "But that'll all have to wait for Monday, buddy."

"Yeah, yeah. It's quitting time. I know."

"Dude, it's beyond quitting time already."

Nick grinned. "Go on. I'm just going to update my notes and then I'll be right behind you."

Andy laughed out loud. "How many times have I heard that from you, partner? Ain't nobody buying it." He stuffed his notebook into his bag and headed for the door. "Please don't sleep here. My wife thinks you're a workaholic as it is, and she worries about you."

"Very funny. Tell Jen I'll sleep in my own bed tonight, so she doesn't have to worry."

Andy waved a hand and gave Nick a parting shot as he left the office. "And call me if you need me."

Nick's grin faded when he went back and sat down at his

desk. It had been less than a week, and they had not one but two murders on their hands and very little to go on for either. He could only hope that the financial information and a search of Henrietta Stone's residence would give them better footing and a path to follow.

Because at the moment, he felt like they were just spinning their wheels.

10

It was just after one o'clock on a gray Sunday afternoon. They'd had another bout of rain overnight and were expecting more later in the day. Lydie had gone up the coast to take care of a few errands and check out some new essential oils at one of their wholesale distributors. She had hoped to be back before they got the next round of showers, which her Spidey-sense said would begin around the three o'clock hour. That left Vanessa to hold down the fort at Lavender Fields.

Of course, the shop wasn't technically open on Sunday or Monday, though they tried to accommodate any of their regulars who came out to the property on either of those days. But Sundays weren't normally a day that customers raced out for herbs or lotions, so it tended to be a workday for staff. With no pressing Enchanted Affairs events on the schedule for another few weeks, business was in a bit of a lull. Vanessa was making the best of her time by putting together some more of their most popular herb packets to plump up the shop's inventory, which Lydie had started on last Thursday.

Vanessa had just finished another two batches and shelved them in the shop's storeroom with the first few sets when the workroom buzzer sounded, and she heard a car pull into the lot. Thinking Lydie was back earlier than expected, Vanessa stepped out into the storefront to meet her with Circe close on her heels. However, she was surprised to see Barbara Drake getting out of her Mercedes in the parking lot.

"Now what do you suppose she wants, Circe?" Vanessa asked as she lifted the Russian Blue cat into her arms and gave her thick ruff a scratch. Going behind the counter to wait for the woman to come into the building, she frowned. "She knows damn well that we aren't open on Sundays. And she never buys anything when she comes out here, anyway."

Circe meowed in agreement and then began to purr, as together they watched the high-maintenance socialite saunter toward the building.

The old-fashioned bell over the door jingled as Barbara entered and gave Vanessa a brilliant grin. "Hello, Vanessa. My goodness, it's soggy out there."

"Good afternoon, Barbara. Yes, it seems like we got quite the deluge overnight, and Lydie says we're in for more rain in a couple of hours. But we can use it, or at least our gardens can use the extra water, I suppose." Vanessa tilted her head and gave the woman a puzzled look. "What brings you this far out of town on a wet day like today? You know, we're not actually open on Sundays—and Lydie isn't here right now—but if there's something you need, I'll be more than happy to help if I can."

Barbara waved a hand in the air and then removed her stylish rain hat, smoothing her platinum, collar-length bob as she approached the counter. There was a crafty look in her baby-blue eyes that made Vanessa wary right off the bat.

"Oh, yes, I know your shop isn't open, darling. I'm actually here to see you."

"Me? Whatever for?" Vanessa sputtered, taken by surprise,

then backtracked. She hardly knew Barbara but didn't want to seem rude. "Uh... what I mean is—"

Barbara laughed out loud, a harsh, husky sound that Vanessa was sure was meant to be sultry but fell quite short in her opinion. The woman shook her head, her bob swinging artfully just below her jawline. "Oh, don't apologize, for God's sake. It's not like we're the closest of friends, so your surprise is acknowledged and appreciated."

Barbara rubbed her hands together and gave Vanessa a smile that didn't seem to quite reach her eyes. "Do you think we could sit down somewhere cozy? Maybe have a cup of your excellent tea?"

For the love of...

"Um, sure, okay," Vanessa replied. "I've got several more herb packets to put together today, but you caught me in between batches. Come on back."

Vanessa led the way to the back room where she set Circe on the worktable. She struggled to keep the smile from her face when the cat—an amazing judge of character—gave a low growl in the socialite's direction.

"Now, Circe, if you are going to be like that, maybe you should go into the casting room and take a nap," Vanessa murmured.

Conveying her displeasure, the cat gave the socialite one of her infamous cat stares, then jumped down and threw another growly meow over her shoulder as she slipped into the darkness of the casting room.

Turning back to Barbara, Vanessa made a face. "Sorry about that. Circe is normally good with people."

Barbara shrugged. "No worries. It is odd, though. Animals usually like me."

With a non-committal 'hmm', Vanessa motioned for the woman to follow her into the office. "Why don't you have a seat in here, and I'll make us both a cup of tea. It'll only take a jiff. The kettle's already hot. Do you take anything in it?"

"Honey and a drop or two of cream if you have it," Barbara replied as she dropped her Prada shoulder bag onto the settee and pulled off her Hermès scarf.

"You bet. Be right back."

Leaving Barbara there, Vanessa hurried into the small workshop kitchen and made quick work of the tea, wishing that Lydie was here for back-up. She didn't like what she'd briefly seen in the socialite's aura and didn't relish spending any more time alone in the shop with her than necessary.

But before long, she returned to the office with two steaming cups in hand. "Here we are."

Since Barbara had settled on the settee, Vanessa took a seat on the adjacent chair after giving the woman her cup. "Now, what did you want to see me about?"

Barbara took a tentative sip of her tea and then closed her eyes and sighed. "Oh, yes. That really hits the spot." She sat back and glanced out the side window with a pensive look on her face. "I had an interesting visit from your cousin and his partner on Friday," she murmured after a moment.

"Oh, really?" Vanessa wondered where this was going but nodded. "As have half of the Garden Society members, I'd wager. Nick and Andy have been out here a couple of times as well, so count yourself lucky it was just the once."

"Yes, I thought they may have been out here," Barbara replied with a smirk. "Especially with Henrietta being done in by aconitine in her tea at the garden party." She paused briefly, then took another sip from her cup and smiled. "And with Enchanted Affairs providing the tea and all."

Vanessa narrowed her eyes and gave a terse response. "Our tea had nothing to do with Henrietta's death, Barbara."

The socialite was quick to put up a hand. "Oh, I know that.

I'm not saying y'all were responsible. Just that it stands to reason that you, Lydie, and your team, would be some of the first to be interviewed. And hopefully cleared, of course." Her look was again sly. "Do they have any idea of how the aconitine got into Henrietta's tea?"

"Now, how on Earth would I know that?"

Barbara shrugged. "Well, Detective Sutton is your cousin. And you did say that they'd been out here a couple of times already. To be honest, I guess I just assumed that you would have the inside track on the investigation so far."

Ah. So that's why you're here… a reconnaissance mission. Snooping for intel.

Vanessa laughed out loud. "Yeah, well, believe me when I say that Nick wouldn't tell me even if he knew. We don't have that kind of relationship, Barbara."

"I see."

"Plus, he's very persnickety and tight-lipped about his investigations. Nick doesn't like meddling. But with so many women milling around as the event was getting underway, it seems like it would be near to impossible to figure out how the poison got into her tea. It would've had to have been done quickly, but just about anyone could have gone by Henrietta's table, dropped the aconitine into her pot, and then moved on."

"So, they *have* established that it would have happened at her table and not in the pavilion beforehand?"

"Again, I'm not privy to what they have or haven't ruled out or established. That's just my take on how it could have been done."

"But in broad daylight? And like you said, with so many women milling about?"

Lydie's voice was loud and clear in Vanessa's head as she replied. "Yeah, well, sometimes in plain sight is the best cover."

Vanessa watched the woman carefully. Her aura was all over the place, and she was sure there was something just a little bit sinister lurking right beneath the surface. "But it does make sense that if Henrietta's teapot was the only one where the aconitine was found, it would've had to happen at the table, don't you think?"

"I suppose that's true."

"And for that matter, with so many master gardeners present at the event—yourself included, if I'm not mistaken—the suspect pool seems pretty wide." Vanessa threw the statement out as if it had only just occurred to her, then nonchalantly waved a hand in the air. "Anyway, who knows? It may just come down to asking the right person the right question. In my experience, there's always somebody watching everything. Maybe someone saw something they don't realize is important, but I would think that *somebody* would have seen something."

She smiled to herself at the narrowing of Barbara's eyes, but went on in a slightly baffled fashion. "What I don't get is what Henrietta Stone could've done that was so terrible that someone would want her dead because of it."

As Vanessa had hoped, the socialite took the bait, and her brash laughter filled the office again. "Oh, dear, sweet Vanessa." Barbara gave her a pitiful look. "The reasons are as wide and varied as the suspect pool."

Vanessa blinked innocently. "Really? I know that Henrietta wasn't well liked by some, but did she have that many enemies?"

"Darling, that heinous cow was *disliked*—and I use that word lightly—by too many to count. Yes, there were quite a few with very clear reasons to want to see her, shall we say, put out to pasture?"

"Seriously?"

"Oh, yes. And many of those have the capacity and expertise to do the deed in this very fashion—me included." Barbara set her cup on the side table and leaned forward. "Take for instance, Anna Ingram."

"Why Anna?"

"Anna was the Society treasurer when Henrietta was elected the first time, had been for almost a decade. They did not see eye to eye or agree on anything. But the biggest problem, as I heard it, was the way Henrietta played fast and loose with the Society's finances. Anna is a top-notch CPA. So, Henrietta made sure that Anna was replaced with Kathryn—who is not a CPA, and I'm doubtful can actually run a calculator—the minute Anna's term was up. Anna was furious, made a huge stink about it. It was quite the free-for-all."

"Wow."

"Indeed." Barbara grinned. "Then there's Letitia Edwards."

"Letitia?" Vanessa chuckled. "You're joking."

"Not in the least. The hatred between Letitia and Henrietta goes way back. Letitia was the event coordinator for the Society for years, and I will say, she wasn't bad at it. But more importantly, she enjoyed the position." Barbara made a face, and Vanessa could literally feel the anger behind the look. "Well, Henrietta put the brakes on that in her first term as well. Gave the position to Winnie Douglas, poor thing. Winnie didn't even want the job, but Henrietta knew she could browbeat her into it and then call the shots, something she couldn't do with Letitia. No, Winnie was just another poor member Henrietta could beat down, not that Winnie needed any help in that area. She does a decent job of self-flagellation on her own."

"But again, that doesn't seem a likely reason for murder."

"Oh, honey, you have no idea." Barbara laughed out loud again, and then narrowed her eyes in thought. "Although, there is something else from the past between Henrietta and Letitia that nobody talks about. Something deeper and uglier, but I've yet to find out exactly what that was." Sitting back and picking up her tea, she smiled. "Anyway, Letitia may seem a bit scattered at times and so sweet as to make your jaw ache just to be around her, but that woman can carry a mean grudge. Trust me on that."

"The Society seems like a really toxic environment." Vanessa shook her head. "But both Anna and Letitia are still Society members. If it was me, I'd be out the door, and then bathing in rosemary and sage to rid myself of all that negativity, probably smudging my entire surroundings, as well."

Barbara nodded. "That's because you and Lydie don't *need* to be part of something like the Society. Some of these women? It's all they've got in their tiny, miserable lives. Just look at Doris Mayfield."

"Doris?"

"Yep. Doris should have topped the suspect list."

"You've got to be kidding. I mean, I know she ran against Henrietta for president, and that there was talk of election-tampering, but she seems so nice, so... unassuming."

"Mmm, you'd think, right?" Barbara shook her head. "Listen to me, the meek ones are the ones you have to keep an eye on. Doris was completely unhinged about the whole thing, actually filed a complaint alleging the wrongdoing. She and Henrietta had a crazy screaming match. It was pretty explosive, and the allegations hung over the Society like a thundercloud for over a month before Henrietta finally put an end to it. But that's neither here nor there now."

"What do you mean?"

"Well, darling, hadn't you heard? Doris was found dead in her kitchen on Friday afternoon. Another suspicious death."

"*What?*" Vanessa just about spit out her tea. "Oh my gosh! That's horrible. No, I hadn't heard. Lydie and I went down the coast to her grandmother's house yesterday morning and didn't get back until late. How did she die?"

"From what I've heard through the grapevine, it's looking like anaphylaxis."

Vanessa frowned. "But why would that be suspicious?"

"Because Doris had an extreme peanut allergy and was very careful about it. As I understand it, she'd eaten some stew for lunch that turned out to be just chock-full of peanut oil."

"Who would've wanted to kill Doris? Maybe it was just an accident, and she couldn't get to her medication. Or it came on too fast to call 911."

"Did I not mention that Doris made the stew herself? Unless it was a suicide, Doris would never have had peanut oil in her kitchen, let alone made stew with it. No, though I don't have more of the details, you mark my words. This will turn out to be yet another murder and not just a suspicious death. And I would look at Anna Ingram there as well."

"Why?"

"Dear *unassuming* Doris was having an affair with Anna's husband, as well as several other members' husbands, I might add, and all at the same time. I know for a fact that Anna knew about the affair. Don't know how many of the other members knew, though. They all could be a nice addition to the suspect pool."

Vanessa could do nothing but stare at Barbara with her mouth open. What the hell kind of town were they living in? It all sounded like something out of a bad soap opera. And how was it that none of this had ever crossed her radar?

"It's really hard to believe," Vanessa murmured. "So many ugly secrets in such a small town."

"We all have secrets, darling. Some are just worse than others."

"Where did you hear all of this?"

Barbara just smiled again but said nothing.

"Never mind. This latest news about Doris is just so sad. I can't wrap my mind around it." She gave the woman a pointed look. "However, that's the one thing about my cousin, Barbara.

Nick will find out exactly what happened... in both cases. You can take that to the bank."

An hour later, Lydie came breezing into the shop with a huge smile. "I had a very productive trip, my friend. Talked Denny Mason into giving me a good discount on a shipment of essential oils that will be delivered on Thursday." She glanced over her shoulder at the parking lot where rain was just beginning, and then turned back with a smile as she set a small box on the counter. "I cut that pretty close. Wasn't sure I was going to make it back before the showers started. Got caught up at the warehouse. Anyway, Denny gave me this box of samples to try along with our order. Also picked up some more supplies for the herb packets and charms."

She stopped abruptly when she got a good look at Vanessa's face. "What's wrong? What's happened? Were the police here again?"

Vanessa shook her head. "Not Durham County's finest, but I did have an interesting visit from... wait for it... our local socialite, Barbara Drake."

"Barbara? She rarely comes out here and never buys a thing when she does. What was she doing here on a Sunday?"

"She wasn't here to buy anything, Lydie. She specifically came to see me."

Lydie's mouth dropped open, and Vanessa watched her struggle with how to respond. "What on earth for?"

Vanessa chuckled. "Almost the exact words that came out of my mouth before I could drop my filter into place."

"Well, don't keep me in suspense. What did she want?"

"It was an information gathering trip, as far as I could tell. She wanted to know what I knew about Nick's investigation into

Henrietta's death. She was quite disappointed when I told her that he didn't share that kind of information with me."

"Ha! I can well imagine." Lydie pursed her lips. "Interesting. Did you get anything from her? Ask her any questions?"

"As it turned out, I didn't have to. She just started doling it out." Vanessa began filling Lydie in on all the sordid details of Barbara's visit and the conversation she'd had with the woman as they went into the workroom.

Lydie plopped down in one of the armchairs and shook her head. "This is just unbelievable. I mean, how does she know all this stuff about these women?"

"I asked her that, but she just smiled. There was something really sinister hovering in her aura, too. If you ask me, she's a pretty good suspect herself. And surprisingly, she actually acknowledged that."

"Yes, but that could just be a ruse. Something to throw us off. But she's moved up to the top of my list, for sure. At first, I was thinking that she was possibly one of the three victims that Winnie was talking about in my visions. But what if she killed Henrietta, and this was just her trying to find out how close Nick and Andy were getting in their investigation? If they were looking in her direction?"

"Yeah, well, stick a pin in that thought." Vanessa sank down into the other armchair and glanced over at Lydie. "All of this muck she was doling out? It was just a warmup for a nice little sucker punch in the end."

"What do you mean?"

Vanessa sighed. "When Barbara was giving me all the dirt on Doris, she said that Doris should've been at the top of the suspect list but that really didn't matter now."

Lydie sat up. "Oh my gosh! Please don't tell me..."

Vanessa nodded. "Doris was found dead in her kitchen on Friday. Evidently, she had an extreme peanut allergy, and according to Barbara, that's how she died. Peanut oil in her stew. It was all I could do not to freak out when she told me, considering your visions and what we already knew." She scrubbed her hands over her face. "I mean, Doris was also one of the women in your visions, Lydie. We were thinking possible suspect then, too, but she was another victim instead."

"Yes. And if 'three's a charm,' Doris is only number two. And we have no idea who could be next."

"Or who is responsible for either death."

11

Lydie stood up with a determined glint in her eyes. "Okay, I think it's time we start getting serious about meddling in Nick's investigation."

Vanessa crossed her legs and gave Lydie a considering look. "You are talking about meddling without his knowledge, correct?"

"Yes... and no," Lydie replied with a grin, then added quickly, "mostly, yes."

"I do not like the sound of that. Exactly what are you suggesting?"

Lydie knew her partner wasn't going to like her next proposal but plowed ahead. "So, hear me out before you blow a gasket. Yes, we will work under the radar like we've been doing, but we have got to step it up and get serious before someone else dies. And we both know that's what's coming, right?"

"Right," Vanessa replied slowly. "And?"

"Well, I was thinking that one of us should at least give Nick a heads up about what we learned from Barbara. I'm pretty sure she didn't unload on him the way she did with you. And, you know, we could maybe learn a few things from him along with it."

"Huh. So, let me get this straight. You think one of us should have a chat with my favorite cousin and give him the skinny on *his* investigation. Shall I guess which one of us you think that should be?"

"Come on, Van," Lydie pleaded. "Giving Nick what we've learned is the right thing to do. It's important information. And it may help us to figure out who's next on the hit list."

"And I don't totally disagree with that logic, Lydie. But Nick's not going to take kindly to me showing up and basically admitting that we've been snooping behind his back. You know how he gets. I don't relish getting my head bitten off for encroaching on his investigation, even if it's the right thing to do."

"It's not admitting to anything if we're just passing along what we've heard," Lydie insisted, then blew out a breath. "Okay, okay. I'll do it. Considering your contentious relationship, it's probably best that I do it, anyway."

"Please." Vanessa giggled. "You don't fool me, girlfriend. You were just hoping I'd put up a fuss so that you could volunteer because you've always had the hots for him."

"What? That's just so juvenile and patently untrue." *At least, not completely true*, she thought. "Anyway, we should probably go over everything beforehand and decide exactly how much of it to tell him."

"I beg your pardon? Not tell Nicky everything we know?" Vanessa asked with a gasp. "Why, Lydie Charles, I'm shocked, I tell ya. Just shocked."

"Ooo, you're so funny. You know very well how he feels about my visions and your runes. All I'm saying is that we only tell him the pertinent stuff that may help his investigation. If we approach it for what it was—Barbara stopping by to pick your brain to see what you knew, and then giving you the information without us asking for it—then like I said, we're not actually the ones meddling. He can't accuse us of interfering if we're just doing our duty by telling him what we've heard."

Vanessa burst out laughing. "Yeah, you keep telling yourself that, sista. Let me know how that goes for you."

Before Lydie could respond to Vanessa's sarcasm, they heard the sound of a car pulling into the parking lot. Frustrated with the interruption, they went out to see who else had decided to visit the shop on a Sunday.

Both were surprised to see Lydie's Aunt Wilma getting out of her car and racing through the rain toward the building. Wilma came into the shop and pushed the hood of her black raincoat back with one hand and dropped the small valise she was carrying with the other.

"Hey, girls. Geez, Mother Nature is giving us a good dumping out there. The flora and fauna will be so happy."

Lydie came around the counter and shook her head. "Aunt Wilma, what are you doing here?"

"Now, is that any way to greet your favorite auntie?"

"I'm sorry. I'm just surprised to see you, is all."

"Surprised?" Wilma frowned. "Why are you surprised? We talked about me coming to stay with you for a week or two when you were down at your grandmother's yesterday. I need to use your industrial kitchen for testing some of my new recipes."

Lydie's aunt owned and operated The Magick Baker Boulangerie in Sunset Harbor down on the south coast within a mile of Lydie's grandmother's greenhouse and nursery. A talented baker, Wilma's magical concoctions were very popular with locals and tourists alike, and she managed a thriving business during the season.

Every year about this time, she spent a month or two working on new recipes to add to her menu as specialties for the upcoming season. Her own industrial kitchen was getting a much-needed overhaul with new state-of-the-art appliances, and she'd asked

Lydie if she could use theirs for her trial-and-error period until the remodel was complete. With Enchanted Affairs in between events, Lydie had agreed. But she hadn't expected her aunt so soon, and definitely not in the middle of a murder investigation, which had now been compounded with Doris Mayfield's death as well.

"Aunt Wilma, I thought we talked about you coming at the end of the month."

"Oh, we did." Wilma made a face. "But I really need to get these new recipes on their feet. I'm getting antsy. We're already into fall and Halloween is right around the corner. I want to have the new menu ready to go before the winter slowdown. The regular season will be back in full swing again before we know it, and I need to be organized and ready. Is this a bad time? I just really hate to have to wait until the end of the month. I could come back next weekend, I suppose, if that would be better."

"No, you most certainly will not," Vanessa said giving Lydie a nudge. "Don't be silly."

"Vanessa's right. You're here now, and you're not driving all the way back down to Sunset Harbor only to come back next week or the week after." Lydie sighed and felt like a terrible niece. "I really am sorry, Aunt Wilma. I didn't mean to make it sound like you weren't wanted here. There's just a lot going on right now, so my mind is on other things. You know you're always welcome."

Wilma gave her a studied look. "Okay, kiddo. What's going on? I swear I could feel the dark energy the closer I got to Seal Cove. I can literally see the stress in your aura and feel it pouring out of you from where I'm standing." She stepped forward and took Lydie by the arm, then started for the workroom pulling her along. "Vanessa can make us all some nice chamomile tea, and you can tell me what's got you so stressed out."

"I do believe we can all use some de-stressing right at the

moment," Vanessa murmured as she went into the workroom kitchen to make more tea.

Lydie and Wilma continued on into the office where Circe had been snoozing in the window seat and sat down on the settee to wait. At the sound of their voices, the feline stretched and yawned before jumping down and making a beeline for Wilma.

"Well, there's my dear Circe," Wilma cooed as the cat jumped up into her lap and began a furious meowing chatter. "Yes, yes, absolutely. I am just hearing about all the troubles, sweet thing. But I am so comforted knowing that you are here to support my girls."

Circe gave another string of meows before settling down and beginning to purr, then giving Lydie the stink-eye.

"Don't look at me like that, missy," Lydie said. "You know we've been doing everything we could."

"So?" Wilma began and made a come-on gesture. "Give. What is this all about?"

Lydie hesitated, not sure how much to tell her aunt. She hadn't said a word about the deaths to anyone in her family. She knew her mom would pop a vein when she found out, especially if she heard it from someone else. But she didn't want to trouble her aunt, either.

She took a breath and dove into the deep end. "Well, you know Enchanted Affairs handled the Seal Cove Garden Society's yearly awards party just last Sunday."

"Yes. I know. You borrowed the table linens for the event from mom."

Lydie nodded. "Gram has the best linens. Anyway, it was a lovely garden party, just like it's been every year, but Vanessa and I had been getting some disturbing omens in the days leading up to it."

"Like?"

"My runes and divination pool were both a mess the day

before the party," Vanessa said as she came in carrying a tray with a pot of tea and three cups. "The pool started out cloudy—which you know is never a good sign—and gave me pause. But then it went very, very dark."

"And I had a pretty disturbing waking dream on the heels of that," Lydie added.

Wilma frowned and put a hand on Lydie's knee. "You had a waking dream? But Lydie, sweetheart, you haven't had one of those for quite a while, have you?"

Lydie shook her head. "I hadn't, no. But then it was followed that night by an actual visionary dream, a prophesy."

"And these visions, both waking and other? What was in them?"

"Portents of death, Aunt Wilma."

"Oh, my. Do you know whose death? Were there any details?"

"Both visions were pretty vague to start with." Lydie sighed. "But they each included women from the Garden Society."

Vanessa poured out three cups of the fragrant chamomile tea. "All we could do is stay vigilant, keep a close eye out for anything seeming or feeling somehow off."

"I think partway through the afternoon we both figured that maybe it wasn't as bad as we'd originally thought, because the party seemed to be going so well," Lydie said.

"Until it wasn't," Vanessa added.

Wilma leaned forward and took the cup that Vanessa handed her. "So, what happened?"

Lydie and Vanessa exchanged glances.

"Girls? What happened?" Wilma pressed.

"The Society president was poisoned with a tincture of monkshood," Lydie replied. "Someone put it in her teapot. And of course, Enchanted Affairs catered and provided the tea and the pots, so we've had several visits from law enforcement."

"Well, it's obvious that Enchanted Affairs would have had

nothing to do with that. The thought that y'all would is just ridiculous. Was the monkshood found in any of the other pots?"

"Not a one," Vanessa said.

Wilma waved a hand in the air. "There you go. I rest my case. I sure hope you set these provincial cops straight."

Vanessa snickered. "You remember my cousin Nick, don't you, Aunt Wilma?"

Wilma tilted her head and smiled. "You mean that hot, young hunk that's always giving you a hard time about the craft?"

"Aunt Wilma!" Lydie sputtered.

"Lydie, dear. I'm middle-aged, not dead. I can appreciate a pretty face," her aunt replied with a wink.

The comment had Vanessa snickering again. "Nick is in charge of the investigation."

"I see." Wilma took a sip of her tea. "Well, he seemed like an intelligent sort, so I'm sure he knows that y'all were not involved in any way."

"That remains to be seen." Lydie hesitated. "Unfortunately, there have been some recent developments."

"What kind of developments?" Wilma asked, looking back and forth between them.

"There's been another death," Vanessa said. "We only just found out. Evidently, it happened on Friday."

"Oh, well, that's definitely a development."

They took turns then filling Wilma in on the details from Lydie's visions and Vanessa's runes, and everything that had happened up to the present, including what they'd just learned about Doris Mayfield's death from Barbara Drake.

"And you think that these two deaths are connected?" Wilma asked when they'd finished. "I mean, beyond the Garden Society link?"

Lydie shrugged. "There's not enough evidence to say for sure, but with everything Vanessa and I have been shown, everything we've heard? My gut says yes."

"Mine says the same," Vanessa added with a nod.

"The Society may be part of this whole thing." Lydie shook her head. "But I think there's more to it than that, something deeper that I haven't been able to see yet in my visions."

"I feel that way, too," Vanessa agreed again. "My divination pool has been very stingy with info, and my runes keep telling me the same thing over and over, that this isn't done. Unfortunately, I get a little peek here and there, but nothing solid to go on."

Lydie frowned. "My main concern at the moment is that Doris' death won't be the last, if my visions are correct."

"Which they have been so far, Lydie," Vanessa added. "You know Henrietta and Doris are just numbers one and two."

Wilma nodded. "Mmm, yes. And as Lydie's vision indicated, three's the charm."

"Exactly," Vanessa said, jabbing a finger in Wilma's direction.

"All right. So where do we go from here?"

Lydie and Vanessa exchanged glances.

"We?" they asked in unison.

"I'm intrigued, and I can lend a hand where needed in between test bakes while I'm here."

"Aunt Wilma, like we told you, we have to be very careful," Vanessa said. "Nick will have a meltdown if we get caught meddling in his case."

"Then don't get caught," Wilma replied.

"Look, we're not trying to conduct our own investigation here, Aunt Wilma," Lydie insisted. "But after what I've seen in my visions, I just don't want anyone else to die."

"I understand that, sweetheart, but I don't see how you can avoid doing more digging, especially if the investigators won't listen to you about what you've been shown. I know how closed-minded some folks can be about the craft, so please tell me that you have a plan."

"We'd just been discussing sharing some of the pertinent information that Barbara gave Vanessa with Nick when you arrived," Lydie replied. "But we hadn't gotten much further than that."

"That's a good start. Passing on that information is the right thing to do. That should be the first order of business. And it's also possible that you can glean some information of your own at the same time, hopefully without him realizing it. Might give you an idea of who to keep an eye on or what that 'something deeper' may be."

Lydie nodded. "That's what I was thinking."

"Stealth will be the name of the game after that. However, you really do need to come up with some kind of a plan, girls."

"I so love the way you think, Aunt Wilma. Maybe you can help us do that," Vanessa said with a grin. "Lydie's gonna take what we decide to share to Nick and see what she can pick up from him as well."

Wilma frowned. "Why Lydie? Nick's your cousin, right?"

"He is, yes. But she volunteered to do it on account of having the hots for him."

"Oh, for the love of... seriously? Would you just give it a rest, already?" Lydie muttered in frustration. "You know that had nothing to do with it. Listen, I don't relish the idea of getting my head bitten off either, but you wouldn't be able to keep a cool head for more than ten seconds to do this, and you know it. You'd probably end up in the clink for abusive behavior toward a police officer."

Vanessa laughed and put up both hands in surrender. "Okay, okay. Take it down a notch. I was only joking. And yes, you're absolutely right. I'd probably wrestle Nick to the floor and punch his lights out the minute he said anything offensive, and then he would gleefully charge me with assault, cousin or not."

"No, he wouldn't." Lydie gave her a reluctant smile. "But only because the day that you can wrestle Nick Sutton to the floor and punch his lights out is never going to come. However, that doesn't mean that he wouldn't throw you in a cell for trying."

"Fair enough."

"Uh girls, can we get back to the issue at hand now?" Wilma asked as she obviously struggled to hide her grin at their antics.

Vanessa giggled. "Oh yeah, the plan. Right."

"The plan, yes. But first things, first," Lydie replied. "We have to decide on what I'm gonna tell Nick tomorrow. Because I want to get it over and done with the first thing in the morning, and I need a clear script, so I don't get tripped up."

Wilma smiled. "Well, then. Let's get started."

The constant deluge of rain showers finally moved off to the east overnight leaving a well-watered landscape and partly sunny skies the following morning, though the temperature had started to dip.

With the birds chirping, Lydie got up long before her alarm. She hadn't slept well, tossing and turning all night with snippets of visions swirling in her dreams. Unfortunately, there wasn't much new there. She had half expected Henrietta to show up again and berate her for not figuring out what was happening yet. Or that perhaps Doris would make an appearance now that she'd crossed over, but neither of them were anywhere to be seen, at least not that Lydie remembered.

She, Vanessa, and Wilma had spent several hours the night before going over what she would tell Nick this morning, as well as deciding on several avenues to explore for information going forward. Lydie was on her second cup of tea in the workroom and was just about to leave for the station when Wilma came downstairs looking about as chipper as she felt. Obviously, her aunt hadn't slept any better than she had.

"Good morning, Aunt Wilma. How are you feeling?"

Wilma ran a hand through her short hair. "Darlin', I feel like I've been beaten with a stick. Tossed and turned all night long. I had some weird dreams but can't remember much of them. Something about missing money and blackmail payments."

"That's weird. But I know what you mean. I didn't sleep well either. Sounds like we had the same night, though probably for different reasons."

Wilma yawned and rubbed her eyes. "You about to head out for your pow-wow with Nick?"

Lydie sighed and set her teacup in the sink. "Yes. I'm not looking forward to it, so I better get going before I change my mind. You know where everything is out in the industrial kitchen. Call me if you need anything. I should be back in a couple of hours."

As she headed out to the car, she dearly hoped that it wouldn't take that long.

The drive to the station only took about ten minutes, and as she pulled into the parking lot and turned off the engine, Lydie went over the list in her head of the things she was going to tell Nick. Finally, she made herself get out of the car when her anxiety level started to rise. She did some deep breathing exercises on the way into the building and by the time she reached the front desk, she'd centered herself.

"Can I help you?" the desk sergeant asked.

"Yes. I need to speak with Detective Sutton. My name is Lydie Charles."

The sergeant pointed to the hard plastic chairs along the wall. "Have a seat. I'll see if he's available."

Opting to stand rather than sit in the uncomfortable-looking chairs, Lydie used her cell phone to check her emails while she waited.

Nick didn't make her wait long.

"Lydie?" Nick called her name when he came around the front desk ten minutes later. "What are you doing here? Has something happened?"

She licked her lips and tried to give him a pleasant smile, which felt stiff and anything but pleasant. "I need to talk to you. I have some information that you should know. Information that pertains to your investiga—"

Nick frowned. "Lydie?" he asked again. "What's wrong? Are you okay?"

The vision came over her so rapidly and with such ferocity that she had no time at all to prepare. The station lobby faded away, replaced by a dark room with silhouettes of souls just out of clear sight. It stole her breath, and she felt the blood drain from her face. Her knees wanted to buckle as she tried desperately to hold off the vision.

No, no, no. Not here, not now...

But there was a cacophony of voices in her mind coming at her with the speed of light, and it seemed that Henrietta Stone would not be put off or silenced, either. The woman's grating voice boomed over the lot of them.

"You're wasting time, missy," Henrietta complained.

Lydie shook her head. "No. We're doing what we can. You haven't given me much to go on."

"Lydie? Talk to me, darlin'."

She heard Nick's voice, heard his confusion, but there was too much. Too many voices scrabbling for her attention.

"Blackmail, girlie," Henrietta boomed.

Lydie shook her head. "Blackmail? What does that even mean?"

"Who's being blackmailed?" Nick asked.

"Follow the damn money," Henrietta instructed. "That's the key…"

"Follow what money?" she asked, but the vision was already fading around the edges. "Wait! Henrietta, tell me what blackmail, what money?"

But the darkened room, the silhouettes, Henrietta, they were all gone in a wink and she was left in the too-bright lobby staring up into Nick's concerned green eyes. He had a grip on her arms and was literally holding her up.

"What the hell was that?" he asked, alarm coloring his words.

"I…" She felt the flush of embarrassment when she realized that the desk sergeant was also staring at her as if she was a bit touched.

"Lydie, answer me. What just happened? And what's this about blackmail?"

She sighed and rubbed her temples where a doozie of a headache was beginning. "Look, Nick, I'll explain what I can, but can we go to your office. I need to sit down but not here. Please."

He searched her face and seemed not to notice the desk sergeant's interest. "Are you sure you're okay?"

No, not even…

Still, she nodded. "I will be," she murmured as she let him lead her down the corridor and away from curious eyes.

12

Nick kept a tight hold on Lydie as he led her down the hallway and back to the office. He didn't know what had happened to her for those brief moments in the lobby, but it had scared him half to death. She'd gone pale as a wraith, and her eyes had taken on a distant, glassy look as if a very essential part of her had fled into the ether. For an instant, he'd thought he could almost feel a vibrating hum emanating from her.

It was unnerving.

He helped her into a chair by his desk as if she were made of glass, and frantically searched her face again. Her color had begun to return, for the most part, but now there was a fragile, exhausted look about her.

"Can I get you something to drink, Lydie?" he asked quietly. "You look like a strong breeze would blow you down."

"Yes. A little water would be helpful. Thank you."

"You bet. Hang tight. I'll be right back."

He hurried down the hall to the breakroom and returned a few minutes later with a bottle of water. Standing in the doorway, he watched her, unobserved, while she sat with eyes closed, gently rubbing the intricate medallion she wore around her neck between her thumb and fingers.

Her eyes popped open when he cleared his throat, and he went to her then with an apologetic smile, holding out the bottle of water.

"I can get you a cup, if you'd like."

"No, no, the bottle is fine." She gingerly took the bottle from him, and cracking it open, literally guzzled a third of it before giving him a sheepish look. "Sorry. Sometimes the visions just drain me dry with their severity, even the short ones." She dug in her bag and came up with a small compact of little white pills. Downing a couple, she nodded. "That should head off the migraine I can feel hovering, at least for a while."

Nick pulled a chair over and sat down opposite her. He still had concerns, but she was definitely looking better by the minute. "Visions?" he asked. "Is that what you're telling me that was? Some kind of vision?"

She gave him a wry look. "Don't sound so skeptical, Nick. I told you about my visions that day you and Andy came to interview us. Would it help if I called them waking dreams?"

"Not really." He chuckled and then sobered. "Seriously, what happened to you out there? One minute you were present, talking to me, and the next... well, it was like a part of you had disappeared."

Lydie's feelings were always right out there for all to see, and this was no exception. Normally, Nick enjoyed watching them parade across her lovely, expressive face, but it was obvious now that she was struggling with something—something she was hesitant to tell him. The thought gave him pause.

"Lydie?" he prompted.

"Oh, Nick. We've been over this. It's not something you really want to hear. You've made that clear."

"Come on, Lydie," he said with a sigh.

"No, Nick, I get it. You need to stick to facts and concrete proof. My visions are certainly not that. But then there was the whole 'witchy hoo-doo' thing, remember?"

Nick frowned. "So, how many ways do I have to pay for that stupid remark? It was years ago and just a joke, but it's like I never hear the end of it from Vanessa."

"But you are aware of how your family feels about our life-style, about the craft. It hasn't been easy for her." She looked down at her hands in her lap, turning her thumb ring around and around. "You hurt her feelings, Nick," she murmured. "You made fun of the essence of who and what she is."

And by extension... you, he thought. Sometime humans could be so cruel without even realizing it. "I've apologized over and over. Are you going to continue to punish me, too?"

She looked up at him then, and he was struck by the emotions swirling in the turquoise depths of her eyes. Regret, hope, uncertainty... possibly a good dollop of distrust?

"Lydie, you're not wrong. I do need to keep to the facts in this investigation, but instinct and intuition are always a part of the mix. I know what I said before in the interview, but talk to me. I promise to keep an open mind. You said something about blackmail and following a money trail in your... vision. What did you see? Who were you talking to?"

She paused briefly, and the look in her eyes was resolute. "Henrietta Stone."

Her words hung like a thunderclap in the air, and at first, he was unsure how to respond. Part of him rejected what she was suggesting, yet he'd seen something come over her, heard her say the Stone woman's name. "Lydie, Henrietta's dead."

She let out a cross between a gasp and a laugh. "Really, Nick? You think I don't know that? I was the one who gave her CPR before EMS arrived at the scene, remember? All I know is that she hasn't moved on yet. She's mad as hell, and I gotta tell you, as unpleasant in death as she was in life. She seems to want my help in finding her murderer, yet she's as cryptic as always and very little help."

Nick shook his head. "Wait... you said 'always.' Has this happened to you before? With Henrietta specifically?"

Lydie's gaze bounced around the room, looking everywhere but directly at him, and he could tangibly feel her unease.

"Yes. She's been in several of my waking dreams since the garden party, but only interactive in the last two."

"Interactive. You mean, you think she's talking to you from the grave?"

Lydie finally turned to him and shook her head. "I don't *think*, Nick. I know."

The shadows in her eyes made him want to make this easier for her. But he had a job to do and was compelled to understand all of the crazy things she was telling him. However, it wasn't easy for him, either.

Scrubbing his hands over his face, he blew out a breath. "Okay, how about we put a pin in that for a minute. Tell me what Henrietta said to you. What was the blackmail comment about? Did she mean that she was being blackmailed?"

"I don't *know*!" Lydie blurted and pushed up out of the chair. Walking to the window next to Andy's desk, she leaned on the sill, her forehead against the glass. "Like I said, Henrietta has not been very forthcoming with details. All she said was the word 'blackmail' and to follow the money. She said that was the key." She turned back to him then. "Does that make any sense to you?"

He frowned. "There is a possible embezzlement aspect of this case, but nothing's been confirmed, and there's been no evidence of blackmail... as of yet."

"Embezzlement? From the Society?"

He should have known that she would pounce on that small comment. So much for being tight-lipped about his investigation.

"Lydie, you know I can't elaborate. I shouldn't have said that much."

"Of course, not." She made a face.

"Anything else you can remember from this waking dream?"

"That was all Henrietta said, other than the fact that I was wasting time." She paused and pinned him with a stony look. "But I will say this, just so we're clear. I don't have any control over when these waking dreams come over me. And knowing how you feel, if this latest vision hadn't happened here in the precinct, I would never have told you about it."

"Lydie, that's not—" he began, but she put up a hand and cut him off, clearly finished with the subject.

"Besides, this isn't what I came to talk to you about in the first place."

Nick sighed again and gave a resigned nod. "Okay. What do you have for me?"

"We've come across a few things we thought you should know."

He gave her a narrow-eyed look. "We?"

"Vanessa and I."

"I see. And when you say that you came across this information? Came across it how?"

"Well, is wasn't from another vision," was her snarky reply. "This was word of mouth from the living."

When he just continued to stare at her, she threw up her hands.

"It was from a conversation with Barbara Drake, okay?"

"Oh, Lydie." Nick leaned back in his chair and frowned. "Please tell me that you and my nosy cousin haven't been snooping around in this investigation. Because Vanessa and I have had that conversation on several occasions."

He watched in fascination as fire sprang up in her eyes with her annoyance. Lydie was a beautiful woman, especially when she was mad.

And boy, was she mad.

"Now, you just listen to me, Nicholas Sutton. We didn't go looking for this information. Barbara just showed up yesterday afternoon wanting to talk to Vanessa. *She* came snooping around thinking to get the skinny on *your* investigation, which your nosy cousin shut down almost immediately, I might add."

"All right," he said quickly, hoping to stem her tirade. "Take it easy."

"I didn't have to come down here, you know. We could have just kept it all to ourselves, and then you wouldn't have had the embarrassment of having to witness my visionary spectacle right here in your precious precinct."

Oh, man, he thought. Yeah, not handling this very well at all, buddy.

He got up and went to her then, taking her hand and holding it tight even as she tried to pull it from his grasp. "Okay, okay. I apologize. Look, I guess I can be a little territorial with my investigations."

"You think?"

He grinned. "Be fair, Lydie. How many times do you want me to say I'm sorry?"

She made a face and managed to finally yank her hand free from his grasp. "Maybe a few more times, because I know you're going to backslide. You just can't help yourself," she grumbled. "You know, Vanessa said you'd react just this way—which is why I'm here instead of her—but I told her that giving you this pertinent information was the right thing to do. Don't make me sorry I came down here, Nick."

"Look, how about this." He crossed his heart like a child. "I promise to *try* to hold onto my tongue. Best I can do."

He watched a reluctant smile tug at the corners of her perfect lips before mentally shaking himself and dragging his attention back to her gaze. "So, what is this information that Barbara imparted? We were just out to interview her last week."

"Yes, she did mention that to Vanessa. We're not actually open for business on Sundays, so I was up the coast running errands while Vanessa was working on inventory in the shop. When Vanessa told her that I wasn't there, that's when Barbara said she'd come to see her and not me. Vanessa got the feeling it was a reconnaissance mission."

"Reconnaissance?"

Lydie nodded. "She was looking to find out from Vanessa where you were in your investigation. Wanted to know if you knew how the aconitine had gotten into Henrietta's teapot. Vanessa made it clear that she had no idea what you did or didn't know—that you were very tight-lipped about your cases." She smirked at him with the comment.

"I appreciate the back up."

"Vanessa also suggested there were quite a few women at the party who had the know-how and could have spiked Henrietta's tea, including Barbara herself."

Nick laughed out loud. "Geez, I can just hear how Van would have said something like that, in the most innocent of ways, of course. What did Ms. Drake have to say about that?"

"Barbara actually agreed." Lydie grinned. "But she said that while any of the master gardeners had the expertise to poison Henrietta, there were several who had it out for her for a myriad of reasons. That's when she started throwing out specific names and other interesting tidbits."

"Really? Such as?"

"Well, she started off with Anna Ingram."

"Anna Ingram? If memory serves, she's on our list to interview, but we haven't gotten to her yet."

She nodded. "Well, evidently, Anna, being a CPA, had been

Society treasurer when Henrietta took over as president. She and Henrietta didn't see eye to eye over the financials from the start, and Henrietta forced Anna out when her term was up, appointing Kathryn Wilks-Raymond in her place. Kathryn, who according to Barbara, has very little skill in the area of finance."

"Lydie, I'll admit that this is all weirdly interesting in a gossipy kind of way, but it's basically just that, little more than tongue-wagging. How is it a motive for murder?"

She held up a finger. "No, no, I'm not done with what she said about Anna. But let's move on to Doris Mayfield first."

Nick shook his head. "No need. I guess you haven't heard that—"

"That Doris is dead? Oh, yes, that was another tidbit that Barbara offered during her visit." Lydie closed her eyes and rubbed her temple as she spoke. "She evidently took great glee in relating the news that Doris had died from anaphylaxis from peanut oil in her stew. She said that Doris had been highly allergic to peanuts and would never have used peanut oil in anything she cooked, let alone ingest it." She opened her eyes and gave him a knowing look. "So, according to Barbara, Doris' death was murder as well."

Nick felt his anger rise. "How in God's name did she know any of that? Doris was just found on Friday. We haven't made any details public, let alone gotten final confirmation for cause of death."

"She said she'd heard it through the grapevine. So, it's true?"

"Lydie, again, I can't confirm or deny anything about either case. But no, I haven't heard back from the M.E. yet." He didn't think Lydie would repeat anything he told her, but he'd be damned if he was going to take any chances.

She nodded. "Fair enough. Then, as you said, let's put a pin in that for a minute. Not to speak ill of the dead, but the other tidbit that Barbara dropped on Vanessa involved both Doris and Anna."

"I'm listening."

"Well, I'm sure you've heard about the bad blood between Henrietta and Doris over the election for Society president."

"Yes."

"Well, Barbara said that if Doris hadn't died, she would have been at the top of Barbara's list of suspects for Henrietta's death. But Anna Ingram was next in line, as Doris had been having affairs, at the same time, with several Society members' husbands. Anna Ingram's included. And Barbara said she knew for certain that Anna had found out about the affair."

He nodded. "We did know about Doris' affairs, or at least the accusations. Could present motive for Anna in both deaths, but again, hearsay and gossip."

Lydie crossed her arms. "Then there was Letitia Edwards."

"What about her?"

"According to Barbara, Letitia and Henrietta hated each other. Letitia was the event coordinator for the Society, and by Barbara's account, not bad at it. But Henrietta ousted her as well."

When Nick started to shake his head, Lydie again put up a finger.

"I know, I know, more gossip, but Barbara said there was something more between the women from their past, something that nobody talked about, and it was deeper and uglier."

"And what was that?"

Lydie grinned. "She didn't know, which Van said obviously really frustrated her. Barbara said that she hadn't been able to find out what it was yet."

Nick stared at her with a frustrated look of his own, but her smile grew into a grin. "Well, you're the detective... go detect," she suggested as if she could read his mind.

"Very funny." Nick crossed to his desk and made a few notes in a file to look into some of what Lydie had told him. Then he looked over at her. "So, was that it? Anything else you want to tell me?"

The smile she gave him at the question was innocent enough, but he found the look in her eyes just a bit too smug for his liking, but then she shook her head.

"Nope. I've done what I came to do and more. All unburdened."

She grabbed her purse and started to leave but turned back at the door. He thought she'd say something more, but then she just shook her head. "Good luck with your investigations, Nick."

"Well, how did it go?" Vanessa asked from behind the counter when Lydie entered the shop twenty minutes later. "How did my dear cousin take the proffered information?"

Lydie made a face. "The whole thing started off on the wrong foot with some really bad timing."

"Bad timing? What do you mean?"

"Well, I had a waking dream right there in the lobby of the precinct, just as Nick came out to get me." Lydie related what had happened, what Henrietta had said to her in her vision, and then how Nick had reacted at first to her information.

"Ah ha!" Vanessa stabbed a finger at her. "I told you that's how he'd react, didn't I?"

"You did, and I told him so." Lydie grinned. "Right after I chewed him up one side and down the other."

"You didn't."

"Yep. Of course, my head was starting to throb, and I wasn't in any mood after the vision to make nice, so I kind of let him have it."

Vanessa's mouth dropped open. "What did he say?"

Lydie gave her a sheepish look. "He apologized several times. Then he actually listened to what I'd come to tell him."

"Really?"

"Yes, but unfortunately, he pointed out that, while interesting, most of it was gossip, hearsay, or conjecture, which is all true."

"But did you learn anything?" Aunt Wilma asked as she came in from the workroom. "Get any helpful leads?"

Lydie sighed and shook her head. "Not much. But I did get confirmation on a couple of things. First, that there is an aspect of embezzlement to one of the cases, or maybe both, I'm not sure."

"Nick *shared* that with you?" Vanessa asked in a shocked tone.

"He totally didn't mean to. When I told him what Henrietta said in my vision, I asked if it made sense to him. He said, and I quote, '*There is a possible embezzlement aspect of this case, but nothing has been confirmed, and there's been no evidence of blackmail... as of yet.*' When I pressed him for more, he clammed up."

"Well, that goes right along with my weird dreams from last night. Missing money and possible blackmail. You said you got confirmation on a couple of things," Wilma said. "What else?"

"Everything Barbara told Vanessa about Doris' death is true, for one thing."

Vanessa looked gob-smacked. "I can't believe that Nick actually told you that, either."

Lydie grinned. "Oh, he didn't. His reaction to what Barbara told you was enough. He was really ticked off, wanted to know how she'd found it all out. But, of course, when I asked if it was true, he started the whole backpedal deal. Can't comment on an active investigation, don't have confirmation of anything yet. Yada, yada, yada. But my gut says it's all true."

"What else?" Wilma asked.

"They already knew about Doris and her affairs but not that

Anna Ingram's hubby was one of the bunch or that Anna knew about the affair."

Vanessa rubbed her hands together with glee. "Ooo, a sordid mess. How de-lish."

"So, where do we go from here?" Wilma asked.

"I think we need to find an inconspicuous way to have a chat with Anna Ingram." Lydie narrowed her eyes in thought. "Nick said she was on his list to interview but that they hadn't gotten to her yet. If we could somehow talk to her before he gets around to it, that would be ideal. Now that I brought her to his attention, we'd have to be quick." Distracted by Circe's chattering, Lydie bent down and lifted the feline into her arms. "Yes, you're absolutely right, sweet girl. With embezzlement in the mix, we should definitely talk to Kathryn Wilks-Raymond as well. Nick deflected when I asked if the embezzlement was connected to the Garden Society, but my money says it is."

"Just how are we going to do either of those things inconspicuously? We don't know either woman very well. I mean, we can't just drop by and say, 'Hey, do you mind if we have a quick heart-to-heart about murder?'" Vanessa pointed out. "And if Nick gets wind of what we're doing, he'll blow his top."

"Then we'll just have to come up with something," Lydie replied. "So, put on your thinking caps, ladies. We need a plan."

13

Standing on Anna Ingram's front porch Tuesday just after the noon hour, Vanessa felt a bit of anxiety begin to rise. She had no idea how she was going to get the woman to talk to her, let alone give her sordid details about any of the things Barbara Drake had told them or insinuated. It had worried her all morning. However, Lydie and Aunt Wilma had nominated her to try, and since Lydie had taken the uncomfortable meeting with Nick the day before, Vanessa didn't think it would be wise to complain. Besides, Lydie and Wilma were hoping to meet with both Letitia Edwards and Kathryn Wilks-Raymond today, so would have their hands full with double duty.

Vanessa had to admit that together they'd come up with a pretty clever ruse to get a foot in the door with each of their targets, but after that, it was gonna be a crapshoot.

Anna had seemed surprised by Vanessa's call but was quite receptive to winning 'one of three door prizes' from the Society's garden party drawing. Lydie had put together three small bags of herbs, teas, and lotions from Lavender Fields to pass off as the prizes, but even that would do no more than get the trio through the respective doors. Vanessa had no idea how they would get the information they were looking to find, but she would give it a try.

Thinking she'd better get it over with before she lost her nerve, she reached out and rang the doorbell. It didn't take long for the woman to answer. Anna Ingram, an older woman in her mid-fifties, was kind of a plain Jane, but made up for it with her tasteful fashion sense and warm personality.

"Hello, Vanessa," Anna said with a cheerful smile, holding the screen door wide open. "Come on in out of the cold and wet."

"Thanks, Anna," she replied as she entered the foyer. "I was hoping that we weren't through with the lovely late summer weather we'd been having, but Lydie reminded me this morning that we already had a foothold on fall, and winter wouldn't be too far behind."

"Here, let me take your coat."

When Vanessa handed it over, Anna gestured to the adjacent room. "Have a seat in the living room. I'll hang this up and then bring in the refreshments."

"Oh, no need to go to any trouble."

But Anna just waved a hand in the air. "No trouble at all. I have coffee brewed, but if you'd rather have tea, the kettle's hot as well."

Vanessa considered a moment. "Actually, tea would be lovely."

As Anna headed into the kitchen, Vanessa took a turn around the living room. It was a large, bright room decorated with a blend of creamy colors in beiges and pale blues. Very calm and inviting, with touches of family paraphernalia and photos scattered throughout.

She set the prize bag on the big, round coffee table and sat down on the sofa. Moments later, Anna was back with a tray that held a teapot, a plate of sugar cookies, two cups, and all the necessary trimmings. She placed the tray on the coffee table next to the gift bag and sat down with Vanessa on the sofa.

"Now, here we are." She poured out two cups of steaming, fragrant tea and handed one to Vanessa. "This won't come close to matching Enchanted Affairs' blend, but it's not bad."

Vanessa chuckled. "It smells wonderful." After taking a careful sip, she smiled. "And it really is delightful. Is that just a hint of ginger I taste?"

Anna nodded. "I've been meaning to get out to Lavender Fields and pick up some of your house blend tea. I absolutely love it, but I just haven't had the time to get away."

"Well, that's a happy coincidence then because this prize bag contains a full tin of the house blend, along with some herb sachets and a couple of my favorite lotions."

"Oh, isn't that wonderful!"

Picking up the gift bag, Vanessa passed it over to Anna. "I'm sorry this is so late. We had planned to hand the prizes out after the awards ceremony, but... well..."

"No worries," Anna said quickly as she took the bag from Vanessa and looked inside. "And, yes, it's understandable that you had to wait with the party ending so abruptly the way it did." Looking up at Vanessa, Anna grimaced. "I mean, with Henrietta up and collapsing like that. Just terrible."

"Yes, and then... her death. Well, it really was just shocking."

Anna nodded in agreement. "I heard that the police are treating her death as suspicious."

"That was true, but unfortunately, now it's looking more like it was intentional. Her teapot was spiked with an extract of aconitum napellus. So, I rather think it is more than suspicious at this point."

"Monkshood?" Anna whispered with a shocked look. "Who on earth would do such a thing intentionally? I mean... that would make Henrietta's death... well... a possible homicide."

Vanessa thought the woman was either a terrific actor or really shaken by the news. It was as good a place as any to slide into the awkward conversation she'd come to have, but Anna went on before she could get into it.

"I don't know what this world is coming to. Letitia Edwards called me this morning to tell me she'd heard from Margot Beaumont that Doris Mayfield had died on Friday." The woman shook her head. "And Doris' death seems to be suspicious as well. Do you believe that?"

"Yes, I had heard that on Sunday from Barbara Drake when she stopped by Lavender Fields."

"Barbara Drake?" Anna asked with raised eyebrows. "She came by on a Sunday? I thought Lavender Fields wasn't open on Sundays."

"Oh, we're not. But sometimes folks just pop by, although Barbara never has before." Vanessa shrugged. "Anyway, Barbara said Doris had died from anaphylaxis from peanut oil that she'd ingested, which I thought was just awful. Evidently, Doris was highly allergic."

"That is terrible. Did Barbara say how she'd found that out?"

Vanessa shook her head. "No. All she would say was that she'd heard it through the grapevine." She paused for a moment, and then gave Anna a hesitant look. "Anna... I don't usually engage in or give much thought to gossip—and forgive me for bringing this up—but I think there are a few things that you have a right to know. Things that Barbara shared with me during her visit. Things that included you."

"Me?" Anna blurted, looking a bit stunned. "What in the world would she have to say about me? I hardly know the woman."

"Well, I got the feeling that she was on a fishing expedition when she came out to the shop."

"What do you mean?"

"See, my cousin Nick Sutton is the detective in charge of both investigations, and it seemed like Barbara was poking around for information on where he was in his inquiries, that sort of thing."

"And my name came up?"

"In a roundabout way, yes." Vanessa took a sip of her tea and then plunged in. "The conversation started out with her asking me if Nick knew how the toxic extract could have gotten into Henrietta's teapot, since hers was the only tainted pot. That's what I mean by fishing." Vanessa sighed. "Nick's very proprietary about his investigations. So of course, I told her that he would never share information from his cases with me, though, I did give her my personal opinion."

"Which was?"

"That it would be close to impossible to figure that out with so many gardeners milling around with the expertise to do the deed, including Barbara."

"Oh, my. What did she say to that?"

Vanessa smiled to herself, knowing that the woman was now hooked into the storyline. "It did surprise me, but Barbara agreed. However, she did say that any of the master gardeners would have the expertise as well as a myriad of reasons for wanting Henrietta gone, so to speak. I guess Henrietta was not all that well liked. Anyway, that's when she started throwing out names and possible motives. That's also when she told me about Doris' death."

"I see," Anna murmured. "And that's when my name came up? Because I'm a master gardener?"

"I'm afraid so. You weren't the only one, but she did start with you and had quite a bit to say, not only about your relationship with Henrietta, but with Doris as well."

Anna was quiet for a few moments, then looked up with anger ablaze in her eyes. "I can well imagine what that nasty woman had to say. So, let me just clear the air."

So much for hardly knowing the woman, Vanessa thought.

"First of all, I did loathe Henrietta Stone. The woman was the worst president that the Garden Society has ever had. Incompetent, corrupt, completely unsuitable. I'd been the Society's treasurer for a number of years. I'm an accountant. It's what I do for a living. But Henrietta replaced me as soon as she could after taking office. She didn't want anyone with a decent accounting background looking over her shoulder as she pilfered from the Society."

"Oh, my word! Was Henrietta embezzling from the Society?"

Anna nodded. "Mind you, I don't have physical proof, but I would wager a year's salary that a scan of the books will tell the tale. It's the reason that Kathryn Wilks-Raymond is now treasurer. She and Henrietta were bosom buddies."

"Well, I have no doubt that my cousin Nick will turn up all the details in his investigation soon, if he hasn't already. He's incredibly meticulous."

"If he hasn't gotten there yet, you make sure to point him in the right direction."

"Unfortunately, you can probably point him in that direction yourself," Vanessa said cautiously. "I have a feeling he'll be dropping by very soon. The one thing I do know about Nick's investigation for sure is that he has a long list to get through. I think Lydie and I were his first interviews, and he and Andy have come back out to Lavender Fields again since then for a second round."

"Hmm. I'll keep that in mind." Anna picked up her cup and took a sip, then gave Vanessa a considering look. "In light of Doris' recent death, I suppose the other thing Barbara shared with you was my history with Doris as well. It's a bit sordid, and something you never expect to happen to you, but several years ago she and my husband had an affair. And yes, before you ask, I found out about it. This is a very small community."

"Oh, Anna, I'm so sorry. I really didn't mean to upset you."

Anna waved away her comment. "As I said, it was several years ago, and Vern wasn't the only man Doris was messing around with back then. She had a number of men on a string at the time, including husbands of various Society members. Though Doris and I were never, ever going to be friends after that, we made peace with the whole nasty business not long after it happened. I made it clear to her at that time that she'd need to find her flings elsewhere and with someone other than my husband." Anna shrugged. "And then we both moved on."

"I really do apologize for bringing up this whole mess, but I just felt you had a right to know what Barbara was saying about you."

Anna put a hand on Vanessa's arm. "No need to apologize. It's nothing to do with you. And I do appreciate the heads up. Look, I have nothing to hide, and I'll gladly speak to the police should they show up on my doorstep." She sat back with her tea and a sly look. "In the meantime, it sounds like Barbara is doing a little deflecting of her own."

Vanessa frowned. "What do you mean?"

Anna's smile seemed just a touch evil to Vanessa. "I mean that Barbara Drake may come off as squeaky clean, and oftentimes as if she just wants to help, but don't let her fool you. She has no problem spreading lies and gossip or sticking the knife in wherever she finds a vulnerable spot. She's a nasty piece of work with skeletons of her own in those massive closets of hers."

"Oh... well... I—" Vanessa began, but Anna cut her off.

"But then, I'm sure you don't want to hear all the gossip. Suffice it to say that there's a reason Barbara comes poking around and keeps an ear to the ground. She's the queen of collecting information about others, all the dirty little secrets she can find. The secrets we all have can be a very profitable business. And for Barbara, business is always good."

Earlier that morning, while Vanessa was only contemplating her meeting with Anna Ingram, Lydie and her Aunt Wilma had intended to meet with Letitia Edwards, another one of their three 'door prize winners.' Unfortunately, Letitia was on her way out of town when Lydie called, so she and her aunt switched gears and headed out to meet with Kathryn Wilks-Raymond at the Garden Society offices around nine-thirty with the third prize.

"Oh, this is just so unexpected," Kathryn said as she escorted them back to her office. "I had no idea there were door prizes for the garden party. Winnie didn't say a word."

"Actually, Winnie didn't know," Lydie replied as the three of them entered the office and sat down. "It's something Enchanted Affairs does from time to time, especially with repeat businesses. We thought it would be a fun extra since we've handled the Society's annual awards party for the last few years. We had planned to hand out the door prizes after the awards ceremony, but unfortunately, we didn't make it that far," Lydie finished with a sad look.

Kathryn nodded slowly. "Yes. It was a really terrible way to end what had been a delightful afternoon. Enchanted Affairs came through with a fabulous event, as y'all always do."

"That's really nice of you to say." Lydie handed Kathryn the gift bag and smiled. "Anyway, Vanessa and I thought we should get the prizes to the winners as soon as possible."

"I see." Kathryn looked to Wilma. "And who is this you have with you today, Lydie?"

Lydie slapped a hand to her forehead. "Oh, Lord. Where are my manners? This is my Aunt Wilma. She runs *The Magick Baker Boulangerie* in Sunset Harbor down on the south coast. She's having her kitchen renovated and needed an industrial kitchen to do some recipe testing, so she's using Enchanted Affairs' kitchen for a couple of weeks."

"How fun is that?" Kathryn beamed. "It's a pleasure to meet you, Wilma."

"And you as well," Wilma replied with a smile.

"Kathryn, I just want to tell you how sorry I am about Henrietta," Lydie said. "I understand that you two were close."

"Yes. We were not only colleagues but friends as well." Kathryn sighed. "And actually, I may have been Henrietta's only true friend. I mean, she wasn't terribly well liked, you know, but to think that someone would do something so heinous... well, it's just mind-boggling, isn't it?"

"It is." Lydie frowned. "And to make matters worse, Barbara Drake stopped by Lavender Fields on Sunday and had some awful things to say about Henrietta."

Kathryn narrowed her eyes. "Did she really? Like what?"

Lydie hedged a bit. "Well, I don't like to spread gossip or innuendos, especially when Henrietta is gone and can no longer defend herself."

"Like I said, Henrietta was my friend. If Barbara Drake is saying terrible things about her, then that's really unfair. Someone should be able to step up and defend her, right?"

"I guess that's true," Lydie murmured. "Look, other than a couple of really ugly personal attacks that I won't mention, I think the worst thing was the insinuation that Henrietta was... possibly stealing from the Society's funds."

Kathryn nodded. "I suppose she said that was why I'm now the treasurer instead of Anna Ingram? No oversight?"

Lydie sighed and nodded. "Again, I'm sorry to have to tell you this."

"It's all right, Lydie. I hate to say it, but there is some truth to what Barbara told you about the Society coffers. I'd been working on Henrietta, trying to get her to replace some funds that she'd...

temporarily borrowed. Though I don't know how Barbara found out about it." Kathryn put up a hand. "You have to understand. Henrietta was in some pretty steep debt and struggling. She wasn't a bad person... just in dire straits, and it made her difficult at times."

Difficult at times? Lydie thought. That's an incredible understatement.

"The poor thing. There was also a tough personal issue pressuring her that she couldn't get away from," Kathryn continued. "And that made it almost impossible for her to dig her way out of the situation she was in. So, it just continued to get worse and worse. Unfortunately, we didn't have time to clear up the discrepancy before she died. And now I'm afraid I'm going have to report it all to the Society Board of Directors."

Wilma shook her head. "That's just so sad. Didn't she have family? Someone to assist her in her time of need?"

Kathryn shook her head. "She has a sister up north somewhere, but they weren't close. Other than that, Henrietta was on her own."

"So sad," Wilma murmured again. "I'm an outsider here, but it almost seems like the Garden Society is being targeted for some reason, what with this other death now, I mean."

"What other death?" Kathryn asked.

"Well, that was another thing we heard from Barbara. Doris Mayfield died on Friday," Lydie replied. "And it seems that her death is being treated as suspicious as well."

"Really?" Kathryn looked surprised. "You heard that from Barbara? Did she say why?"

Lydie shook her head. "Barbara said that Doris was deathly allergic to peanuts and peanut oil, and that's what killed her. Anaphylactic shock."

"But why would that be suspicious?"

"Because, evidently, peanut oil was found in the stew that

she'd had for lunch. Barbara said that she'd heard that the police think someone else was there and spiked her stew with the peanut oil."

"Oh, my. That's just terrible."

"I know." Lydie stared at the woman for a moment and blinked a couple of times. She could have sworn that Kathryn's aura—which had been a friendly orange for the entire visit—flickered briefly between red and green, before fading back to orange. Red was obviously a warning sign, and green could indicate envy, jealousy, guilt. But it happened so quickly that Lydie wasn't sure she'd read it correctly or if she'd just imagined it.

"Lydie? Are you all right?" Kathryn asked with concern, bringing Lydie back to the moment. "You look a bit flushed."

"I'm fine. Just a bit of a headache brewing, I think." Lydie looked to Wilma. "I suppose we should get going and let Kathryn get back to her workday."

"Yep." Wilma nodded. "I've got some baking to do later this afternoon and need to pick up a few supplies this morning, so we probably should get a move on."

"Well, thanks for dropping my door prize off, Lydie," Kathryn said as she followed them out to the office lobby. "I really do appreciate it and can't wait to try some of these lotions."

"You bet. Enjoy." Lydie waved over her shoulder. "Have a good day, Kathryn."

In truth, Lydie couldn't wait to get to the car. There was suddenly something about Kathryn that made her a bit uncomfortable, but she had no idea what it was, and the woman has been nothing but pleasant for their visit.

As she and Wilma climbed into the car, Wilma voiced her concerns as well. "Okay, that was just weird."

Lydie frowned. "What?"

"Well, didn't you feel it? And her aura?"

"You saw it, too? It happened so fast that I wondered if I'd imagined it."

Wilma barked out a laugh. "No, ma'am. There was a blip there that had the hairs on the back of my neck standing on end. But you're right, it was a quick flash and gone."

"Red and green. Could be that she was just feeling some anger over all Barbara's gossip, for disparaging her friend."

"True. Or maybe it was just her discomfort with the conversation about death. Some folks can't handle that." Wilma shook her head. "She seemed fine. Just something a bit off, in my opinion."

As Lydie pulled the car out of the parking lot, she was conflicted. Kathryn had been in her visions with Henrietta and Doris. But Barbara, Letitia, Anna, and Margot were all there as well. Kathryn obviously had strong feelings when it came to Barbara. Was that what Lydie and her aunt were feeling? Or was it something else, something deeper. In any case, they needed to uncoil this knotted mystery, and quickly. Because a third death was looming, Lydie could feel that as well, and she feared that Henrietta had been correct. They were running out of time.

14

Nick was in the office early again on Wednesday morning. There were just so many questions to sift through with these two cases and not nearly enough answers to move the investigations along at a decent clip.

At this point, it was obvious to him that Henrietta Stone's and Doris Mayfield's deaths were entwined in some way. But other than the fact that they were both members of the Garden Society and apparently hated each other's guts, he just couldn't get a grip on what his inner voice told him was an important hidden connection.

He would get to the bottom of it all, he promised himself. He always did. His partner often called him obsessive, and though the accusation always annoyed him, Nick supposed it was a fair observation. Once he got a hold of a puzzle—and murder was definitely that—he couldn't let it go until it was solved to his satisfaction.

At just after nine o'clock, said partner arrived. Andy stopped in the doorway and shook his head. "Oh, buddy, come on. Really?"

"What?" Nick glanced behind him as if Andy might be looking at something other than him. "What's the matter?"

His partner continued to shake his head and gave Nick a pitying look as he went to his desk and deposited his small backpack. "I'm not kidding, Nick. If you're not careful, people are going to start to talk about the sad and pitiful detective who's homeless and lives in his office."

Nick made a face. "Ha. Ha. You're killin' me here."

"Seriously. How early did you get in this morning? And don't lie to me. It's obvious that you've been here for quite a while."

"Don't start nagging. Geez, we're only a couple of weeks in. And besides, seven-thirty isn't that early. I had a few things bouncing around in my head that I needed to get out and examine. Couldn't sleep anyway, so thought it was best for my own well-being, and yours for that matter, to come in and get to work."

Nick went over to the board and stared at Doris Mayfield's photo for a moment before looking over his shoulder at his partner. "Stopped by my grandmother's house briefly on my way home last night. Had a round-robin conversation—off the record —about Doris Mayfield with several of Gran's friends that were there for a hen party. They all—reluctantly— said much the same thing. In various ways, they confirmed the info we received in that package on Friday about Doris' multiple affairs. One of them said Doris was, and I quote, 'quite promiscuous.' She said it in a whispered hush, like someone might overhear her and report back to Doris."

"I'm not surprised. If you want the basic dirt, that's the place to get it—in a hushed sort of way. About the package, are we any closer to finding out where it came from?"

Nick shook his head. "Len on the front desk said he found it on one of the chairs in the lobby. I guess Friday was pretty chaotic midafternoon when we were out interviewing Barbara Drake. He didn't see who left it there, so he brought it in and put it on my desk. He's gonna check the limited video feed for the lobby as soon as he gets time, but I'm not optimistic. Too many dead spots."

Andy pulled out his notebook and ran a finger down a page. "Well, I've got Anna Ingram on the docket for us to interview today about her part in Doris' promiscuity, or should I say her hubby's part in it. So, we may be able to get some on-the-record firsthand confirmation there." He looked up at Nick. "We also need to have that chat with Kathryn Wilks-Raymond about the funny business at the Society that Barbara Drake alluded to."

"Yeah. I've got both on my list, too. I'm hoping the requests I submitted for the bank statements of the two deceased women will finally come through today as well. I'm counting on those giving us a better connection between Stone and Mayfield. There has got to be something."

Andy narrowed his eyes. "Are you thinking about that vision thing that Lydie had? The possible blackmail aspect?"

"Maybe," Nick replied absently, looking back at the board. "There is definitely something that put these two specific women into somebody's crosshairs. I'm betting their bank statements are gonna give us some clues as to what that something may be."

"Any reports back from the lab yet about the forensics from Doris Mayfield's house? I know the peanut oil bottle that Dr. Landon found in the trash was obviously wiped, but any other prints or DNA they may have found in the house would really be helpful. Maybe at least give us a direction to follow?" Andy blew out a breath. "I mean, I feel like we're getting nowhere fast and can't catch a break."

"I'm so with you on that, partner. It is really frustrating. And so far, the lab's got nothing. They did find a few partials prints, but nothing they can match. The phone used to make the 911 call was wiped clean as well, along with almost every surface in the kitchen. Someone spent some quality time cleaning up after themselves before putting in that call and leaving the premises."

Andy ran a hand over his face. "I just can't believe that the neighborhood canvass turned up zip. I mean, in today's tech filled world, how is it possible that no one saw anything or anyone? I know that it was midday on a Friday, but not one witness? Nothing? Really?"

"Yeah. Again, frustrating. But someone saw or knows something. We *will* catch a break. We're getting closer. I can feel it coming in my bones."

"Well, it can't come fast enough."

"True." Nick looked at his watch. "Let's give it another thirty minutes to see if Kathryn Wilks-Raymond is in the office at the Garden Society, and then maybe head out there around ten-thirty. I'd like to get a clearer picture of what Barbara Drake was talking about."

"You mean that bit about malfeasance, about what Kathryn and Henrietta were up to? She did say they were thick as thieves, and that Kathryn would have quite a bit of dirt to share."

"That's exactly what I'm thinking. I'll check on the warrants. If we can at least get those, they would really make things go smoother."

"Now you're talkin'."

"Then later this afternoon, hopefully, we can hook up with Anna Ingram. Get the skinny there."

It seemed like their luck was beginning to turn when Andy called out to the Garden Society at ten o'clock and found out that Kathryn was in the office. Then, just before they could grab their gear and go, the warrants for the victims' bank accounts, as well as the Society's books and offices came through.

"What did I tell you, pal? We can look at the victims' accounts later. Let's get a team together and get out to the Society offices first. Do a search and confiscate the books, see what else we can find out from Kathryn Wilks-Raymond."

Andy grinned. "I do love it when a plan comes together."

By the time they'd gathered a small team for the search and got out to the Garden Society offices with the warrant, it was almost eleven. Kathryn Wilks-Raymond, a curvaceous, attractive woman in her mid-forties with big, chocolate-brown eyes and a stylish chestnut bob, met them at the door.

"I wondered how long it would take before you came out here with questions," Kathryn said with a sigh as they followed her back to her office.

"There have been some revelations in our inquiries, as well as suggestions of possible fraudulent activity concerning the Society's finances. Hence the warrants." Nick replied.

Kathryn nodded when she sat down behind the desk. "I completely understand. I will help in any way I can."

"Were you aware of any problems with Society funds?" Andy asked when he and Nick were seated.

Again, the woman nodded. "Sadly, all too aware."

"You want to tell us about it?" Nick asked quietly. "What are we going to find when we have a look at the books, Mrs. Wilks-Raymond?"

"Call me Kathryn, Detective." With a heavy sigh, she began her tale. "Henrietta was in some financial difficulty—had been for a while. I ran across her... misappropriation of funds quite by accident early on during an internal audit."

"Misappropriation of funds?" Andy asked. "What are we talking about here? Embezzlement?"

The woman pressed her lips together and slowly nodded.

"How much money?" Nick asked as he watched her fiddle with a pen on her desk, as if she needed something to do with her hands.

"Henrietta had taken a little over fifteen thousand dollars

from the money market fund when I stumbled across discrepancies."

"And do you know how long she'd been at it? Over what period of time?"

"I do," Kathryn said quietly. "I'm pretty sure it started not too long after she'd been elected to her first term as president."

"So, for several years at least." Andy looked up from his notepad. "Is that why she replaced Anna Ingram with you as treasurer?"

Kathryn looked over at him with surprise before acceptance crossed her face. "I suppose. We were friends. I don't think she thought I'd find the theft, or if I did, that I'd tell anyone."

"And to be clear, you didn't. Isn't that right?" Nick asked.

"Detective, Henrietta was my friend, but I didn't want to be part of anything illegal." The woman closed her eyes for a moment, and when she opened them, her resignation was evident. "No, I didn't tell anyone. I should have informed the Board immediately, but instead, I tried to help my friend out of the mess that she'd made. I begged her to let me help her replace the money—I have the means—but she was resistant. In the end, we just ran out of time. I had planned to come clean with the Board this week. I'd started preparing a packet with all the evidence on Monday."

Nick glanced down at the gift bag sitting on Kathryn's desk. "Lavender Fields. Are you a frequent customer?"

Kathryn laughed. "Oh, no. Lydie Charles and her aunt were by here yesterday morning. It seems I won a door prize for the Society's garden party that I had no idea they were giving out. Because of what happened with Henrietta, the party was cut short, so Lydie came by to deliver my gift."

Nick narrowed his eyes. "Did she now?"

"She did. Isn't that sweet?"

"Sure." He was going to have another talk with 'sweet Lydie Charles' at his first opportunity.

"Unfortunately, she also told me that Doris Mayfield died on Friday. You know, Doris was also a Garden Society member. I was really stunned when Lydie told me that. Do you know how it happened? She said it may have been intentional like Henrietta's death."

Oh, yeah. Lydie and I will definitely be having a little chat... and soon.

"The investigations into both deaths are ongoing, so I can't discuss them. I'm sorry."

Kathryn blinked away tears. "I understand. This whole thing is so disturbing. Just breaks my heart."

"It is that." Nick nodded, then switched gears. "I apologize for the intrusion this morning, but my team will be as fast as possible with the search, and then we'll be out of your hair. We'll be taking all financial documentation. Is this the only computer on the premises?"

"Yes," Kathryn replied, dabbing at her eyes with a tissue, then pointing to some cabinets behind them. "There are hard copies of bills, invoices, and that sort of thing, in the file cabinet over there, but all the financial statements and apps are on the hard drive. Do you know how long it will be before we get everything back? I'll need to give the Board an approximate timeline. They're going to be anxious about this whole mess, to say the least."

"We'll try to get through everything as quickly as we can. It will probably be within the next couple of weeks, though I can't give you any guarantees," Nick said. "We're a bit short on manpower right now, like everyone else, I guess. We'll be in touch when we're done."

As he and Andy got up to let the team into the office to do their job, Nick turned back at the doorway. "One last thing,

Kathryn. Can you think of anyone who'd want to harm either Ms. Stone or Ms. Mayfield in this way?"

The woman looked as if she was contemplating something, then she sighed. "Henrietta and Doris were not friends. There was extreme animosity there. And there was something bad, something that happened between Henrietta and Letitia Edwards many years ago that had festered over time. But if you're looking into who may have wanted to see both Henrietta and Doris suffer, you may want to look at Barbara Drake. She was not a fan of either woman. But then again, neither was Anna Ingram. That's all I'm going to say."

"Fair enough," Nick replied.

It took about an hour and a half for the team to go through the Garden Society offices and collect all the pertinent documentation. The electronics division, which consisted of two computer techs, had been given the Society's hard drive with instructions to put a rush on it. The rest of the team would sort through the three boxes of files they'd confiscated.

Nick and Andy would handle the warrants for the victims' financials and go through those bank statements later. In the meantime, they had a meeting with Anna Ingram, who it seemed, was not shocked to hear from them.

"Come on in. I've been expecting your call, Detective Sutton," the woman said as she answered the door and led them into the living room.

"You have?"

Anna smiled. "Your cousin mentioned that you would probably be in contact."

"My cousin?"

"Yes. Vanessa Deerborne is your cousin, isn't she?" At his nod, she went on, "Vanessa was here yesterday delivering my door prize from the Garden Society's awards party. Of course, Henrietta's untimely death came up during the visit."

I'll just bet it did. Apparently, a conversation with my nosy cousin as well as one with her business partner was warranted.

"I see. Well, then you probably know why we're here, what information we're looking for," Nick said, trying to keep the annoyance out of his voice. He was getting really tired of having to reiterate the phrase 'stay out of my investigations' to Vanessa. And lately, Lydie, for that matter.

"I imagine there are a few things you'd like to ask me about, so why don't I go first," the woman replied. "You'll want to know what my relationship with Henrietta Stone was like. I can tell you that I despised that woman. She was hateful, corrupt, and useless. If you haven't already, you should take a look at the Society's financials. I'm certain you'll find that she was embezzling from the organization, which is why she ousted me from the treasurer post that I'd held for several years."

She put up a hand when Andy started to speak. "And before you ask, yes, I am a master gardener, so I definitely have the knowledge to distill an extract of aconitum napellus—or monkshood to the novice. However, while I hated her for what she was doing to the organization, I didn't poison Henrietta. I was seated on the opposite end of the lawn and never went near her table during the entire event. You can ask any of the women who were seated at my table."

"Okay," Andy said. He looked up after scribbling down some notes on his pad. "Can you tell us a bit about Doris Mayfield?"

"I figured my relationship, or lack thereof, would be the next item on your list," Anna replied. "Several years ago, Doris had an affair with my husband, Vern, which I'm sure you already know or you wouldn't have asked. Not to speak ill of the dead, but Doris got around, if you know what I mean. She was *getting around* with a whole list of men at the time. And Vern wasn't the only Society member's husband on Doris' list."

"And you found out about the affair when?" Andy asked.

"Oh, it didn't take me long. This is a small town, Detective. And I'm not stupid."

Nick leaned forward. "Did you confront her when you found out?"

The women's smile was almost chilling, but her response was quite cordial. "Of course. I invited her out for coffee, and we had a discreet conversation about it. I made it clear to her that I didn't care who else she diddled but that my husband was off limits. I told her that I'd spill the beans to every other wife and ruin her but good if she ever came near Vern again." Anna crossed her legs and leaned back in her chair. "We were never going to be friends after that, Detective, but she and I came to an accord that day."

"Thank you for your candor, Mrs. Ingram," Nick replied. "We may have more questions at a later date."

"Any time, Detective. I have nothing to hide."

As they got to the door, Nick turned back to the woman. "One last thing, Mrs. Ingram. Is there anyone else you can think of who may have wanted to harm either Ms. Stone or Ms. Mayfield?"

If Anna's smile was chilling before, Nick thought it was deadly now.

"A few come to mind, but the top of the list is Barbara Drake. That woman is completely vile and thrives off of others' pain and misery. She loathed Henrietta, and I don't know what was between them, but she was constantly hateful to Doris."

"Okay. Thanks again for your time," Nick said as he and Andy escaped to the street.

As they drove back to the station, they went over what they'd learned from both Kathryn and Anna.

"Well, that was uncomfortable. She really didn't hold back. She was really nasty about it all… in a creepy, yet pleasant sort of way," Andy said making a face. "But I do find it interesting that both she and Kathryn immediately threw Barbara Drake under the bus."

"Yeah. There wasn't even a second thought in either quarter. Kathryn did add Anna and Letitia to the list. Though she said Letitia's problem was with Henrietta only and not Doris."

Andy nodded. "And Barbara pointed her finger at both of them. Seems like they're all throwing shade at everyone else."

Back at the office, Nick updated the board with everything they'd learned and then printed off the bank statements that had come through for both victims. After the Society's financials, they would be the next order of business.

His phone rang as he retrieved the statement copies from the printer. Hoping it was the lab with more info over the forensics, he answered quickly.

"Sutton."

"Nick, this is Kelli Landon."

"Hey, Doc. What's up? You have something new for me?"

"Well, you could say that, though it's nothing you're gonna want to hear."

"Okay," Nick said slowly.

"You should come out to Barbara Drake's residence right now."

Nick felt his stomach drop. He really didn't like the sound of this. "What's happened, Kelli?"

"Barbara Drake is dead."

15

Nick hung up the phone after a short and disturbingly sketchy conversation with the medical examiner. He stared at the phone for a moment, trying to piece together what little information Kelli had just given him.

"What was that about?" Andy asked with a frown. "I can see by your face that it's not good news."

"Yeah, that's a bit of an understatement. Grab your gear, partner. We need to head out to Barbara Drake's residence."

"Uh-oh. What's happened now?"

Nick slipped on his coat, then turned to Andy. "Evidently, Ms. Drake was found dead a few hours ago. Don't know a whole lot more than that, but it doesn't sound good."

"Oh, geez," Andy muttered in a resigned tone. "Cause of death?"

Nick shook his head. "Kelli said she was found in the attached pool house... floating in the pool."

"What?" His partner gave him a hopeful look. "Please tell me this was an accidental drowning and not connected to our first two homicides."

"Well, you can hold onto that hope, buddy, but I'd say it's

fairly doubtful." Nick sighed. "That was the reason for Kelli's call. Evidently, the housekeeper came in around noon and found Drake—fully clothed—face down in the pool. So, unless she got a sudden urge to take a dip and was too lazy to change into a swimming suit, this sounds more than suspicious to me. I guess we'll just have to get out there and give the whole thing an eyeball."

Andy followed him out of the office and down the hall to a side door. "No matter what we find, our suspect list seems to be dwindling. And shoot, I was leaning in Drake's direction, too. Kinda liking her for the garden homicides, you know?"

Nick stopped and gave his partner a squinty look. "The 'garden homicides?'"

Andy laughed. "That's how I've started thinking about them. You know, the Garden Society, garden homicides. Anyway, for that reason alone, it's hard to see Drake's death as a coincidence, right?"

Nick barked out a humorless laugh. "Could be an unrelated death, but the little voice in the back of my head is shouting that there's not a chance in hell this isn't connected to Stone and Mayfield somehow. Of course, that would just muddy the water even more than it already is, but again, let's hold our theorizing until we get a look at the scene and Kelli's tentative ruling."

"Well, I'm gonna keep positive thoughts, because that's how I roll," Andy said, sarcastically, with a cheesy grin.

Nick shook his head, before turning and leaving the building.

Barbara Drake lived outside of town in a beautiful park-like setting. Lush, fragrant, and very secluded, which had Nick's mind humming. Yeah, maybe this was a coincidental death, but then again, he didn't believe in coincidence... especially when it came to death.

Turning into the long, winding driveway up to the Drake residence, Nick stopped halfway up the hill to orient himself and get a feel for the place. They'd been here the week before to interview the victim about Henrietta Stone's death, but he was now looking at the place with a more critical eye.

"Perfect place for someone to park and sneak up unseen, even if she has security cameras," Andy murmured, then turned with a smile. "Not that I'm thinking along sinister lines or anything."

"Yeah, I was thinking the same thing," Nick replied as he took his foot off the brake and continued up the driveway to the house. Pulling in next to the ambulance, they got out of the car, and Nick took a few more moments to scan the front of the huge, Tudor-style mansion with its lovely front gardens. The house and gardens could have been taken right off the pages of Elegant Living magazine or some such similar thing.

Barbara Drake was divorced—it was said that she got the house in the divorce settlement—and lived at the property alone. He knew from their earlier interview that she was a master gardener herself but used a landscaping service to maintain her grounds. He found it odd that she would live in this massive house alone, secluded as it was. She didn't even have a pet, but then, a lot of people liked solitude and to have space around them. Nick thought he would have found it incredibly lonely.

When they finally headed into the house, they stopped in the foyer to glove up and pull on protective booties over their shoes. Barbara's death might end up being accidental and not a homicide, but until they knew for certain, they would make sure not to contaminate the scene either way.

They found Kelli and the EMS team in the pool house where they had removed Barbara Drake's body from the water and were preparing her for transport.

"Hey, Kelli. Meeting this way is becoming an unpleasant bad habit," Nick said with a grimace. "You pulled her from the pool already?"

Kelli sighed. "Well, she was halfway out when we got here. Linelle Reynolds, Barbara's housekeeper, tried to save her but only got her to the steps. Damage was already done by then. We got photos of how we found her when we arrived, for what it's worth."

"Okay. So, what do you have for us so far?"

The M.E. sighed and shook her head. "Not much more than I told you on the phone. I can confirm that she's deceased—as you can see for yourself—but not a specific time of death, because unfortunately, the pool is heated. That messes with my timeline a bit, but I'd say it was sometime within the last twenty-four hours."

She nodded to the EMS team and watched as they zipped up the body bag and lifted Barbara's body onto the gurney. Then Kelli turned back to Nick as the team started out of the pool house to transport the body back to the morgue.

"And I can estimate that timeline right now because Linelle actually talked to her on the phone yesterday afternoon around four-thirty. She cleans the house every other Monday, but Barbara was planning a small dinner party for Friday and wanted her to come out early."

Nick walked around to the end of the rectangular pool, looking for anything out of the ordinary. "So, Linelle found her out here?"

"Yes. She was actually supposed to meet Barbara at noon. She said that Barbara wanted to discuss a few specific things she wanted done for the party. But when Linelle got here, the front door was slightly ajar, so she came in with some of her equipment."

"Yeah, we saw it in the foyer where she obviously left it," Andy said.

Kelli nodded. "Evidently, she called out to Barbara a couple of times but got no answer. Anyway, when she found Barbara, she freaked out and jumped into the pool to try and save her. But she said when she turned her over, Barbara's eyes were open, and she knew then that it was too late. She towed the body to the pool steps and got out, then immediately called 911. She's waiting in the living room so you can take her statement."

"What about Barbara? Was there anything—besides the drowning, of course—you saw that was concerning or that would indicate something suspicious?" Andy asked.

Kelli smiled thinly. "I wouldn't jump to conclusions just yet, Detective, simply because she was found in the pool. This *may* have been a drowning, but I won't know exactly how she died until I get her on the table. But to your question, I saw no contusions or bruising in my very limited examination after she was pulled from the pool."

"Okay then, I guess we'll have the team come out and give the house a look-see, and in the meantime, have a chat with Linelle," Nick replied.

"I'm on it," Andy said as he pulled out his cell phone and made the call.

"You said she's in the living room?" Nick asked.

Kelli nodded and stripped off her latex gloves, dropping them into a plastic bag in her satchel. "Go easy on her, Nick. She's young and severely shaken up. I'm pretty sure she's never seen a dead body before today, let alone found one. Carla's shadowing me this week. She's my intern, and I've had her sitting with Linelle while I finished up out here. But I'm done, so I'll head in with you and grab Carla on my way out, unless you need anything else from me."

"Nope. That's fine. Just give me a call when you have a definite cause of death or anything more for me."

"Of course," Kelli replied. "Ms. Drake will be my first priority. I'll send the digital pics of how she was found and then give you a shout as soon as I know something."

Once Andy was finished with his call, Kelli led them out of the pool house and back toward the front of the main house to the living room where she addressed the waiting and waterlogged housekeeper. "Linelle, I know this is a difficult situation, but this is Detective Sutton and his partner Detective Gilmor. They'll need for you to go through the timeline like you did with me. Can you do that?"

Linelle was a pretty little thing in her mid to late twenties. Now, traumatized and wrapped in a towel, she looked more like a twelve-year-old. With wet hair and teary eyes, she looked over at Nick and nodded.

"Do you want Kelli and Carla to stay with you while we talk, Linelle?" Nick asked.

She gave him a hopeful look. "Can they?"

"You bet." He turned to Kelli. "That is, if you have the time."

"Absolutely." Kelli took a seat on the sofa next to the trembling housekeeper, bracketing her between herself and Carla.

"I-I'm sorry," she said to Kelli. "I'll get you all wet. Oh, geez, I'm getting the sofa all wet, too." She looked around, as if not really sure what to do.

Kelli took the young woman's hand. "Don't you worry about that. You're fine. And we'll both dry out eventually, as will the sofa."

Nick sat in a wing chair opposite them and spoke gently. "Okay, Linelle. Just start at the beginning and take us through how you found Ms. Drake. Kelli said that you were supposed to meet with her around noon and found the door open when you got here?"

Linelle nodded. "I wasn't scheduled to clean until Monday, but Ms. Drake called me yesterday afternoon and wanted me to come today."

"She was having a party on Friday, is that right?" Andy asked softly.

"Yeah. She's not always here when I come to clean, but she

wanted to talk about a few extra things she wanted done before the party."

"So, what did you do when you got here?" Nick asked.

The housekeeper took a deep breath and blew it out slowly. "Well, like you said, the door was open a little. I could see that when I came up the front steps. I was carrying some of my stuff and had my hands full, so I kinda nudged the door with my shoulder. I called out for Ms. Drake, but there was no answer." She looked at Nick as a tear trickled down her face. She swiped at it with the back of her hand and went on. "Like I said, she's not always here when I come. I have a key and know the codes, but the door was open. I knew she wouldn't ever leave the door open if she'd gone somewhere, so I went looking for her."

Andy looked up from his notepad. "But she wasn't in the house?"

"I didn't go upstairs. I suppose I should have. I mean, she could've been in her bedroom, but I guess I didn't think about that. Anyway, I finally went out into the pool house because I noticed that door was open, too, and it never is when I come to clean. I don't do the pool house. Ms. Drake has a pool service that handles the area."

"And that's when you found her?" Nick asked quietly.

Linelle nodded and began to silently cry. "She-she was fully dressed and floating face down."

A sob escaped her, and Nick watched Kelli rub Linelle's back and murmur words of encouragement. After a moment, the housekeeper nodded again and wiped her eyes.

"I-I'm sorry," she stammered. "This is just so awful."

"I know. Take your time," Nick replied.

"The thing is, I know you're not supposed to mess with the body in situations like this," Linelle said. "I mean, I've watched those CSI shows on TV. But I was just so stunned at seeing her there. I jumped in without even thinking about it. I thought maybe I could help her. And then when I turned her over... oh my gosh, I saw that she was... that she—" She broke down again and turned to Kelli.

"It's okay, Linelle. There was nothing you could've done," Kelli said rubbing a hand up and down Linelle's arm. "It's a natural instinct to want to help someone like that."

"Totally understandable," Andy added.

"So, what did you do then?" Nick asked.

"Well, I pulled her over to the stairs, but couldn't get her any farther. I just got out of the pool as fast as I could and ran back to the foyer to get my cell phone out of my pack. And then I called 911. I got water all over the floors."

"No worries. It's just water," Andy replied with a smile. "Did you go back to the pool house after that?"

Linelle vigorously shook her head. "I sat out on the front steps until the EMS guys came. And then Dr. Kelli came, and I've been sitting in here with Carla ever since." She looked at Nick and then Kelli. "Can I go home now? I don't want to be here anymore."

"You bet," Nick said, and then put up a finger. "Just one more question. Did you notice anything, inside or out, that seemed off to you? Anything other than the front door being ajar and the pool house door being open?" Nick gave her an intent look. "Think carefully, Linelle. Was there anything else that you thought was out of the ordinary? You know Ms. Drake's habits, what she likes, doesn't like. Was there anything that stands out in your mind?"

The young woman started to shake her head and then stopped, blinked a couple of times, and then looked up at him with surprise.

"You know, yes, there was something, but I just kinda passed over it."

Nick sat forward. "And what was that, Linelle?"

"So, when I was looking for Ms. Drake, the first place I went was the kitchen. Sometimes she sits at the little table by the window overlooking the back gardens. She has an office upstairs, but I think she likes... liked to do bills and stuff with the garden view."

"Go on."

"Well, there were two drink glasses, you know, like, I guess you would call them highball glasses, on a towel by the sink."

Andy frowned. "What's so odd about that? Why would that stand out to you?"

"Ms. Drake never, and I mean, *never* did that. She was really OCD about it, too. She jumped all over me when I did that with a couple of glasses when I first started cleaning for her. I mean, I'd washed them out with dishwashing soap and everything, so they were clean. But it didn't make any difference to her. Trust me, I've never done anything like that here again. She always rinsed her dishes and put them straight into the dishwasher. Always."

"Okay. Good catch," Nick said. "Anything else?"

Linelle slowly shook her head. "Not that I can think of."

"Okay. Well, if you think of anything else, no matter how small or insignificant it may seem, please give me a call." Nick handed her his business card.

"Thank you. I will."

They all stood as the sweepers arrived. Andy met the team to give instructions while Nick walked Kelli, Carla, and Linelle into the foyer where Linelle grabbed her pack. Then they headed outside, and Nick tagged an officer along the way.

"Linelle, I'm going to have Officer Davies here drive you home. I don't think it's a good idea for you to drive yourself after what you've been through."

"If you like, we can drop her off at home, Nick," Kelli offered. "Officer Davies will probably be needed here, right?"

"Thanks, Kelli. Linelle, we'll load the rest of your cleaning equipment into your car, so if you want to have someone come get it or bring you back later, that would be fine. I'll make sure it's secure."

"Okay," the young woman murmured quietly. "Thanks, again. I'll have my brother come and get my car later."

Nick watched them climb into Kelli's Volvo, then he and Officer Davies went back into the house where the sweepers had begun their work.

It was after five o'clock by the time Nick and Andy got back to the office. Nick was frustrated and beat-tired. They had collected everything they'd found, which wasn't as much as he would have liked. The two glasses from the kitchen, found exactly where Linelle had said they'd be, the garbage, both inside and out, and a handful of damp towels from the laundry room that had obviously been rinsed out. It wasn't much, but then the sweepers had collected prints from the kitchen and laundry room, so maybe that would pan out with something substantial. He could only hope that Kelli would find something that would tell them conclusively, one way or another, about Barbara Drake's death. Was it another death connected to the first two? Or was this just mere happenstance?

Nick was leaning toward the former—that Barbara's death was no accident. Something about those glasses on the kitchen counter was a red flag for him. Whoever had been there obviously didn't know about Barbara's OCD issue or they would never have left them there. They would have put them directly into the dishwasher as Barbara herself would have done. The towels in the laundry room indicated that something had been cleaned up. But what, when, and by whom? These were the questions that were buzzing around in his brain.

In the meantime, they had the financial information for Stone and Mayfield to go through. Because his instinct told him there was something more connecting those murders than just hard feelings, he hoped the financial statements would give him that something.

When he sat down at his desk and opened the first file on his computer, Andy came in and made a point of looking at his watch.

"Dude, you do know what time it is, right?"

Nick squinted at the computer screen and tried to ignore his partner, but Andy was having none of it.

"You can't ignore me because I'll just keep yammering." Andy came over and leaned down next to Nick. "We've had a very eventful day. We've put in a request for Drake's financials in anticipation of her death being connected to Stone and Mayfield. The lab has everything that the sweepers collected. We've done all we can for today. We're both done in and need some rest."

"Yeah, I'll go in just a minute."

"No, you won't. Nick, you'll obsess. Please. For my sake, if not for your mental health. Turn that thing off and go home. You'll not do either of us any good staying here all night, pouring through computer files."

Nick shook his head. "It's just so frustrating. We're right on the edge of finding that thing that will crack these cases, or at least start the dominoes falling. I can feel it."

"So, what? You're psychic now? Lydie Charles rubbing off on you?"

"Very funny."

"Come on, Nick. Let's go home and come back fresh in the morning. Please."

With a sigh, Nick knew his partner was right. "Okay. In the morning. But if you're late, no whining about me being early, deal?"

Andy laughed out loud. "Deal."

Nick gave one more look at the screen before shutting down the computer. Lydie may just be rubbing off on him, he thought, because there was something in those bank and financial statements for Stone and Mayfield. That something would give them the break they were looking for. And *that* he knew in his bones.

16

Lydie was a bit surprised when she got back to the shop and found it closed at half past two on Friday afternoon. She'd had an issue with a large essential oil shipment they'd received from a wholesaler up the coast, so she'd driven back up that morning with the erroneous shipment to correct the order rather than waiting another week to get the amended batch. It was a beautiful fall day with a snap in the air, perfect for a drive up the North Coast Highway, which also saved her from having to ship the incorrect order back and pay the freight.

Vanessa had gone over the hill to the valley to pick up an old high school friend from the airport and would be staying overnight to catch up. Aunt Wilma had offered to watch the shop while Lydie was gone, since she would be testing recipes in the industrial kitchen all day long, anyway. She'd probably run out for a bite to eat or to pick up more baking supplies.

Evidently, she hadn't been gone long, as the sign on the front door said she'd be back by three-thirty. And it wasn't really a problem, since business on Fridays tended to be slow in the first place.

Digging for her keys, Lydie used the first box to push through the shop door, and then made two additional trips with the updated merchandise. Along with the rest of her purchases, she hauled everything back to the workroom to sort. She was dying for a nice cup of tea, and got a pleasant surprise in the form of a basket of chocolate berry brownies that Aunt Wilma had obviously left on the workroom table. She decided that the brownies would go nicely with that tea.

Putting on the kettle, she proceeded to open the boxes one by one, unpacking her new goods while she waited for the kettle to heat.

Once she'd emptied the boxes and bags and stacked the goods on the workroom table, she scooped some loose tea into a small pot. Filling it with hot water, she covered it with a tea cozy and put it on a tray with a cup and a plate with two of the yummy-looking brownies. She grabbed the packing slips from the shipment and the receipts from the rest of her purchases, taking them all with her into the office.

Sitting down at her desk and pouring the tea, she picked up her cup and had barely taken a few bites of brownie when she felt the change in the air. She set the cup down on the saucer with a clatter as her vision began to blur and the sound of white noise rushed into her head. A strong odor of chlorine filled her nostrils. And as certain scents will often do, it immediately brought back old childhood memories with vivid clarity—memories of the summer fun she and her friends had splashing around in the swimming pool at the Y.

But this definitely wasn't the Y.

Nor was it fun.

However, this vision did feature a swimming pool, long and rectangular, clearly in a pool house of sorts. The air in the building was humid, and thick with it. The water of the pool was mirror-calm.

With the exception of the woman's body floating face down in the center.

Lydie hadn't had a prophetic dream, waking or otherwise, for several days. Not since her full-on vision in front of Nick at the police precinct on Monday. But with previous visions indicating that there would be three deaths, her breath came in huge gasps as she tried to make sense of what she was seeing before her. Did she know this woman in the pool? With the victim face down in the water, it was hard to tell, but she suddenly had the feeling that she should, yet she couldn't quite get a hold of a name.

Until the voice next to her spoke.

"Seems you were too slow, Lydie. Yet again." There was a long sigh. "And now look at me."

Lydie turned to find Barbara Drake standing next to her staring down at the body in the water. *Her* body. She was wearing the same clothes as the woman in the pool, though she was dry as a bone, with makeup and hair all in place and just so.

Barbara turned to her, the look in her eyes wistful. "I wasn't ready. I was having the time of my life... and making a sly bit of coin on the side." She turned back to gaze sadly at her body floating there. "I guess we never know when our time is up, but I *really* don't appreciate my time being helped along. *That* annoys me to no end, you know? Definitely not fair play."

So, Barbara was number three? Lydie swallowed hard and then cleared her throat. "Barbara, what happened to you?"

"You were warned, weren't you, Lydie?" Barbara asked. "That cow Henrietta. She told you that you were acting too slowly, but you obviously didn't listen."

"Barbara, Henrietta hasn't given me much to go on. She—"

Barbara waved her answer away. "Oh, I don't blame you, Lydie. Trust me, I know exactly where to place the blame. They'll get theirs in the end. Because karma is a bitch."

"Who'll get theirs? Who did this? Tell me who's responsible, Barbara."

The dead woman turned then, and the look in her gaze was fierce and mean. "This wasn't an accident, you know. I didn't drown. So, you watch yourself, Lydie Charles. You're not safe, either. You're a target now, too, but for very different reasons."

Lydie blanched. "What do you mean? What reasons?"

"Well, you've poked and prodded, haven't you. Nosed around where you shouldn't. I have to say, I do admire that. You're resourceful and you've got grit, but that will only go so far if you don't watch your step."

"What are you talking about? A target for whom?" Lydie cried. "I've only tried to stop what was happening, to prevent more death. But my visions aren't always clear."

Barbara tilted her perfectly coifed head and pursed her lips with a considering look. "You are a smart one, Lydie, but you're not looking closely enough. Or, I dare say, at the right things. Henrietta told you to follow the money, didn't she? The witch. But that really doesn't matter now. So, do as you were told, and *follow the damned money*."

Barbara's voice was starting to fade. The pool house, the entire scene was beginning to waver slightly.

"Wait! Tell me what to look for. What money? Barbara, please, I need more information. At least point me in the right direction."

Barbara just smiled and shook her head. "Like I said, you're a smart one. You'll figure it out, along with that handsome detective of yours. He's following the money, so at least he's on the right track." She turned to walk along the side of the pool, stopping to take one last glance at her body floating there. Then she looked back at Lydie as her image began to fade along with her voice. "You know, I have quite an extensive library here. You may want to take a page from one of my books. Paris is so nice this time of year. After all, a picture is worth a thousand words, right?

You'll need geraniums to find the way. Geraniums hold the key. But a reminder, be quick and watch yourself, and I mean it. There's danger coming. And it's moving in your direction..."

Then the entire vision evaporated in a blink, leaving Lydie alone in her office, breathless, filled with unnamed terror, and with Barbara's last words ringing in her ears. She didn't know how long the vision had lasted, but the tea she'd poured was now almost cold. She was so parched that she drained the entire cup in a few quick gulps and immediately poured another.

What on earth were they going to do now? Should she tell Nick about this? Perhaps he'd have an idea about what it all meant.

Not only did she feel dehydrated, but she was suddenly ravenous. She picked up the brownie that she'd started and nearly shoved the whole thing into her mouth, following it with half the fresh cup of lukewarm tea from the pot. She was about to do the same with the second brownie when the phone on her desk rang. With a sigh, she set the brownie down, licked the sticky from her fingers, and took a quick sip of tea before picking up the receiver.

"Good afternoon, Lavender Fields," she answered breathlessly.

"Hey, Lydie. This is Nick." There was a slight pause. "Everything okay? You sound out of breath."

"Oh, Nick. I've just had a... um... yes, I'm fine," she replied, amending her answer, and stemming her instinct to tell Nick about her vision just yet—and certainly not over the phone.

But he seemed to sense her distress and pushed.

"You sure? You don't sound fine. What's going on, Lydie?"

She yearned to tell him, to blurt it all out, to at least share the burden with someone. "Actually, there is something that I really do need to tell you, something distressful that's just happened. I think it may be important but it's not something I want to talk about over the phone."

"Okay," he murmured slowly. "I can swing by later, if that works for you."

"Yes, that works." She felt relief flood her system. Later would be good. It would give her time to settle, get the terror out of her system. Nick may not believe in her visions, but she knew that telling him would help with her anxiety. "So, what were you calling about?"

"Well, a couple of things. First, after our chat on Monday— and your... uh... vision about three deaths—I wanted to tell you that Barbara Drake was found dead on Wednesday."

"I know," she replied without thinking, then nearly bit her tongue in two. "I mean, about her dying but not when."

"You know?" he asked in confusion. "How? Who told you?"

After a brief pause, Lydie all but whispered, "She did. About twenty minutes ago."

"Lydie..."

She sighed. "I had another vision, Nick. Look, this is what I didn't want to discuss over the phone. I know you don't believe in my visions, but she died in her pool, right? And, Nick, just so you know, she didn't drown."

"Okay, I just found that out this morning, along with the actual cause of death. And that hasn't been released to anyone yet. How could you have known that, Lydie?"

She laughed out loud, but it held no humor. "Come on, Nick. Do you really think that Barbara doesn't know exactly how she died? She didn't say how it happened, but she did tell me that it wasn't an accident and that she didn't drown."

There was silence on the other end of the line, and Lydie could almost hear Nick's thoughts racing in that silence.

"Nick, there were a few more pretty disturbing things that Barbara told me. One of which is that it's possible I'm being targeted now, too."

"Targeted? By whom? And why?"

Lydie rubbed her forehead where she could feel a headache brewing. "She didn't fill in many of those blanks, either. But she did mention that I've, and I quote, 'poked and prodded.'"

"For the love of God, Lydie. This is exactly what I've been trying to tell you and Vanessa, which was the other reason for my call. I had two interviews this week, Lydie. Two, that specifically mentioned you and Vanessa coming by to 'chat' under the guise of handing out door prizes. What were you two thinking? What did you expect? That it wouldn't ruffle any feathers? That the killer or killers wouldn't mind?"

"We were just asking a few questions, just trying to confirm what my visions have shown me."

"Listen to yourself," he said, his voice filled with anger on the other end of the line. "We're talking about *murder* here, Lydie. You have got to leave this investigation to us. If what you say is true, you could be in real danger."

"I know, I know. I'm sorry. Again, this was why I wanted to have this conversation face to face."

"This is not good. You should have come to me first."

That comment and the tone he used struck an unpleasant chord and had Lydie's anger rising to match his. "Oh, yes. Fine. Like that would've been accepted without a smirk? *You* listen to *yourself*, Nick. It's so easy for you to berate and point fingers. But remember our conversation on Monday? You briefly humored me, but you made it perfectly clear early on that you had no time for whatever 'information' I gleaned from my so-called waking dreams or visions."

"Lydie..."

"Do you even understand how terrifying it is to have these prophetic visions? Being told what's coming, and yet knowing that there's no one I can tell who will take me seriously other than Vanessa and my family?"

"We went over it all on Monday, Lydie. I thought we'd gotten past this." Nick said, calming down a bit. "Look, I'm in the middle of something here, but give me an hour to wrap it up, and I can come out there. We can go through everything, including any new information you might have gotten with this last vision."

There it was again. Relief. Just the thought of Nick coming out and listening was like a balm to her terrified psyche, and it took the edge off of her anger which she knew was fueled by her fear. He would know what steps to take, what to do next.

"Okay," she said taking a deep breath and letting it out slowly. "I'll be waiting."

"In the meantime, is Vanessa there?"

"No. She's in the valley and staying there overnight. Aunt Wilma was watching the shop today doing some recipe testing in the industrial kitchen. She obviously ran out for something, because she wasn't here when I got home. But she must have gotten delayed. She was supposed to be back by now."

"Okay, good. When she gets back, both of you stay put. Give me an hour." Nick paused. "We'll figure this out, Lydie. I promise."

She said goodbye and had barely hung up the phone when she felt the first nip of nausea begin to rise to go with the headache that was now pounding behind her eyes. Both happened from time to time with her visions, but they usually passed with a cup of tea and a bite to eat. So, she freshened her cup and took another bite of the second brownie. Then turned back to her packing slips and receipts.

Unfortunately, after twenty minutes the headache was passing but the nausea was getting worse. She thought to go splash some water on her face and see about taking something to settle her stomach, but as she started for the workroom, she slapped a hand over her mouth as her stomach roiled. Her quick walk became a fast jog toward the bathroom, and she barely made it there before the vomiting started.

Nick tried to put his conversation with Lydie and concern for her safety out of his mind, but he couldn't quite get there. She and Vanessa had been messing around in his investigation even while telling him that they weren't. Now, if what Lydie had seen in her recent vision was true—and he still couldn't believe that he was beginning to consider her visions in those terms—then she and his cousin could very well be in real danger. And the fact that they were no closer to figuring out who was committing these murders, or why, made it impossible to know which direction the threat may come from.

He shook his head and tried to put the situation aside again as he cross-checked the financial records between Henrietta Stone and Doris Mayfield one more time. He'd already found a pattern. There were $1,000 monthly withdrawals on the same day, or close to it, from both women's accounts going back for several months. He'd started out looking for an indication of embezzlement. But after Lydie's vision on Monday with the supposed hint from Henrietta Stone about blackmail and following the money, his instincts had him looking for evidence of that blackmail instead. And now he had a hunch that these were the extortion payments he'd been looking for.

Was Barbara Drake paying too? They'd put in for her financials the minute they'd gotten back from her house on Wednesday but hadn't received them yet. They'd done that even before he knew for certain that her death was connected, in anticipation that hers was the third death from Lydie's visions.

He hadn't told Lydie directly, but he was becoming more and more certain that her visions or dreams, or whatever she wanted to call them, had merit—or at least some validity. He wasn't sure how that whole thing worked, but after what he'd seen and heard so far, he was willing to go on a little faith.

The M.E. had conducted the autopsy on Barbara on Thursday, and afterward, Kelli had run some very specific tests, as her radar had been up. She'd called him once she'd had her answers. It seemed that Lydie had been correct. Barbara Drake hadn't drowned.

Kelli had gone through an in-depth explanation about mucus mixing with water creating foam in the lungs when a person drowned, but really all she'd needed to say was that she'd found no water in Barbara Drake's lungs. That would've been enough for Nick.

What was really interesting, though, was the actual cause of death. Barbara Drake had died of cardiac arrest brought on by an overdose of digitalis. And not just a run of the mill overdose, either. Evidently, Barbara took digoxin for her heart, so having digitalis in her bloodstream was not unusual, and testing for it wouldn't normally be done. But digoxin was derived from Digitalis lanata, a species of the Foxglove plant. And because the M.E. was a master gardener and had a degree in toxicology—and since they'd already had two suspicious deaths inside the Garden Society by botanicals—Kelli had run those very specific tests. What she'd discovered was that Barbara Drake's toxicity level of digitalis in her system was four to five times higher than it should have been. Which resulted in digitalis poisoning.

"I can't say conclusively that this wasn't an accident, Nick," Kelli had told him. "But she would have had to have taken way over her prescribed dosage in one sitting. And there's no way to differentiate between the digoxin that she was prescribed for her heart condition and a possible extract of digitalis surreptitiously given, as was the case of Henrietta Stone and the monkshood in her tea. Or in Doris Mayfield's circumstance, with the peanut oil introduced into her stew. But the level of toxicity in her blood-work could have easily caused cardiac arrest."

"So, not a suicide, either?" he'd asked, tongue-in-cheek.

Kelli had laughed at that. "In my opinion, not likely."

So, there was no way to prove that Barbara Drake been intentionally overdosed, but the scene—which had obviously been cleaned up by someone—had definitely put that scenario in his head. But how it had been done and by whom, were the questions. He was still waiting on anything the lab could give him from the meager evidence they'd collected from Barbara's house. Maybe they'd get lucky there.

Nick checked his watch. He was late. He'd asked Lydie to give him an hour, and he was fifteen minutes past that now. Reluctantly shutting down his computer, he turned to his partner. "Hey, Andy, I'm gonna need to head out a little early today. Lydie wants to talk to me. I told her that I'd come by, and I'm already late."

His partner gasped dramatically. "*What?* Stop the presses. Nick Sutton is leaving early for the first time in—probably *ever*?"

"Very funny. You're killing me here."

"Tell Lydie 'hey' for me. Now, get outta here and let me enjoy the moment."

Nick laughed and grabbed his jacket.

It was a ten-minute drive from the station to Lavender Fields, and as he pulled into the parking lot, he noticed that the door to the shop was standing wide open.

He parked and climbed out of the car. Stretching the kinks of the day out of his long frame, he started toward the shop.

"Hello?" he called as he entered. "Lydie? Anybody home?"

Before he could get much farther, Lydie's Aunt Wilma came running from the back room.

"Oh, Detective Sutton! Thank God. You have to come quickly. I just got back from my errands, and it's Lydie. I was just about to call 911. She's really sick and needs to go to the emergency room. Can you take her? I think she's been poisoned."

17

Nick raced after Wilma to the office where Lydie was lying on her side on the small sofa with her eyes closed. She was so incredibly pale. It nearly stopped him in his tracks, and he felt something in his chest hitch. After their earlier phone conversation, seeing her so sick made his blood run cold.

"What the hell happened here?" he demanded. "I just talked to her on the phone a little over an hour ago. You said that she'd been poisoned. Why did you think that?"

"Don't talk about me like I'm not here," Lydie muttered, opening her stunning turquoise eyes, which were made all the more so next to the deathly pallor of her face. "It was the brownies, Nick." She gestured toward the desk where the second brownie was still sitting on the plate where she'd left it.

"Brownies? Where did they come from?"

"The rest of them are in a basket on the workroom table," Wilma explained. "I found them on the shop doorstep when I went to leave around two this afternoon." She was wringing her hands and clearly feeling guilty. "I should have known, should have left a note, something. But I just assumed they were for the girls. I never thought they would be poisoned. I mean, why would I think that?"

Nick shook his head. "Wait, let's back up a second. Why do you think it was the brownies that were poisoned?"

"Because of her symptoms, and because I examined one, picked it apart with a fork." Wilma put up a hand before he could say anything. "Don't worry. I knew better than to contaminate it as I looked. I just used the fork to inspect it more closely. Anyway, it looked to me like Ilex opaca—holly berries. They're very toxic."

"They won't kill me, Aunt Wilma," Lydie said. "I'm an adult and only ate the one brownie, not enough to do any real damage. Just made me sick, is all."

"But these are baked, Lydie," Wilma insisted. "The fresh berries contain only trace amounts of cyanide. But they also contain amygdalin. When you cook holly berries, the amygdalin transforms into hydrogen cyanide. You know that."

Nick took Wilma's hands in his to stop her from wringing them raw. "Look, we'll get to the bottom of this. You can give me a detailed explanation of what happened, and you two can argue about it later, but right now we need to get Lydie to the ER."

He handed Wilma the keys to his cruiser. "Grab the basket of brownies and then go open the back door of my sedan. We'll follow."

As Wilma left the office, Nick knelt down next to the sofa. "How you doin', pal?"

Lydie gave him a wan smile. "Not gonna lie. I've been better."

He tenderly smoothed her hair away from her face. "Can you sit up? I'm gonna carry you out to the car now."

"I can walk," she protested weakly.

Nick shook his head. "Not likely, and not on my watch, darlin'."

He helped her into a sitting position, and then gently lifted her into his arms. She seemed to weigh no more than a child, and a sense of urgency seized him hard as he carried her out of the office. But before he could take her down the hall to the shop, she pointed at the workroom table. "I'll need my purse. It's there on the table, and my cell phone is on the office desk."

He kept walking. "We'll send your aunt back for them while I'm getting you settled in the car."

It seemed to take an eternity to get Lydie comfortable in the back seat of the cruiser and for Wilma to retrieve Lydie's purse and cell phone, but in reality, it was probably only a matter of minutes. Nick's sedan was unmarked, but he used the siren and lights all the way to the hospital, which again seemed to take forever. Lydie sounded confident that the berries she'd ingested wouldn't kill her, but he wasn't taking any chances by dallying along the way.

He put in a call to his partner to meet them at the hospital, and then another call to Kelli letting her know that they were on the way. After giving her a brief rundown of what was happening on the call, she was waiting for them with Dr. Emmet Case, the chief trauma specialist at Seal Cove General, when Nick pulled the cruiser around the circular drive and right up to the sliding doors of the emergency room.

"This is Lydie's Aunt Wilma," Nick said with a nod toward Wilma. "She thinks that Lydie's been poisoned with holly berries," he said, as they got Lydie out of the car and into the waiting wheelchair.

"Well, she's not the first one seen in the ER today," the M.E. said as she moved a little to the left to allow Nick to push the wheelchair through the sliding doors and into the ER.

"What do you mean? Someone else came in with the same thing?" he asked with a shocked look.

"Yes," Dr. Case replied. "Dr. Landon may be the M.E., but she's also the toxicology expert here, so I tagged her when that first case came in about an hour ago."

"Emmet and I had been discussing your cases and the toxic botanicals used. So, he was on alert for anything remotely similar. But let's chat about that after he gets a look at Lydie, and we get her taken care of, okay?"

At the front desk, Kelli gently moved Nick out of the way. "Emmet will take her from here, Nick. You and Lydie's aunt need to give the front desk whatever info you can. I'll let you know when we have everything sorted."

"I wish everyone would stop talking about me like I'm not here," Lydie whispered.

"Hush now and let Dr. Case take care of you." Kelli shook her head and then smiled at Nick as the trauma specialist wheeled Lydie toward the door at the end of the front desk. "I'll be back out in a bit. We can talk then."

As Kelli turned, Nick grabbed her elbow before she could follow them back to the exam rooms. He wanted to ask if Lydie was going to be all right, wanted Kelli to allay his concerns but his throat wouldn't let him utter the words for fear of what the answer might be.

"Don't worry, Nick," Kelli said, patting his arm. The look she gave him said she understood what he'd left unspoken. "She's going to be fine. She's in good hands with Emmet. I promise."

Then she disappeared through a door at the end of the front desk, and Nick was left praying that she was right.

To take his mind off all kinds of dire thoughts, he helped Wilma fill out the intake forms for the front desk as best they could. After Wilma gave them Lydie's insurance card and ID from her purse, and the paperwork was sorted, Nick guided Aunt Wilma to one of the uncomfortable chairs in the waiting area just as Andy came through the sliding doors.

"What the heck happened, Nick?" Andy asked. "You said that Lydie was poisoned?"

"Seems so," Nick answered. "This is Lydie's aunt. She found

her. Aunt Wilma, this is my partner, Andy Gilmor."

"Nice to meet you, ma'am," Andy said. "Wish it was under better circumstances."

Nick turned to Wilma. "Okay, like Kelli said, Lydie's in good hands, so can you walk us through what happened today? Where did the brownies come from?"

Lydie's aunt closed her eyes for a moment, obviously using the time to center herself. There was worry in her gaze when she reopened them. "I don't know, Detective."

"Call me Nick," he said with a reassuring smile. "So, you found them on the shop steps but didn't see how they got there? Is that right?"

"Yes. I have no idea who sent them. Vanessa and Lydie both left fairly early this morning. Vanessa went over the hill to Maple River in the valley, and Lydie went up the coast to exchange an order. They left within ten minutes of each other."

"And obviously the basket of brownies wasn't there then, right?" Nick asked.

"Correct. I went out to my car for one of my recipe books just after I ate lunch at eleven, and it wasn't there then, either."

"What time did you find them?" Andy asked.

He'd taken out his little notebook and was making notes. By the look on his face when he glanced up, Nick knew his partner was thinking the same thing as he was. This was connected to the Garden Society cases they were working. He didn't know how... yet. But he felt it in his bones.

Wilma rubbed her forehead and frowned. "I found them as I left to go get some more baking ingredients at the supermarket on Main. That was about two o'clock. I should have left a note, but I thought I'd be right back—and definitely before Lydie got home. So, I just left them on the workroom table. I never guessed that I'd get sidetracked by the strip mall across the parking lot with the specialty kitchen shop." She shook her head in disgust.

"And you didn't hear anything between eleven when you went to your car for your recipe book and when you found the brownies at two o'clock? A car? A knock on the door? Anything?" Andy asked.

"No, I didn't. But then, I listen to music with my ear pods when I'm prepping." Her smile was a bit sheepish. "I'm a head-banger from way back, Detective. So, I wouldn't have heard a thing."

"You were baking with ear pods in your ears? Isn't that a little dangerous?" Andy asked cautiously.

Wilma chuckled. "I take my ear pods out when I have some-thing in the oven. Have to hear the timer, you know. But I didn't bake today. At least, I hadn't planned to bake until this after-noon." She frowned then. "There is a driveway buzzer that lets the girls know when someone pulls into the parking lot. But that sounds only in the main building workroom for the shop and not in the detached industrial kitchen, so even without the ear pods, I wouldn't have heard that, either."

"So, someone could've pulled up, dropped off the basket and drove away without you knowing." Andy said with a nod. "But then, that would be pretty risky if they didn't want to be seen."

Nick nodded. "I was thinking the same thing. Unless they knew that both Lydie and Vanessa were gone but not that Aunt Wilma was on the property."

"Yeah, but with Aunt Wilma's car parked in the lot in plain sight, it would have been obvious that someone was there. I guess it could've been just their dumb luck that Aunt Wilma had her ear pods in and didn't hear them."

"Their dumb luck and Aunt Wilma's saving grace. No telling what could have happened if whoever did this had gotten caught."

"Oh, no," Wilma gasped. "I never even thought of that."

"Lucky stars, Aunt Wilma," Nick said, and watched the faint

smile cross her face.

"Either way, this was intentional," Andy mused. "Maybe not to kill, but to incapacitate?"

"And maybe a warning," Nick murmured, gazing out the window to the parking lot beyond.

"A warning?" Andy asked. "What do you mean?"

Nick glanced back at Wilma. He didn't want to upset her any more than she already was by talking about the disturbing vision that Lydie had described.

But Wilma obviously wasn't going to be put off.

"What is it, Nick?" she asked, her steely gaze boring into him. "A warning about what? The girls' involvement in your case? Lydie's visions? Vanessa's runes?"

He should have known that Lydie's aunt would know a whole lot more than she should have about what was happening. This was why she was so upset that she hadn't left a note with the brownies. He guessed that she thought she should have known better after learning what Lydie and Vanessa had been up to.

He shook his head and told them both, "I called to talk to Lydie this afternoon between three-thirty and four. When she answered the phone, I could tell something was wrong, though she was reluctant to tell me just what that was." He blew out his breath. "She'd had another interactive vision."

Wilma clucked her tongue. "Oh, my poor girl. She's had visions all her life, but the interactive ones are fairly rare. I know she's had several over the last few weeks."

Andy put up his hand as if he were in a classroom. "Question. What is an 'interactive' vision?"

"Just what it sounds like, Detective," Wilma replied. "From time to time, my niece can speak to the dead."

"Uh... okay," he murmured, and went back to scribbling in his notepad.

"Anyway, she knew that Barbara Drake was dead and that

she'd been found in her pool. She also knew that Barbara hadn't drowned," Nick went on.

"How the heck did she know that? We just found that out this morning," Andy blurted, and then waved the question away. "Let me guess. Barbara Drake told her in this vision she had?"

"Nailed it in one, partner." Nick gave Andy a thumbs-up gesture. "Barbara evidently also said that Lydie was now a target as well."

Andy frowned. "Wait—why would Lydie be a target?"

"She said that Barbara told her it was because she and Vanessa had been poking and prodding."

"And asking questions?" Wilma asked quietly.

Nick nodded slowly. "What do you know about that, Aunt Wilma?"

The woman sighed. "I'm sorry, Nick. I was with Lydie when we went to talk to Kathryn Wilks-Raymond on Tuesday."

"Uh-huh," Nick muttered. "And was this the 'you've won a door prize from the garden party' visit?"

Wilma nodded but was obviously embarrassed. "But in our defense, we were very careful. And we were just trying to confirm some of the information that Lydie had been told in her visions. She would've come to you with anything we found out."

Nick scrubbed his hands over his face in frustration. "Aunt Wilma, this is a murder investigation. The three of you can think you're being careful, but you have no idea who's involved in this mess or where a threat may come from. I've told both Lydie and Vanessa this too many times to count."

"I understand. I was the one who told Lydie that she needed to go to you after the last vision, when she came to talk to you at the precinct. Anyway, things sort of spiraled from there."

"I'll say," Nick replied. "Anything else that we should know; more revelations that you haven't told us about?"

Wilma began to shake her head, but then hesitated.

"What is it, Aunt Wilma?"

"Well, it was mostly a feeling, and I know you don't want to hear about that. It's subjective and not really any concrete evidence."

Nick sighed. "Humor me… please."

Wilma stared at him for a moment, as if trying to decide whether or not to trust him, then she gave a brief nod. "I don't know what it means, but when Lydie and I were talking with Kathryn on Tuesday about the two deaths and what Barbara Drake had told the girls about the Stone woman, well, Kathryn's aura changed colors, and not in a good way."

"I beg your pardon?" Andy looked up from his notepad. "What does that mean? And why would that be important?"

"For most of our visit that day, Kathryn's aura fluctuated between orange and yellow, which usually denotes balance, happiness." Wilma frowned, and her eyes took on a distant look. "But toward the end, when we were discussing Barbara Drake, her aura flashed from a pleasant orange, first to a dull red—a definite warning sign of anger—and then to a forest green, which can mean jealousy, resentment. It happened very quickly, and it was over just as fast, but not before both Lydie and I saw it. We left soon after. It made us both really uncomfortable. We even talked about it in the car."

"I see," Nick said slowly, though he really didn't get it at all. Visions, conversations with the dead, and now auras. How the hell did he quantify any of it?

"And I can see that you really don't," Wilma said with a chuckle, echoing his own thoughts. "All I will say is that I came away with the feeling that there was something not right with that woman. I don't know what, but there's more to her than meets the eye, mark my words. And whatever it is, I don't think that it's good." She waved a hand in the air then. "But that's just me. And like I said, subjective."

Before Nick could reply, Kelli came out from behind the front desk and joined them in the waiting area.

"Well?" Nick asked, unable to contain his concern. "How is she?"

Kelli smiled. "Like I told you earlier, she's going to be fine. As it turns out, she didn't ingest enough to do more than make her sick." She turned to Wilma. "Dr. Case treated your niece for the poisoning, and she'll be right as rain in a day or two."

"Oh, that's so good to hear," Wilma said. "What a relief."

"If she has any problems, just bring her back in. However, I really don't anticipate any lasting issues. She's mostly just wrung out, which a good night's sleep will go a long way in addressing. Dr. Case wanted to admit her and keep her overnight for observation, but she's refused."

"What do you mean, she's refused?" Nick frowned. "If she needs to stay the night, she'll damned well stay."

Kelli put up a hand. "Take a breath, Detective. Emmet's suggestion to stay was just a precaution. She'll do fine at home, probably better in her own surroundings. He gave the same advice to Kathryn, who's thinking over the option as we speak but will probably go home as well."

"Kathryn?" Nick asked. "Kathryn Wilks-Raymond is the other victim of poisoning with holly berries?"

The M.E. nodded. "Yes. Evidently, she came in about an hour before you got here with Lydie. Emmet called me as soon as she got here."

"And she's still here?" Andy asked. "Can we talk to her?"

"I suppose. She's also doing much better, although she wasn't as sick as Lydie. But that was because she consumed less of the brownies than Lydie did. Anyway, she's in exam room five. Come on back with me. Aunt Wilma can sit with Lydie for a bit while you two speak with Kathryn."

They followed Kelli back to the exam rooms, and Wilma

slipped into Lydie's room as Nick and Andy went on down the hall and into exam room five.

"Kathryn, Detectives Sutton and Gilmor are here to ask you a few questions about how this happened to you," Kelli said as they entered the small room. "Dr. Case will be back in a bit, and you can let him know if you're going home or are going to take him up on the overnight stay. Alright?"

A pale Kathryn nodded. "That's fine. Thank you, Dr. Landon."

Kelli turned to Nick. "I have a couple of things to take care of in my office downstairs, but it won't take long. I have samples of both brownie batches. I'll let you know if there's anything else I find."

"Thanks, Kelli," Nick nodded, then turned to Kathryn.

"So, how are you feeling, Kathryn?" Andy asked once Kelli had left the room. "Do you feel up to telling us how you ended up here in the ER?"

The woman nodded. "This has been such a strange day. I usually don't go to the office on Fridays, but I went in this morning for several hours. I'm still going through some of my notes and trying to put together a report for the Board. It has to be done very soon, as I don't know when we'll get the files back that were confiscated by your office on Wednesday. The Board will need some sort of explanation in the next week or so."

"Understandable. So, you went into the office this morning. Go on," Nick prompted.

"Well, I went out for lunch and to run some errands about twelve-thirty, and when I came back an hour or so later, there was a little basket of brownies sitting on my desk with an unsigned thank you card."

"Thank you for what?" Andy asked without looking up from his scribbling.

Kathryn shook her head. "I have no idea."

"And you don't know how the basket arrived?" Nick asked.

"I don't know that, either. I assumed at the time that Margie, my part-time assistant, had accepted the delivery and put it on my desk. She was gone when I got back from my errands."

Nick frowned. "Was the door locked when you got back from lunch?"

"No."

"Is that normal when no one's in the office?"

"We lock up at night, but usually there's someone there during the day. I don't always lock up when I'm just going out for lunch. And Margie rarely thinks about it."

"So, what did you do when you got back and found the basket of brownies?" Andy asked. "I'm assuming you ate at least one, considering you're here in the ER."

Kathryn gave him a slight smile. "Very astute, Detective. I thought a brownie would be a nice partner to the single cup of coffee that I allow myself in the afternoons. Of course, I don't usually eat sweets, so it was a double treat."

"So, just the one brownie, then?" Andy asked.

"Actually, I only ate half of it. It just didn't taste right, which should have been a red flag, especially with everything that's happened in the last couple of weeks, starting with Henrietta's death."

"How long before you began to feel the effects?" Nick asked.

"Just thirty minutes or so. I started to get queasy, and then it progressed quicky into vomiting. My husband is a director for the Coastal Trauma Institute and is out of town at a conference for two weeks, and the kids have been at Henry's parents' house in San Francisco for the summer. I called Margie on her cell because I wasn't sure I could drive myself here."

"And where is the basket of brownies and the thank you card now?" Andy asked.

"I brought them both in with me. I gave them to Dr. Case."

Nick nodded. "Okay, good. We'll get with him later. Just one more question, Kathryn. Can you think of any reason you'd be targeted this way or anyone who would want to do this?"

There was a slight hesitation before Kathryn looked up at him with wide eyes and shook her head. It was brief but it did not go unnoticed.

"I have no idea why someone would do this, Detective. This is all just so confusing. First, Henrietta and then Doris." There was another pause. "And now this? I hope you find whoever's doing this soon before more people get hurt."

Nick noticed that she didn't mention Barbara Drake. It had been two days since they'd found Barbara's body floating in her pool. He'd learned the hard way that news traveled very quickly in this little coastal town, especially when it came to the Garden Society. He thought it hard to believe that Kathryn hadn't heard about Barbara Drake's death. But stranger things had happened. Nevertheless, he was starting to get a feeling that he had missed something vital somewhere along the way, but had no idea what that something was.

"Alright, then. I think that will do for now," he finally said. "If you think of anything else, please give us a call."

Nick gave Kathryn one of his cards before he and Andy left her room and headed down the hall to where Lydie was resting with Wilma by her side. As they stepped into the little room, Lydie looked up and their eyes met. Most of her color had returned to her face, which went a long way in easing Nick's concerns, but he could tell that she still wasn't feeling great.

"How ya doin'?" he asked with a half-smile.

She returned his half-smile with one of her own. "Much better than the last time you asked me that, I can tell you. Guess I'll live after all."

"Oh, Lydie," Wilma admonished. "What a way to talk. This could have been much worse. You're lucky you didn't eat that second brownie."

Lydie reached out and took her aunt's hand. "I know, Aunt Wilma. I'm sorry I gave you such worry. I'm just so glad that Vanessa was over in Maple River and out of harm's way."

"Speaking of which, pal," Nick began with a shake of his finger. "This is just what I was worried about on our phone call earlier. You and my cousin putting yourselves in danger by 'poking and prodding.' Remember?"

Lydie nodded. "I know, I know."

"Kelli said that you won't stay the night for observation like Dr. Case suggested. I would feel better if you did."

"There's no point, Nick. I'm not a hundred percent, but I'm already feeling better. I'll be back to my old self in a day or two. I want to sleep in my own bed."

Nick narrowed his eyes and studied her. "Okay, but I'm leaving a squad car in your parking lot." Before she could complain, he put up a hand. "That wasn't a question and it's not negotiable. I'm going to do the same for Kathryn because her husband is out of town for two weeks."

"Kathryn?" Lydie asked. "Kathryn Wilks-Raymond? What happened to her?"

Nick could have bitten his tongue in two. This was not information that Lydie needed to know right now. She'd just stew over it and try to figure out why they'd both been targeted by obviously the same person.

He sighed. "She also got a basket full of brownies. But that's not something you need to worry about right now. Do you hear me? We're gonna spring you from this place as soon as Dr. Case says you're good to go. Got it?"

She gave him a begrudging nod, but Nick could almost see the wheels turning in that pretty little head of hers. Even surviving an attempted poisoning, he could tell that she wasn't going to let this go.

The question now was, where did they go from here?

18

By the time Lydie's ordeal was all said and done at the hospital, it was close to eight o'clock before Nick had finally driven her and her aunt back to Lavender Fields. Nick had hovered for another thirty minutes or so before reluctantly heading home himself. Of course, not before he'd made certain that the security detail was in place, which Lydie had thought was overkill and made no bones about telling him that more than a few times. She would hardly be alone with Aunt Wilma staying with her for another week and a half, and according to Dr. Case, in a day or two, she'd have no lasting effects from the whole thing. But Nick had been adamant, and she'd been too worn out to argue.

After Nick had finally gone. Lydie called Vanessa and spent another thirty minutes, first trying to convince her friend and business partner that she was fine, and then giving her an update on the latest vision featuring a very chatty Barbara Drake. To say that Vanessa had been royally freaked out about the whole thing would've been a huge understatement. In fact, she'd been ready to race back to Seal Cove, but to do what, Lydie had no idea. There was nothing to be done.

"Seriously, Van, I'm going to be okay," Lydie told her. "I'm already feeling much better, just incredibly wrung out and ready for a good night's sleep. But I did want you to be aware of what had happened so you wouldn't lose your mind when you got back to find a police car parked in the lot at Lavender Fields."

"Well, thanks for the update and the backstory. I guess forewarned is forearmed, right? So sad about Barbara, though. I would never have thought she would have been the third victim. I was really hoping we'd figure it all out before anyone else died, or maybe that Nick would get a break in the case."

Lydie sighed. "Me, too. To be honest, I was leaning toward her as possibly being behind the deaths. I never thought of her as one of the victims, even though she was in my visions along with the others. Guess I let her personality color my thought process."

"Well, you weren't the only one. Barbara was a lot to take, most of the time. It's just too bad that this latest vision didn't happen earlier. Maybe you would've been more cautious about the brownies. Although, with Aunt Wilma using the industrial kitchen, I guess that may not have helped."

"Yeah, probably not. Oh, but here's another weird twist. It seems that I wasn't the only one who got the tainted brownies. Someone also left the same type of brownies at the Society offices. Kathryn Wilks-Raymond was at the ER about an hour before I even got there."

"What? Are you kidding?" Vanessa blurted, losing it all over again. "Lydie, this is getting scary. I mean, we knew there were going to be three deaths, but now this? How did we not see it coming? There was nothing in my runes, and you hadn't had any indication in your visions."

"I don't know, but Nick thinks this may have been a warning since—like Barbara said—we'd been poking and prodding, asking questions. And holly berries are toxic but not deadly to an adult unless you eat a boatload of them. So, he doesn't think they were meant to kill, just... discourage."

"Well, it's discouraging all right, to say the least," Vanessa muttered. "So, if it was a warning for us because we'd been asking too many questions, what crime do you think Kathryn committed that required her own 'discouragement?'"

Lydie frowned. "That's a good question. I know that she was really defensive about Henrietta when Aunt Wilma and I were there the other day. She was pretty angry about the fact that Henrietta was being disparaged when she could no longer defend herself. Maybe she spouted off to the wrong person."

"Maybe."

"Speaking of Nick, here's another thing I need to give you a heads-up about. He was extremely peeved about our 'poking and prodding.' Evidently, he'd heard about our exploits from both Kathryn and Anna before this brownie event had even happened. I got an earful on the phone just before the brownie took effect and things went sideways. So, you'll probably get an earful, too, the next time he sees you."

"I can just imagine how that whole thing went down. 'This is a murder investigation, Lydie. Are you trying to put yourself in harm's way? What were the two of you thinking? You need to stay out of my investigations,'" she mimicked her cousin, making Lydie giggle. "Blah, blah, blah. That about it?"

"Ha! Almost exactly. At least you'll know what's coming."

They both laughed, and then there was a pause. After a moment, Vanessa's voice took on a somber tone. "Look, I'm really glad you're okay, Lydie. I'm so sorry I wasn't there with you."

"I'm not," Lydie told her. "So, don't be ridiculous. You would've been eating those brownies right along with me, and you know it. Then we both would've ended up in the ER. The timing was just off. That's all. If Aunt Wilma would've been back earlier or I'd been later getting back from the north coast, she could've told me that she hadn't made the brownies—that she'd found them on the front steps of the shop. That would've been a big red flag for me. Aunt Wilma is feeling pretty guilty about forgetting to leave a note, but I told her it wasn't her fault. Sometimes the Universe just decides to be cantankerous. Gotta be careful what you put out there, my friend. You never know what it's going to spit back at you."

"I guess," Vanessa replied, but her tone suggested that she didn't like it much.

"Look, there are a few other things that Barbara told me in this latest vision. But we'll discuss those tomorrow when you get back. Barbara may have been the third victim from my earlier visions, but she had some cryptic advice for me. Looks like we're not clear of this yet."

"Lydie, maybe Nick's right," Vanessa said hesitantly. "Barbara's advice aside, maybe we should just let it all go."

"No! We can't quit now. Please don't fade on me, Vanessa. Please. Just a couple more things to check, and then hopefully, this will all be wrapped up. Okay? I just... I have to see this through, and hopefully before anyone else gets hurt."

Vanessa sighed on the other end of the line. "Okay. But then it all goes to Nick and we're out of it completely, right?"

"You bet."

Unfortunately, Vanessa got back late Saturday afternoon and was none too pleased, either. She'd called Lydie numerous times during the day—just to check up—before Lydie finally had to tell her to quit calling, that she was fine and they would talk when Vanessa got back into town. Lydie was doing some paperwork in the office when her partner came barreling through the door just before six o'clock.

"What the heck are you doing in here?" Vanessa admonished.

"Why aren't you upstairs resting?"

"Well, welcome back, Van," Lydie replied with a cheesy smile.

Vanessa was obviously not amused. "I'm not kidding, Lydie. Someone just tried to kill you. You should be taking it easy."

"Oh, don't be so dramatic." Lydie chuckled, and then put up a hand before Vanessa could argue. "And I am taking it easy, even though I really don't need to. I may not be back to normal quite yet, but I'm really close to it. Besides, I'm just doing a bit of paperwork."

Vanessa gave her a thorough once-over with the stink-eye before sighing and plopping down in the chair opposite the desk. "I'm sorry. I guess I'm still a little freaked out about this turn of events."

"Gee, twenty-five check-up phone calls in five hours? I really didn't notice."

"Ha-ha." Vanessa gave her a reluctant smile. "It was only five or six, and I suppose I got carried away."

"Uh-huh."

"But you're truly feeling okay? Be honest."

Lydie nodded. "I truly feel fine, Van. Cross my heart."

"Alright then. So, what's this about extra cryptic advice from the beauty queen?"

Lydie proceeded to fill Vanessa in on everything Barbara Drake had told her—word for word—in her vision.

When she'd finished, her partner narrowed her eyes. "So, Barbara knew who'd killed her but held back that info? Isn't that just like her." Vanessa shook her head. "At least now we know that Nick is on the right track following the money end of things, but what did Barbara mean about the rest of it? What could her extensive library possibly have to do with anything? And taking a page from what book?"

Lydie smiled. "I think she was giving me directions without *giving me directions.*"

Vanessa frowned. "I don't get it."

"Well, think about it. *Paris is so nice this time of year. After all, a picture is worth a thousand words, right?* Those were *her* exact words."

"But that doesn't make any sense. It doesn't connect to anything in this case."

"Exactly." Lydie leaned forward. "She told me that I wasn't looking closely enough, or at the right things. That's been our problem, Van."

"Lydie, you're talking in riddles."

"Look, I think she was giving me clues on where to look to find the evidence we need to crack this case and expose the killer."

"How so?"

Lydie blew out a breath. "Well, I'm pretty sure she was telling me that there is something hidden in her home library. Maybe a photo or... who knows. Something. But it will make sense when we find it."

"And maybe it's in a book about Paris?"

"I don't know. Maybe."

Vanessa shook her head. "But that means we'd have to get into Barbara's house. How are we going to do that without Nick finding out and blowing his top?"

Lydie smiled again. "Very carefully, my friend."

"I'm serious, Lydie. Nick may toss us both in the clink for obstructing an investigation or some stupid thing. And Barbara's house is bound to be locked up, probably covered in crime scene tape as well. So, how are we supposed to get around all of that without ending up in the pokey?"

"I think that may have been what the 'geranium' crack was all about. Barbara said, *You'll need geraniums to find the way.* We'll look for geraniums in pots or maybe the flower bed. I'm betting we'll find a key hidden somewhere."

"That's a lot of supposition, pal. Especially from a cryptic dead woman spouting weird clues."

"Trust me. I'm totally aware. But I'm trying to look more closely at everything from all angles. However, we won't know for sure until we go out there and see for ourselves, will we? And if we can't find a key or a way in, we simply come back here. No harm, no foul, right?"

Vanessa leaned back for a moment looking thoughtful, then gave another resigned sigh. "Okay. So, when are we taking this little excursion?"

Lydie laughed out loud at the unhappy look on Vanessa's face. "First thing in the morning," she replied, then backtracked. "Well, maybe not first thing. Come out to the shop around eight. We'll have a bit of breakfast, a cuppa, and then we'll head out."

And that was exactly what they did.

By Sunday morning, Lydie was feeling herself again with no residual effects from the holly berries that she could detect. They were in the car and on their way out to Barbara Drake's rambling, secluded mansion by ten a.m.

If Lydie was honest with herself, she'd admit that it felt just a little creepy driving up the long, winding driveway and parking in front of the empty house. Of course, the house was just a house, and the landscape was beautifully manicured, but she still had an eerie feeling, nonetheless.

She and Vanessa got out of the car and stood looking at the front portico as if it might speak to them. Surprisingly, there was no police tape to be seen. But then, when Barbara had been found, it probably looked like an accident on the surface, Lydie thought. She steeled herself for what they might find inside. The creepiness she'd felt driving up to the house held on, and she wondered if her partner was feeling it as well.

Then Vanessa shook her head "This is ridiculous," she muttered and repeated what Lydie had just been thinking. "It's just a house. But let's get on with it. The sooner we're done here, the better. I don't like the vibe."

They went up the walkway to the steps and looked around. Potted plants and flowers were artistically arranged in the alcove by the front door and on the extensive stone porch as well as down each side of the wide steps, though none of them held geraniums. Still, they looked under and around each and every pot just in case.

"Lydie, I don't see any geraniums anywhere," Vanessa said after they'd finished with the porch and stairs. "Are you sure that's what Barbara said?"

"Well, let's check the flower beds. There has to be something here somewhere. I just feel it. And I would think that it would need to be close to the front entrance." She pointed to the beds left of the porch. "You go along those beds, and I'll take this other side."

They split up and each took the separate flower beds. Lydie scoured her side of the house all the way to the end of the bed but to no avail. There were no geraniums or anything resembling geraniums anywhere to be seen within the lush plantings. With a sigh, she turned and went back to meet Vanessa at the porch.

"No luck on your side?" Vanessa asked.

"None. You?"

"Nope." Vanessa frowned. "Okay, let's think about this. What exactly was the phrase Barbara used about geraniums?"

Lydie stared up at the front door entryway from the bottom of the steps and thought back. How had Barbara said it? *You'll need geraniums to find the way*, she'd said. But wait... there was more to it than that, wasn't there? Yes! Lydie narrowed her eyes, and she laughed out loud. "Geraniums hold the key!" she exclaimed. "That's the rest of what Barbara said."

She hurried up the steps to the front door alcove. Hanging to the left of the door was a large, hammered metal sign with the name of *Drake* etched into the surface in large burnished letters. But also, etched around the edges, was a delicate floral design.

"What do these look like to you, Van?" Lydie asked, running a finger over the pattern. "Geraniums?"

Vanessa grinned back at her. "They sure do."

Lydie slipped her fingers behind the back of the sculptured piece and felt around the edges. She found something small attached just above the bottom rim. It came loose with a bit of pressure and dropped into her hand.

"What is it?" Vanessa asked, excitement coloring her words.

Lydie's pulse picked up speed as exhilaration spread through her like wildfire. "It's a magnetic key holder, Van." She slid it open and found a bright, shiny key. Taking it out of the case, she slipped it into the lock on the front door and turned. There was a sharp click, and then Lydie reached for the latch. The door opened seamlessly and the expansive foyer came into view.

She looked over at Vanessa. "Shall we?"

"We shall."

Together, they entered the house and closed the door behind them.

After a moment, Vanessa whispered, "Where do you think the library is?"

"I don't know. And why are you whispering?"

Vanessa cleared her throat and giggled. "No idea. I guess because we're breaking and entering?"

"We're not breaking, Van, just entering. We have a key, remember. Come on, let's find the library and get this done."

The first doorway to the left of the foyer held an elegant, formal living room. It was huge, and felt even more so because it was done entirely in white and cream with only a few pops of color like the accent pillows on the gigantic sofa and a few art pieces here and there. A monstrous fireplace was the centerpiece of the room, but the painting that hung above it dominated.

Barbara herself—in her glory days, Lydie surmised—looked down on them with a knowing smile on her young, beautiful face.

"Geez," Vanessa muttered. "That's unnerving. And just a little self-indulgent, don't you think?"

Lydie snickered. "But that was perfectly Barbara, wasn't it?"

They went back across the hall to the room on the other side. This was a media room of sorts. It held an entertainment center with a huge plasma television and all the accoutrements, another humongous sofa, a few comfortable-looking easy chairs, and several bookshelves with board games and such. They didn't waste much time on it.

Back in the foyer, Vanessa looked up the wide, sweeping staircase that led to the second floor. "Up the steps or to the back of the house?"

Lydie considered. "Let's head to the back. See what's there before heading upstairs."

They continued down the hallway to the right of the staircase and found a large, open kitchen and dining room on one side. The closed door at the end of the hallway opened onto a utility room, and then out to the pool house.

"Okay, I'm good with not going out there," Vanessa said. "I have no interest in seeing where Barbara was found. It's giving me the willies just being this close."

They backtracked to the closed door across from the kitchen and dining area. Here, they found just what they were looking for.

Barbara's library.

"Wow," Vanessa gasped. "Extensive? Is that what she told you? I think that's an understatement, don't you? I mean, how are we going to find anything in here, Lydie? It could take days."

Lydie started to reply but felt the sudden chill as it began to unfold around her and white noise grew louder in her head by the second.

"Lydie? What is it? Oh, geez, another vision?"

Lydie heard the panic in Vanessa's voice, felt her fear as she grabbed her arm, but she was powerless to respond as the vision took over. She heard another voice and turned to find the home-owner sitting in the leather chair by the window, legs crossed, and looking totally at ease. And why not, she thought. After all, this was Barbara's house.

"I'm impressed, Lydie," Barbara said with a delighted grin. "Henrietta said you wouldn't make it this far, but I told her she was a stupid cow." The dead woman burst into roaring laughter. "She really didn't like that, but I enjoyed her annoyance immensely."

"All right, Barbara. You got us here. What are we looking for and where will we find it?" Lydie inquired.

"Barbara?" Vanessa asked. "Lydie, what's happening? What are you seeing? Is Barbara here?"

Barbara ignored Vanessa and shook her head. "Lydie, Lydie, I gave you everything you need to find what you're looking for."

"What you gave me was cryptic gobbledygook."

"What's she saying?" Vanessa wanted to know.

Barbara's smile had an evil edge. "You made it this far on that gobbledygook, didn't you?"

Lydie shook her head and glowered at the dead woman. "I'm not going to argue with you, Barbara. Vanessa and I will not spend days in this place looking for a needle in the proverbial haystack. If you want our help, you'd better start giving us more than cryptic clues and vague comments, or we're outta here."

Barbara tilted her head and drummed her fingers on the arm of the leather chair in obvious irritation. Finally, she nodded. "You really are kind of a buzzkill, aren't you? But you're right, I suppose. I am surprised, though. I didn't take you for the tough negotiator type."

Lydie wanted more information, but she was losing patience. She had a feeling that Barbara would string her along if she let her, and she wasn't willing to spend any more time than she had to in this house. "Just get to the point, Barbara. I've had a rough couple of days. I'm tired and want this damn investigation over. I will also remind you that I'm not your afterlife assistant."

The woman frowned, looking pretty annoyed, and for a moment, Lydie thought she'd simply disappear. But then Barbara wagged her finger. "Now, now. Take a breath and don't be so prickly. What you're looking for is in the travel section on the very back row. I've already given you the basics. In the meantime, here's some expert advice. Don't eat any more tainted goodies."

With that, the woman disappeared with her uproarious laughter echoing in Lydie's head like a funhouse recording as the vision dissolved completely. Her knees nearly buckled, and she would have sunk to the floor in a pile if Vanessa hadn't had a hold of her arm.

"Here now," Vanessa murmured, guiding Lydie to the leather settee opposite the chair in which Barbara had been sitting. "Sit down and catch your breath. Do you want me to get you something to drink?"

Lydie shook her head. "No. Thanks. I just need a minute."

"What was that all about? I'm assuming that Barbara was either giving you more guidance or a hard time. Kinda sounded like a little of both."

"Yes. She does like to play and string you along. That's for sure. However, she did give me a little bit more to go on. With the emphasis on little."

"So, what we're looking for is in here somewhere? For sure?"

"We'll see." Lydie took a few more deep breaths and then got to her feet. "It will be back here somewhere," she said, and started for the back row of bookshelves.

"Ah. I get it now," Vanessa said as they stopped at the travel section Barbara had indicated.

"Yeah, she'd specifically said earlier that Paris was nice this time of year, so look for any books on Paris. You start at that end, and I'll start on this end."

After thirty minutes, they'd found several books each with Paris as a topic. They carried them all back to the leather settee and piled them on the coffee table.

Lydie picked up a book. "Okay, let's go through these. I just hope that this isn't a wild goose chase."

Vanessa took one from her pile and began to flip through it. "With Barbara, you never know, right?"

One by one they weeded through the stack of books. Lydie was beginning to think they were wasting their time when Vanessa let out a squeal.

"Paydirt!" She held up a grainy photo with an accompanying strip club flyer and a yellowed newspaper clipping.

Lydie took the newspaper clipping and began to read. "This article is from the Vegas Herald fifteen years ago. It's about an exotic dancer named Tandy Treat—obviously a stage name— who went missing after a violent encounter with a club patron. Witnesses said that the man was stabbed by the dancer after he'd become abusive and attacked her in her dressing room. The man recovered from his wounds, but the dancer disappeared that night and was never found or heard from again."

"Wow." Vanessa studied the grainy photo. "It's kind of hard to tell from this old photo but the woman does look vaguely familiar somehow."

"Let me see," Lydie said, taking the photo from Vanessa. She looked closely at the photo for a moment. It was obviously taken from the audience while the dancer was on stage. The photo was old and it wasn't a great angle, but Lydie suddenly knew exactly who she was looking at. "Oh, no."

"What is it, Lydie? Do you know her?"

Lydie sighed and looked at Vanessa with a sinking feeling. "Unfortunately, yes. I do know her. And so do you."

19

On Monday morning, Andy was running late due to some sort of plumbing crisis at his house, leaving Nick to continue the tedious job of sifting through the rest of the financial records on his own. In comparing the bank statements for both Henrietta Stone and Doris Mayfield, he and Nick had already identified consistent withdrawals of $1,000 apiece from both women's accounts at virtually the same time each month, which had been going on for some time. Unfortunately, as these had been cash withdrawals, there was no way to trace where the money went or to whom. It was frustrating in the extreme for Nick, as his gut told him that these were the blackmail payments he'd been looking for.

But to whom were they paid? That was the question.

He could easily speculate about the whys. After all, Henrietta Stone had been embezzling funds from the Garden Society's coffers for an extended length of time. Kathryn Wilks-Raymond had been quite upfront about that, and also about the fact that Stone hadn't paid back the fifteen thousand dollars that Kathryn had claimed her friend had taken. Although, when Nick had pressed the woman, there seemed to be a question as to the actual dollar amount Stone had embezzled. In addition, if Lydie's vision was to be believed, Henrietta Stone herself had pointed to someone blackmailing her. Follow the money, she'd said.

So, it seemed reasonable that this could be the motive in her case. All it would've taken was for someone in the Garden Society's membership to catch wind of the stolen funds. It might also be the reason that the embezzled amount had not been paid back. If Stone had been in such dire straits financially before stealing the Society funds in the first place, as Wilks-Raymond had indicated, perhaps she'd been using that same money to pay her blackmailer.

Then there was Doris Mayfield. A thirty-eight-year-old, single woman, who'd been having affairs with numerous Society members' husbands. Nick had received the anonymous package with the surveillance information the day the woman had died. Someone had been keeping tabs on Mayfield's movements and had documented every clandestine liaison in graphic detail. Another clear reason for possible blackmail.

Pay up or we tell everyone what you've been up to and with whom.

To make matters worse for her, Doris came from a prominent family in the valley, one with a stellar reputation. As an only child, she'd inherited just over twenty million dollars as well as the family business empire when her beloved parents had died in a plane crash several years back. So, she had plenty of green, and it would stand to reason that she wouldn't want to tarnish the family name or the company by having all her dirty laundry flapping around in the coastal breezes.

Nick scrubbed his hands over his face in frustration. This investigation was really starting to try his patience. It seemed like the minute they'd get some kind of momentum going, get close to a true break in the case, that break would evaporate just as quickly as it had appeared.

He'd just gotten up to get a third cup of stale office coffee when Andy came bustling in with a huge grin on his face. He was carrying two Java Jive to-go cups in a cardboard tray with his backpack slung over one shoulder and a manila folder under his arm.

Nick made a show of looking at his watch. "It's about damned time. One of those cups had better be for me." He held out his own empty cup. "I've already had two cups of office sludge, and my stomach is pretty angry about it, I can tell you."

"Don't worry. One of these cups is definitely for you, buddy," Andy said, holding out the tray so that Nick could grab his favorite Java Jive latte.

Taking his first sip, Nick savored the rich flavor, the tantalizing aroma, and felt his morning right itself just a little bit. "Okay, I take back all the nasty things I said about you before you got here."

"Ha! Thanks. But I've also got another sweet surprise for you."

He tossed the manila folder onto Nick's desk.

"What's this?" Nick asked, picking up the folder.

"Open it. It will put joy in your heart, my friend. And maybe even settle your upset tummy."

Nick opened the folder and did a quick scan of the contents, then looked up with his own grin, his frustration instantly replaced by anticipation, if not downright excitement. The folder contained Barbara Drake's financials. "Now we're getting somewhere," he said.

"Yep. I stopped by and picked those up on my way in. I'm pretty stoked to see what info we get out of them." Andy set the tray with his own coffee cup down on his desk and dug into the backpack for his notebook before dropping the backpack into the corner next to his chair. "I figured you'd want to dive into Drake's financials right away."

"Absolutely," Nick replied, already perusing the first page of the thick report that came with the financial records. "I'm hoping we'll find the same withdrawal activity in her accounts that we have with Stone's and Mayfield's."

"You think Drake was being blackmailed, too?"

"Maybe." Nick looked up with a frown. "Although, remember, we don't know for certain that Stone and Mayfield were actually being blackmailed, that the withdrawals were for payments. Especially when we're unable to trace where the cash went."

"True. But it does seem logical."

"It does." Nick crossed to the case board where he'd recently added Barbara Drake's photo to the victims' column. "Everything we've uncovered so far points in that direction. If we find the same withdrawal activity in Drake's account, it would go a long way in advancing that theory. And maybe help us find something to track the cash as well."

"I gotta say, Barbara Drake didn't strike me as the type to let herself be blackmailed without some kind of documentation or hidden notes. You know, insurance of some kind."

"You're not wrong. Breadcrumbs, my friend. Hopefully, she left us some breadcrumbs to follow."

Andy leaned a hip on the edge of his desk. "You know, I just don't get it."

Nick grunted. "Which part of this?"

"Well, if the three were being blackmailed, why murder them? Why extinguish your cash flow? I mean, with just the payments from Stone and Mayfield alone, it's $2,000 of income each month. If we find that Drake's included, that makes it a $3,000 payday."

Nick stared up at the faces of the victims, wishing they could talk to him, give him some answers. "Maybe the killer isn't the blackmailer. Maybe it's someone else who snapped to what was happening and took advantage of the situation somehow." Nick shook his head. "But that doesn't do it for me, either. Why kill the ones being blackmailed and not the blackmailer?"

"I know. It just doesn't make sense. But then not much of this case is making sense, so far."

Nick glanced at his partner over his shoulder. "You can say that again. I was just thinking earlier that the closer we get to a break in the case, the farther away it seems."

"I guess it's like you're always saying, something will break eventually. We just have to keep digging, right?"

Nick laughed and crossed back to sit at his desk. "Only way I know how to do what we do, pal."

"Well, while you're digging into Drake's financials, I'll keep sifting through the Garden Society ledgers and files," Andy said, sitting down at his own desk and opening his notebook. "I worked on them for several hours last night until my eyes were starting to cross. I keep finding more questions to which I have no satisfying answers... yet."

With that, they both got busy. For a period of time, the only sounds in the office—other than the occasional ringing phone—was that of muttering from one or the other, and the shuffling of paper.

But after an hour and a half of searching, Nick was beginning to feel his frustration rise again. Just when he thought that nothing was going to pop, he suddenly found what he'd been looking for, though it wasn't exactly what he'd expected.

"Holy crap! Yes!" he shouted. "Gotcha!" Nick tried to tamp down his excitement, but it wasn't easy. "Andy, come here quick and look at this."

Andy dropped what he was working on and hurried over. "What is it? Did you finally find Drake's payment withdrawals?"

"Yes... and not exactly." He looked up at his partner and winked. "I found her payment *deposits*."

"What?" Andy exclaimed. "Barbara Drake was the blackmailer?"

"It would seem so."

"Well, I guess that would make more sense than *her* being blackmailed."

"Agreed. Barbara always seemed too slick by far, and there was something calculating about her that I could never put a finger on. That she was the one doing the extorting, checks all the boxes for me."

"Yeah, that's pretty cold, for sure."

"But here's the kicker, partner. Barbara was raking in three grand a month, not two. Sometimes there are three separate deposits—$1,000 each, sometimes one or two, depending. But the deposits are always listed within a week of the withdrawal dates from both Stone's and Mayfield's accounts. And always for a total of three grand."

Andy's brows drew together with his confusion. "So, she was actually blackmailing someone else besides Stone and Mayfield? But who?"

Shaking his head, Nick got up and went back to the case board. "That would be the thousand-dollar question, wouldn't it?" He looked at Barbara Drake's smiling face, before turning back to Andy. "Didn't the sweep team bring in Barbara's laptop as evidence for the Tech Investigation unit?"

Andy nodded. "The laptop, her cell phone, and a small tablet. You think there may be something on one of those about the third person she was extorting?"

"Could be. You said it yourself, she didn't seem like someone who'd let anyone blackmail her without leaving hidden clues behind. I'm betting that as the extortionist, she has all kinds of documentation. And if so, I'm thinking it could be on that laptop."

"Well, well, well. Looks like things are starting to break after all, right, buddy?" Andy asked with a grin. "Just like you always say."

"Looks like it." Nick chuckled and started for the door. "But don't say that too loudly. Lydie says that the universe has a twisted sense of humor. So, I don't want to jinx our fortune just yet."

"Ha! So, now you're quoting Lydie?" Andy laughed when Nick shot him a lewd hand gesture without even looking back. "Well, I guess that's probably sound advice."

"I'm gonna head down to TID and see if the tech investigators have looked at her laptop yet. That would be very helpful, indeed. You coming?"

"No. I think I'm gonna keep working on this Garden Society stuff. I've found something weird, something I can't explain, and I need to run a few more searches."

Nick stopped at the door and looked back. "Something with the Society ledgers? Financial weirdness?"

Andy started to nod, and then shook his head. "It did start with the financial searches, but this is something else. It may just be a search glitch, though I've run several and got the same answer with each. I need to do a couple more just to satisfy myself that what I may have found is real. Like I said, weird."

"Okay. Let me know what you find. I'll be back as soon as I can," Nick said, and left the office.

Lydie had been very tightlipped about what they'd found in Barbara's library on Sunday until they'd gotten back to the shop, which had frustrated the heck out of Vanessa. But she'd held her tongue until they'd gotten back to Lavender Fields. When Lydie had finally divulged what Vanessa had obviously missed, she was stunned. Tandy Treat, the dancer in the photo, was none other than Kathryn Wilks-Raymond. Vanessa had thought that the woman on stage in the photo seemed familiar when she'd first looked at the picture, but the photo was grainy and taken from the audience a few rows back. However, the moment that Lydie had said Kathryn's name, Vanessa recognized the woman instantly.

Vanessa had wanted to call Nick and turn it all over to him right then and there, but Lydie had dragged her feet. She'd wanted to wait, to sleep on this new information. She'd also wanted Vanessa to check her runes and divination pool, while Lydie herself waited to see if any prophetic dreams or visions would arise overnight.

In the end, though uncomfortable with the decision, Vanessa had relented. And so, here she was on Monday just before noon, checking her runes and her pool for the umpteenth time with little to show for it. They both told her the same thing in a vague sort of way. Danger still lurked. But she had a feeling that said danger was much closer than they knew.

She looked up at Circe, lounging lazily on her cushion on the bookshelf. Their Russian Blue shop mate always liked to lay up high where she could survey her kingdom or snooze the day away without being disturbed.

"So, what do you think, Circe? I don't like this whole scenario. Danger still lurking is not enough information to make a sound decision one way or another, right?"

The feline blinked her bright, green eyes and stretched, before jumping down from her perch and giving Vanessa a meow of agreement.

"Exactly my thoughts, sweet girl. Come on. Let's go tell Lydie."

Vanessa headed out of the casting room with Circe close on her heels and found Lydie in the workroom emptying several supply boxes onto the table.

"Lydie, I've been watching my pool and checking the runes all day with no change. All I keep getting is that there is still danger lurking, and I think that it's closer than we think."

Lydie broke down one of the boxes and started on another. "I know," she said. "I didn't have any dreams or visions last night, either. But I can feel it in the air."

"Then I say we should call Nick and turn this information over to him now."

"Vanessa, I think it's a bit premature, don't you? I mean, we need to talk to Kathryn before we call Nick with wild accusations. We don't even really know what happened with her," Lydie said, stacking the supplies from the box she'd just emptied neatly on the workroom table. "And besides, since when are you so quick to call Nick? You're usually the one to hold back."

Vanessa cocked her hip and crossed her arms. "Uh, since three women have died, someone tried to poison you, and we both promised Nick that we'd stay out of his investigation after your hospital scare. Oh, and, I don't know... since Kathryn may be wanted for stabbing a man? Those all seem like great reasons to me."

"Get serious, Van," Lydie replied. "We don't know that Kathryn is wanted for the stabbing. All that photo suggests is that Kathryn had a very different life back then. And the news clipping said that, according to the witness statements, she'd been defending herself when she stabbed that man after he attacked her in her dressing room. It also stated that he'd recovered from his wounds, right?"

"Yes, but—"

"We don't know what happened after that article ran in the Vegas paper. So, let's not condemn her quite yet, okay?"

"But what if she's the killer?"

"Well, that's a bit of a leap. She stabs someone in self-defense years ago, and suddenly she's a serial killer here in Seal Cove?"

Lydie finished breaking down the last box and slid it onto the recycling pile. "And what would be her motive for killing Henrietta? By all accounts, they were the best of friends. She was trying to help Henrietta find a way to pay back the money she'd embezzled before anyone could find out. She defended her at every turn with Nick, and then again with Aunt Wilma and me."

"I know, however—"

"And why would she want to kill Doris or Barbara, for that matter?"

"I don't know." Vanessa yelled. "That would be a job for Nick and Andy, not us."

"Well, I'm going to call Kathryn and go see her."

"Lydie, I don't think that's such a good idea. I really don't."

At that, Circe leapt up onto the table and gave a sharp meow in Lydie's direction. Then, with a low growl, the cat turned and jumped back down, sauntering away, and disappearing into the casting room.

Vanessa watched Circe go, and then gave Lydie a pointed stare.

"Don't start," Lydie muttered. "She's not always right, you know."

"I didn't say a word. Didn't have to, because she said it perfectly."

Lydie took off her apron and laid it on the table next to the supplies. "Aunt Wilma is baking this afternoon, but she can watch the shop. I'm gonna go change my clothes and run a brush through my hair. Then I'm calling Kathryn, and I'm going to see her. You can come with me or stay here if you're not comfortable going. It's up to you. I'm not forcing you to go anywhere."

"Oh, don't be an idiot. Of course, I'm going. No way am I letting you go alone. But I'm on the record as thinking this is not the best idea."

"Noted," Lydie replied with a grin. "Thanks, Van."

"Yeah, yeah," Vanessa muttered as Lydie left the room. She pulled out her cell phone. "You go ahead and call the serial killer for a meet and greet, my friend. And I'll call Nick with a heads up."

Unfortunately, she got Nick's voicemail after several rings. However, she wasn't gonna let that stop her, and waited for the beep. "Hey, Nick. It's Vanessa. You're gonna want to listen up…"

20

It took Nick just shy of two hours to find the information he'd been looking for down at TID. The Tech Investigation Division had already been over Barbara Drake's laptop with a fine-tooth comb, but he'd had to sift through their catalogued list of folders and files and refer back to the digital data for each item or entry that he thought sounded intriguing. With all the information they'd uncovered, he was very happy with what they'd found—as well as the fact that he hadn't been the one who'd had to dig it all out.

In the end, the data he'd been looking for was saved right in plain sight in a file marked *lucrative projects* along with Barbara's other business ventures. He figured that was just how Barbara probably saw her blackmail scheme. Just another lucrative project. He wondered if she'd started out with only the one victim and then kept adding as she'd found more women with secrets who'd been willing to pay to keep them that way... and if she would've continued to add to the list had someone not taken her out when they did. Regardless, he thought this was just the break they needed to move the case forward.

He hurried back to the office with the report he'd printed to show Andy what he'd uncovered, but he found his partner right where he'd left him, staring at his own computer with a scowl on his face.

"If you keep frowning like that, your face is gonna stick that way." Nick laughed. "At least, that's what my mom used to tell us kids."

When Andy didn't acknowledge him but clicked a few more times with the mouse and continued to glower at the screen, Nick knew something was really wrong.

"What's up, partner? What have you found?"

Andy looked up then and shook his head. "It's not what I've found, Nick. It's what I can't find no matter how deep I go."

Nick went over and leaned in behind his partner to look at the screen. "And what's that?" he asked. "Something important to the case?"

Andy snorted. "I should think so. Like I told you before you went down to TID, I was following a search glitch, or so I thought, and wanted to clear it up."

"Yeah... so?" Nick asked slowly. "What kind of glitch?"

"Well, after two hours of digging, it looks like it wasn't a glitch at all. It was an interesting black hole of missing information."

"Missing information? About what?"

Andy shook his head again. "No, not about what, buddy. About who."

Interested now, Nick narrowed his eyes. "And this mystery person would be?"

"Wait for it," Andy murmured. "It's none other than Kathryn Wilks-Raymond."

Stunned, it was Nick's turn to frown. "What information about her can't you find?"

"I can't find any trace of a Kathryn Wilks beyond fourteen years ago. And I do mean nothing." Andy laughed at the shocked look on Nick's face. "I know, right? Crazy. But it's like she didn't exist before then. Like she popped into existence as a fully formed adult complete with searchable background, most of which looks absolutely legit and normal... until you do some serious digging. That's when it gets a little ragged around the edges. It's not water-tight, but it's all done very, very well. Most run-of-the-mill searches would never look deep enough to start questioning anything."

With thoughts beginning to race in his head, Nick sat down in Andy's visitor chair and leaned on his desk. "How is that even possible? I mean, in this digital age? To completely expunge a background and any trace of it?"

Andy nodded slowly and shrugged. "Difficult, sure, but not impossible if you know what you're doing, or know someone else who does." He leaned back in his chair and grinned. "Come on, Nick. Spies, criminals, and mobsters do it all the time. You know that. They hire hackers, computer geeks. So does the Witness Protection program, for that matter. Well, they have folks on staff with security clearance to create new identities, not bury old ones, but it amounts to the same type of thing." A thoughtful look came across Andy's face. "I will tell you, freelance pays incredibly well. It's all cash, no trace. And this? This would have cost a pretty penny ten or fifteen years ago."

Nick smirked. "You seem to know a lot about this kind of clandestine operation, partner. Anything else you'd care to share with me?"

"Buddy, have you met me? I'm like an onion. I have many hidden layers. Also, I do a boatload of research in countless different areas, but I'm afraid I can't divulge where or how I come by my information, even to you."

Nick laughed out loud at that, but the look on Andy's face was sober and enigmatic, and he wasn't completely certain that his partner was joking, which gave him an uneasy jolt. "Yeah, yeah," he finally said. "So, you think Kathryn fits into any of those categories?"

Andy shrugged again. "Who knows. Stranger things have happened, right?"

"Well, if it's Witness Protection, I doubt we'd have any luck teasing that information out of them. So, what *did* you find?"

Andy looked back at the screen. "The information I can confirm for certain is that she married Dr. Henry Raymond, Director for the Coastal Trauma Institute, and became Kathryn Wilks-Raymond just under a decade ago in a very splashy event up on Seal Point."

Nick whistled through his teeth. "Wow. Snazzy. If said splashy event happened up on the Point, only the cream of the crop attended, I assume." Seal Point was where the rich lived and played. Sprawling estates, exclusive clubs, a very expensive sandbox.

"Yeah, it was a very posh affair with a ton of who's who in the Seal Cove area, as well as from all over the valley. Dr. Raymond has a stellar rep. Anyway, there were a couple of blurbs in the local paper, mostly wedding announcements, parties, dinners, that sort of thing, all pertaining to the upcoming nuptials. But before that, nothing."

"No pictures on the society pages, no awards benefits, phil-anthropic events, nothing else?" Nick asked.

"Nope. Kathryn Wilks arrived in Seal Cove, as far as I can tell, just eight or ten months before becoming Mrs. Dr. Raymond. Before that, she was living over in the valley in Winterhart for a while, working for a Dr. Derek Granger, which may have been where she met Henry Raymond. He and Granger were colleagues at one point. Anyway, before that, I found traces of her in San Francisco and Seattle. And I do mean traces. Just the normal address and work history, that sort of thing. Our Kathryn seemed to like keeping to the shadows as much as possible. Before San

Francisco, it starts to get hazy and then simply comes to an abrupt stop."

"Huh." Nick narrowed his eyes. "I'm wondering if this whole ghost life before she materialized is connected to what I found down at TID."

"You found something regarding her on Drake's laptop?"

Nick smiled. "You could say that. I got some confirmation about the blackmail scheme."

"Really? Was it what we were hoping for?"

"Uh, yeah. That and more."

"So, Kathryn was involved?"

"Well, I found a list of payments—the blackmail payments—associated with initials. HS, DM, and KWR. I'd say it's not too difficult to figure out who those last initials belong to, right?"

Andy's eyes went wide. "Wow. So, Kathryn Wilks-Raymond was the third person Drake was blackmailing? This is all beginning to weirdly intersect in ways I never saw coming."

"Agreed. I'm wondering if Kathryn had something in those missing years, in her distant past, that Barbara somehow found out about. Something big and worth paying blackmail money to keep buried."

"That would make sense." Andy nodded. "Especially if she was hiding from something or someone and wanted to stay hidden at all costs."

"My thoughts exactly." Nick murmured and paused for a moment. "Like something that could jeopardize the status and respect she has now? Something that could destroy this cushy, prestigious life she's built for herself. And what if she got tired of paying? I'm thinking that could be a really strong motive for murder."

"I'll say," Andy replied. "But what about Stone and Mayfield? I can see a motive for Drake, if she was blackmailing Kathryn for something from her past that she's tried desperately to conceal, something that could upend her life now. But why kill the others? I mean, she was supposedly Henrietta Stone's only friend."

"Supposedly. But do we really know that for certain? All we have is Kathryn's statement and the perception of others." Nick rubbed his jaw in thought. "What we know for sure at this point is that Barbara Drake and her two other victims in the blackmail scheme are dead. Kathryn is the last one standing."

"Yeah, but then there's the holly berry poisonings. Kathryn was poisoned right along with Lydie, remember?"

Nick frowned. "True. But was she really? If I recall, she said she'd only eaten about half a brownie, right?"

"That's correct. She said it didn't taste right." Andy sat forward. "Nick, you don't think she would poison herself to throw off suspicion, do you?"

"Maybe not." Nick gave Andy a hard stare. "But what I do know is that people will go to extreme lengths to protect themselves and those they love. So, this all may be just conjecture, but I'm not about to rule anything out at this point. Kathryn isn't listed as a master gardener, but that doesn't mean that she's not well versed in this stuff. She's been in the Society for years. She could have known that a small portion of the brownie wouldn't kill her. Maybe that was her plan. Who knows?"

"So, where do you want to go from here, partner?" Andy asked. "What's our next move?"

"We need to pay a visit to Kathryn before we go any further. Let's find out exactly when she started paying Barbara Drake, what she was paying to hide, and anything else we can figure out from there on."

"I'll give her a call right now," Andy said and picked up the phone.

While he waited, Nick retrieved his cell phone from his jacket pocket. He thought a call to the M.E. with a few clarifying questions about the whole brownie episode was in order. But before he could do that, he realized that he'd had a missed call from Vanessa, and that she'd left a voicemail.

As he listened to Vanessa's message, his anxiety began to rise. By the time he'd finished, his call to Kelli was forgotten as his concern for Lydie and his cousin took center stage. The thought that they may be walking into an unknown situation with someone who may or may not be behind three murders was enough to have his blood running cold. To make matters worse, he tried calling Vanessa back to warn her of what they'd discovered, but the call went directly to voicemail.

"Got Kathryn's voicemail, so I left a message," Andy said, hanging up the phone. "You want to just go out to the Society offices and see if we can catch her there?"

Nick pocketed his cell and grabbed his jacket. "Yep. Like right now. Looks like I missed a call while I was down at TID. Had a message from Vanessa. She and Lydie are doing the same thing we are. Seems they ran across something that may be the reason Barbara was blackmailing Kathryn, though they don't even know it. We need to get out there ASAP. They could be walking into a very dangerous situation."

"Holy Cow!" Andy exclaimed, grabbing his backpack. "Then let's hit it."

With that, they both headed out the door.

Dr. and Mrs. Henry Raymond lived in a very private area nestled in the ritzy neighborhood of Seal Cove Heights, which overlooked the township of the same name. Lydie had called Kathryn to set up a meet, only to find out that Kathryn wasn't at the Society offices today, so she and Vanessa were heading out to the Wilks-Raymond residence.

As Lydie turned off Overlook Drive and drove through the

gates at the bottom of the long, curving driveway, she marveled at the lush, rolling lawns on either side as they continued toward the mansion tucked back into the trees.

The stately, white Southern Colonial with its double-pillared columns at the central entrance was beautiful and impressive as they rounded the final bend and it came into view. Quite fitting for a doctor of Raymond's status, Lydie thought as she pulled the car around the circular driveway and parked.

"Uh, geez," Vanessa murmured. "Now, that's a house. I hope Kathryn has help keeping it clean."

"I'm sure she does, as well as gardeners to handle the expansive grounds. No way would I want to have to take care of this much property, experienced gardener or not," Lydie responded, as they both climbed out of the car and eyeballed the grounds. "I have a hard enough time with my half acre out at Lavender Fields."

"That would be why I live in a townhouse condo with a large back patio. It's just big enough to do small-scale gardening without too much effort," Vanessa agreed.

"It's really lovely up here, though."

Together, they climbed the wide cement steps of the central entrance that led up to a wrap-around veranda with smaller columns which served as support for the second story balcony. The double front doors of what looked like aged oak were elegant and welcoming.

Lydie rang the doorbell.

"This really is magnificent, isn't it?" Vanessa asked, taking in the veranda that ran across the front of the house and the two white rockers sitting just to the left of the entrance. "I bet this thing wraps all the way around the house. I've always wanted a wrap-around porch with rocking chairs just like that. Of course, I don't need or want one this size."

Before Lydie could respond, one of the doors opened, and

Kathryn greeted them. "Lydie, Vanessa, come in, come in. Glad you could find us. The streets up here in the Heights run at odd angles and get a little convoluted. I don't know who designed this neighborhood, but sometimes I think they may have been drunk."

As she and Vanessa stepped into the foyer, Lydie laughed and nodded. "I think you may be right. I had a friend from school whose family lived up here, so I'm pretty good with finding my way, but it can be confusing."

"Well, come on back to the kitchen. We can talk over a cup of tea and fresh scones."

"Awesome," Vanessa replied, and then rolled her eyes and nudged Lydie as they followed Kathryn toward the back of the house.

The kitchen was huge, modern, and spotless, and had a cozy dining nook at one end with windows looking out on a ruthlessly edged back yard already prepped for fall.

"Make yourselves comfortable." Kathryn gestured for them to sit at the table where small plates, cups, napkins, and utensils had already been placed. In the center of the table stood a lovely arrangement of flowers and a basket of scones.

"Your property is really beautiful," Lydie said when Kathryn came over with a pot of tea under a cozy. "And the landscaping is fantastic. I know you're a Garden Society member, but I sure hope you have help with the yardwork."

Kathryn laughed and sat down. "Yes, we have a service that comes every two weeks year-round. I could never handle this much property myself. And Henry has no interest... or time, for that matter. He just about lives and breathes the Coastal Trauma Institute."

"This house is amazing, as well," Vanessa commented. "I do love me a wrap-around porch."

Kathryn nodded. "The house is a Gordon Clairmont. He was a designer in the early twentieth century. The veranda is one of my favorite things about this house. Of course, we had the kitchen and baths upgraded right after we bought it." She picked up the teapot and poured a cup of tea, handing it to Lydie, then did the same for Vanessa, before pouring one for herself. When she'd finished, she looked back and forth between the two of them expectantly. "Now, you said on the phone that you wanted to talk to me about something you'd found. Something I might want to see."

Lydie exchanged a look with Vanessa and then jumped in with both feet. "Yes, Kathryn. We did run across something that we thought you should see before the police also find the information and want to talk to you. We thought you'd want to be prepared."

Kathryn sat back with a smile. "Well, that sounds ominous. What kind of information would this be that the police would want to talk to me about it?"

Lydie turned and grabbed her shoulder bag from where she'd hung it over the back of the chair. She dug for the folder she'd brought with her containing the flyer, photo, and article they'd taken from Barbara Drake's library. Sliding it across the table, she met Kathryn's eyes. "This is what we wanted to show you."

"Wow, how very cloak and dagger, Lydie," Kathryn said with a smile. But when she opened the folder, the smile quickly slipped from her face, and she swallowed hard. "Oh, my God," she whispered as she glanced at the photo, flyer, and the accompanying article. Then she looked up with a tortured expression. "Where did you get these?"

Lydie started to reply, but Kathryn held up a hand. Taking a deep breath, she blew it out slowly. "No, let me guess," she said in a tight voice. "That heinous bitch, Barbara Drake?"

"The woman in the photo is you, isn't it?" Vanessa asked. "And you're the one the article's about?"

Kathryn laughed without humor. "Yes and no. That photo, the

article, they're from another lifetime." She turned to Lydie. "You have to understand, I'm no longer that woman. I have a very different life now. Have had for over fourteen years."

"We understand, Kathryn," Vanessa said. "But if the police find this, well, do you think the Las Vegas police would get involved? What happened fifteen years ago?"

Kathryn shook her head. "The Vegas police aren't looking for me, Vanessa, if that's what you're thinking. But if it became public knowledge that Tandy Treat is still alive, there are worse entities there that would come for me, entities that I've been hiding from since I left Vegas and disappeared all those years ago." She turned back to Lydie. "Obviously, you had to have gotten the copies in this folder from Barbara. But my question is how? And when? How long have you known about this?"

Lydie shook her head. "Not long. And Barbara didn't give us this information, Kathryn. We found it in her library."

"Ah." Kathryn nodded and laughed again. "Of course, you did. I'm assuming on one of your little snooping excursions? But how would you have known where to look?"

"Kathryn—" Lydie began, but the woman cut her off.

"Never mind. You don't have to explain. Besides, you didn't start this. That evil witch did." Anger flared in Kathryn's eyes, and Lydie watched as her aura also flared into a deep red with that anger. "I don't know how she found out about my past, but she did and had been blackmailing me with exposure ever since."

"Blackmailing you?" Vanessa blurted. "Seriously?"

"She was blackmailing Henrietta Stone as well, wasn't she?" Lydie asked in a quiet tone. "About her embezzlement?"

Kathryn looked out the window at the manicured grounds beyond and nodded again. "Yes. It didn't even matter to Barbara that Henrietta was paying her out of the money she'd taken from the Garden Society, the very money she was blackmailing her over. She thought it was funny. She also knew how dangerous it was for me and didn't care that if my past came to light, it would put my marriage, my family, my very life at risk."

"What do you mean, your very life?" Vanessa asked.

"Just what I said." Kathryn glanced back at her with a grim look. "The club I was working in was owned and operated by some very bad people. Think The Syndicate. And it wasn't their only club or business in Vegas, I might add. I started working in that club when I was nineteen years old with a fake ID. The money was great, and I stashed it away as fast as I could, in case of an emergency. But make no mistake, once you were in, they owned you, owned just about every aspect of your life. They had eyes everywhere, and they watched us all the time."

"I'm so sorry, Kathryn. That's just awful," Vanessa said, a stricken look on her face.

"Turns out, it was a good thing that I'd stashed away all that money. That emergency happened a lot sooner than I'd expected, but fortunately, I was ready." Kathryn picked up her teacup and took a sip, and then gestured with it. "To make matters worse, the man in the article, the one I stabbed? He was the one that got me hired, got me the fake ID. He was my husband... and still is."

21

"Uh, come again?" Vanessa's mouth dropped open and she blinked several times. "Did you just say that you stabbed your previous husband... whom you're still married to?"

The look on Vanessa's face was priceless, and if Kathryn's story hadn't been both sad and terrifying, Lydie may have laughed out loud. But she was beginning to get a bad feeling about where Kathryn's story was actually going.

Or where it might end.

"Vanessa, please understand," Kathryn pleaded in a soft voice. "Eddy was a teddy bear when we first met. I was young, just nineteen when we got married. I'd had a fairly sheltered background and so little life experience. To say that my family disapproved of Eddy from the start would be an incredible understatement. And when I married him, they disowned me." Kathryn shook her head and there was a glimmer of unshed tears in her eyes. "Anyway, the first couple of years were, if not the perfect marriage... comfortable. Even happy. But the further up the food chain he went, the meaner and uglier he got. Looking back now, I think

Eddy had plans for me right from the start. He's the one who chose Tandy Treat for my stage name."

Pausing for a moment, Kathryn took several calming breaths before continuing. "After working the stage in that club for two years, being abused mentally, physically, emotionally, I just wanted out. I wanted a fresh start, something normal."

"What happened that night, Kathryn?" Lydie asked. "The article says that he attacked you in your dressing room. Is that the physical abuse you were talking about?"

"Yes. He'd become abusive in every way, but he seemed to especially delight in harming me in ways that wouldn't show. After all, when I was on stage, the costumes—

or lack thereof—didn't leave much to the imagination, you know?" Kathryn pointed to the folder. "Anyway, that was the night I'd had enough. I'd been squirreling away money for months. A little here, a little there, as much as I dared. I had a pretty healthy stash by then."

Lydie frowned. "But how did you get away without a trace? The article said you were never located."

"I'd always kept my eyes and ears open because of the people I was dealing with. I learned as much as I could by listening unobtrusively, watching everything around me with attention to detail." Kathryn laughed, and the look in her eyes gave Lydie a shiver. "After everything I'd seen and heard, I may not have known how to erase myself, but I sure as hell knew how to find someone who could do it for me. And I had the money stashed to do just that."

Lydie glanced at Vanessa. Kathryn's story was beginning to take on quite the different tone.

"I had a new passport and ID made with a new name. A name *I* chose for myself. It was the beginning of my fresh start. But I had to be very careful about whom I asked to help me, and it cost me a boatload of my saved cash." Kathryn stared out the window again, as if seeing in her mind how it had all played out. "Before I went to the club earlier that week, I took a duffle bag, something I could easily carry. I packed just what I thought I'd need to survive —my new ID and what was left of my stash of money, then left the bag in a locker at the Y."

Kathryn's aura had settled some, but there was still some-thing not right there, something dark with a mean edge to it. Lydie could sense it, but she couldn't quite see it. Kathryn had stopped for a moment and got up for a bottle of water from the fridge. When she came back to the table, Lydie put a hand over hers and gave it a squeeze. "Take your time, Kathryn. I know that just telling this story is probably painful, even all these years later."

Lydie waited, and for a moment Kathryn looked as if she would pull away, but then she simply nodded and continued. "The night it happened, I went to the club a little early to get ready for my last night on stage. I was determined to leave Eddy. I had to get away from that life and start over before it destroyed me." She looked Lydie in the eyes. "I think I knew in my heart of hearts that Eddy wasn't going to let me leave without a fight, but at that point, I didn't care. Anyway, I was supposed to go on at seven, and he came into my dressing room just before that. It was probably the worst time to do it, but that's when I told him I was leaving right after the show."

"What did he do?" Vanessa asked.

Kathryn's gaze snapped toward Vanessa, and a tightly controlled anger colored her words. "What did he do? He told me that he would kill me himself before he would let me leave and make him look weak in front of the other bosses. He came at me then, and I just panicked." She stopped and took a deep breath before raising her palms and continuing in a calmer tone. "I don't even remember how the scissors got into my hand. The next moment, he was dropping to the floor and there was blood everywhere. I was in shock. I just grabbed my clothes and purse and ran. I went straight to the Y, cleaned up and changed clothes, got my go bag from the locker, and an hour after it all went down, I hitched a ride out of town. I got rid of the scissors at the first place we stopped for gas."

"That's an amazing story," Vanessa said. "Like something you see in a movie."

Lydie shook her head.

"What?" Vanessa asked, sounding annoyed. "It is."

Lydie sighed. Turning to Kathryn, she gestured to the folder. "So, how did Barbara get what's in that folder?"

"I don't know for sure. I do know why she started looking. That was because Henrietta was angry with me."

"Henrietta?" Vanessa asked. "How would Henrietta being angry with you matter?"

"Because she was already being blackmailed by Barbara by that time, wasn't she, Kathryn?" Lydie asked. "Misery loves company. So, your friend sicced Barbara on you for something you did that angered her."

Kathryn nodded and then explained. "Henrietta blamed me for Barbara finding out that she'd embezzled money from the Society. I told her that I didn't know how Barbara found out, but that I'd never said a word. Henrietta called me a liar to my face, said that I was the reason that Barbara was blackmailing her in the first place. And she knew there was something terrible in my past. Not all the details, of course, but that I was hiding some-thing… big."

"That's just obscene," Vanessa blurted. "I mean, Henrietta was your friend. How could she do something so terrible?"

Kathryn scoffed, and her anger began to rise again, her face turning almost as red as her aura. "Henrietta Stone was never my friend. That nasty woman had no friends at all," she shouted, then shook her head and lowered her voice. "I'm sorry. Like you said, Lydie, misery loves company. The three of us were tethered by misery and blackmail."

"The three of you?" Vanessa asked. "You, Henrietta, and Barbara?"

It was an ambiguous slip of the tongue, but when Lydie met Kathryn's gaze, she understood exactly what Kathryn had meant. And she could see that Kathryn knew she understood. Fear spread its icy fingers up her spine, and she glanced at Vanessa. "No, Van. She means Doris Mayfield. Isn't that right, Kathryn?"

"You are a sharp one, Lydie," the woman replied with an edge to her voice. "Yes, Barbara already had Doris on the hook long before Henrietta and I were brought into the fold. Doris came from a very wealthy and respected family. She'd inherited a vast estate when her parents died." Kathryn sighed. "But the poor thing couldn't keep her hands off of other women's husbands, most of those women, Garden Society members."

"Yes. I spoke with Anna Ingram last week," Vanessa said. "She told me all about that. Evidently, her husband was one of those that Doris had been involved with."

Kathryn smirked. "I'm not surprised. Bet Anna took care of that without delay. She's not easily intimidated and doesn't suffer fools. Anyway, Barbara had a huge file on Doris from a private investigator she'd hired. She even gave a copy of the file to Doris, just to let her know exactly how damning the proof was and the havoc she could wreak with it."

"Did the three of you ever talk about Barbara and the predicament you were all in?" Lydie asked. "Why not go to the police? There were three of you. It would've been your word against hers."

Kathryn laughed out loud, and it sent another round of terror up Lydie's spine. "Are you *joking*? Of course, we talked about it. Going to the police was not an option. For Doris the consequences weren't so dire. Maybe her reputation in Seal Cove would've been damaged, she may have been shut out of the social scene, but she could've started over somewhere else or ridden it out. She had the means."

There was now fury in Kathryn's voice, in her gaze. "For Henrietta and I, not so much. Henrietta would've gone to prison for embezzlement, which is exactly where she should've been, anyway. But my very life would've been at risk, not to mention that I'd committed bigamy. Remember, Eddy survived our encounter." She shook her head. "Look, my Henry is a good man who loves me. And I love him. I could never do that to him. So, no, the police route was never an option."

Lydie cleared her throat and prepared to ask a question for which she was pretty sure she already knew the answer. "What other options did you come up with Kathryn? Did you kill them? Henrietta, Doris, Barbara? Was that your final option?"

Kathryn's resignation was almost palatable, but Lydie sensed no regret in the woman at all. "It was the only option left," she stated defiantly.

"Wait ...what?" Vanessa cried, and then pointed a finger at Lydie. "I *told* you, didn't I?" She turned back to Kathryn. "Why did they all have to die? Why not just Barbara?"

Kathryn nodded. "That was my pitch. The three of us met about a month before the Garden Society awards party. I tried to get Henrietta and Doris to see reason. The only way we were ever going to be free of Barbara's blackmailing scheme was if we got rid of her ourselves. I even offered to do it for the good of the group. All they had to do was have my back, to keep our secrets."

"Let me guess, they turned you down?" Vanessa asked.

"Not only did they turn me down," Kathryn replied with a chuckle. "They were both horrified at the suggestion." She glared at Vanessa and shook her head. "Those two pitiful doormats were willing to continue to pay Barbara Drake, bow down to that heinous woman for years to come rather than take control of their own lives. And let me tell you, it wasn't just the monetary payments. Every time Barbara wanted something distasteful done but didn't want to get her hands dirty, she'd call one of us. So, I did what needed to be done."

Lydie exchanged looks with Vanessa and saw the same terror that she was feeling in her friend's eyes.

But Kathryn wasn't done with her story.

"Look, I know how this sounds, but I couldn't continue to live my life in fear. Been there, done that. Swore I'd never do it again. Barbara Drake was my target right from the jump."

"And Henrietta? Doris?" Lydie asked quietly, alarm spreading through her body.

"I couldn't take the chance that either of them would go to the police the moment I took Barbara out. Instead, I just cleared the table beforehand, so to speak." Kathryn pointed a finger at Lydie as she got up from the table and began to pace. "Oh, and don't give me that look of disappointment, Lydie. I have no remorse over poisoning Henrietta Stone. Actually, I was amazed at how easy it was, that nobody even suspected me even though I was sitting right there at her table."

Vanessa blanched. "But there were over fifty women at that event, witnesses everywhere that could have seen you put the monkshood extract into Henrietta's teapot."

Kathryn stopped pacing and snickered. "Come on, Vanessa. Sometimes, in plain sight is the best cover," she said, repeating the exact words Lydie had said to Kelli Landon when the M.E. had come out to the shop after Henrietta's death. "I made sure to get to the table before anyone else. I chose where Henrietta would be sitting. Your team had just brought the teapots to the table, so I added the aconitine extract to my teapot, and then after a few minutes, swapped my pot with Henrietta's. Easy-peasy."

"And what about Doris?" Lydie asked, realizing just how much danger she and Vanessa were suddenly in here. "No remorse there, either?" She needed to keep Kathryn talking while she worked on a plan to get her and Vanessa out of this house unscathed. Sure, it was a two against one scenario, but Kathryn had just admitted that she'd killed three women.

Kathryn's smile slipped a bit. "I did feel bad about Doris. Let me tell you, anaphylaxis is a terrible way to die. And she'd done nothing to me personally. Probably would've kept my secret, too, but I couldn't take that chance. Don't you see that?"

She turned and walked to the buffet along the opposite wall just as a cell phone began to ring. Vanessa pulled hers out of her pocket and pressed 'talk,' just starting to raise the phone to her ear.

Kathryn swung around at the same time with a small pistol in her hand. She pointed it at Vanessa. "Hang up, Vanessa. We're not done here."

Lydie's heart sank when Vanessa did just that and dropped the cell phone into the breast pocket of her shirt, and then held up her hands, palms out. "Take it easy, Kathryn. It's okay. I hung up. You don't want to shoot either Lydie or me in your own kitchen, do you? I mean, how would you explain that to Dr. Raymond when he gets home?"

"Oh, don't worry, Vanessa. Henry isn't due back from his conference until Saturday, so I'll have plenty of time to sort this all out." Kathryn shook her head at the two of them. "I don't know why you two couldn't just leave things be. Henrietta's death was flawless, there was nothing to lead any of it back to me. I'll admit that I wasn't as clean with Doris. I shouldn't have left the peanut oil bottle in the trash. That was a mistake. But I wore gloves and made sure that I left no other trace, so I don't think your detective cousin had much to go on there."

Vanessa frowned. "How did you get Doris to ingest peanut oil if she was that allergic?"

"I'd called and told her that I needed to talk to her urgently.

She suggested I come by for lunch. She'd made stew, which was perfect. It couldn't have been easier to put the peanut oil into her stew when she went into the bathroom right after I arrived."

"But wouldn't she have smelled it or tasted it?" Lydie asked. "Even in the stew?"

Kathryn nodded. "Unfortunately, that was the problem. I think she smelled it before she took the first bite. When she looked up at me, I could see it in her eyes that she knew what I'd done. So, I had to go to plan B."

"And what was plan B, Kathryn?" Vanessa asked, with a look that said she really didn't want to know.

Kathryn's smile was chilling, and she waved the gun she was holding. "You're looking at it."

"You forced her to eat the tainted stew at gunpoint? Then watched her go into anaphylaxis? That's barbaric."

Anger flared in Kathryn's eyes. "Haven't you been *listening* to me?" she shouted. "I had to protect myself and my family. I had no other choice."

"But Doris was highly allergic to nuts. Didn't she have one of those pens with epinephrine somewhere in the house?" Vanessa pushed with a quick glance to Lydie.

That's it, Van. Keep her talking, Lydie thought, her mind racing to come up with something, anything they could do to get out of this situation alive.

"Of course, she had EpiPens. I took care of that little issue after she... before I left. I went through all the cabinets, anywhere I thought she may have stored them, and took every one I found with me."

"Oh, man." Vanessa whispered with a shake of her head. "You not only watched her go into anaphylaxis, watched her struggle, but you also watched her die, and then took all her EpiPens just in case? That is so cold."

"I'll do whatever it takes to protect what I've built here and to stay off the radar of my former life," Kathryn said with a shrug.

"What about Barbara?" Lydie asked. "She started all of this. You saved her for last."

"Yes. I figured that either Henrietta or Doris would snap to what I'd done if I took Barbara out first, especially if it looked like a homicide. After all, that had been my idea just a month before." Kathryn grinned. "The beauty queen actually made it so easy for me. She realized that I had to be the one who'd killed both Henrietta and Doris. She was gleeful with the knowledge. She *invited* me out to the house to chat."

"Something more to blackmail you over." Lydie said. "I suppose she wanted more money, too?"

"What a greedy bitch," Kathryn replied. "Well, I gave as good as I got. Barbara had a heart condition. She was taking digoxin already. I just helped it along with a vial of digitalis extract that I'd brought with me from boiling up a few of my foxglove plants from one of my back flower beds." Her laugh was harsh and without humor. "So arrogant, she actually trusted me to make the drinks. But then, Barbara always did think she was the smartest person in the room. Of course, she swapped glasses with me after I pretended to drink from mine. Little did she know that I put the digitalis extract in both glasses."

She grinned again, and there was a wildness in her eyes. Lydie couldn't help but think that she was watching Kathryn completely lose her mind in real time.

"It didn't take as long as I wanted it to for the foul woman to die. I'd really wanted her to suffer for all the harm she'd caused. But you take what you can get," she said with a sigh. Then she shrugged again, narrowing her eyes in Lydie's direction. "You never did tell me how you came across the photo and article in the folder. You said you found it at her house. How? And where? I looked all over that house after I got her into the pool and cleaned up the mess she'd made." She made a face. "She vomited all over the kitchen."

They were just about out of time. Lydie was sure of it. So, if Kathryn still wanted to talk, to give them a few more minutes to try to figure something out, Lydie was happy to oblige. So, she started their story.

———

As he and Andy came out of the Garden Society offices, Nick wanted to shout in frustration, which was where he seemed to be living with this case on a daily basis. They'd wasted precious time coming out here because they had been unable to raise anyone on the phone, only to find that Margie, the part-time assistant, had been at lunch.

And that Kathryn hadn't come in today at all.

"This is so damn annoying," he growled as they headed for the car. He climbed into the passenger seat as Andy slid behind the wheel. "We need to get out to Kathryn's house, like, now. Vanessa and Lydie are probably there already, and there's no telling what they've walked into."

"Preaching to the choir, my friend," Andy replied, and punched the gas.

Nick took out his phone and dialed Vanessa's number again. Surprisingly, she answered. At least, he thought she did. "Vanessa? Are you there?"

Then he heard her voice, and his heart nearly stopped. "*Take it easy, Kathryn. It's okay. I hung up. You don't want to shoot either Lydie or me in your own kitchen, do you? I mean, how would you explain that to Dr. Raymond when he gets home?*"

He tapped the speaker mute button on the screen and continued to listen as the conversation in Kathryn's kitchen unfolded for him and Andy.

"Holy crap," Andy exclaimed as he flipped on the vehicle's lights and siren. "So, Kathryn, or whoever she really is, is our killer. She killed all three women."

"Confessed to it in her own words. I just hope we can get there in time to keep Vanessa and Lydie from being victims four and five. Sounds like Kathryn is right on the edge."

Andy nodded. "We'll get there in time, buddy. But call for backup. The more the merrier."

Nick nodded grimly and did just that, trying to get a breath around the weight that had settled on his chest.

And then sent up a prayer.

22

Kathryn laughed out loud. "So, you're telling me that you get some kind of visions. And that both Barbara and Henrietta have given you clues through these visions off and on, yet wouldn't tell you that I actually killed them. You expect me to believe that nonsense?"

Lydie shrugged. "I really don't care what you believe, Kathryn. You asked me how I knew where to find both the article and the photo. That's how I knew. Barbara told me where to look for the spare key to her house, and then where to find what we were looking for. Of course, she didn't make it easy. Her clues were cryptic, and I had to decipher them."

"Well, I have to admit, that does sound like Barbara," Kathryn muttered. "Even on her last breath, she wouldn't tell me anything useful. And believe me, I tried everything to get her to talk. I knew what she had on me was somewhere in the house."

"Once I figured out her clues, the article, the photo, and the club flyer were right where she'd said they'd be—on a shelf at the back of her library in a book about Paris." Lydie confirmed. "Without those clues, I doubt anyone would've ever found them, let alone known what they represented if they had."

Kathryn shook her head with a sour look. "What a waste of space that woman was. I did the world a real favor by taking her out. Who knows how many countless lives she'd already destroyed, or how many more she would have ruined had I not acted when I did." Kathryn brightened then. "On a positive note, all I have left to do now is to get rid of what's in that folder, and I'm home free. There will be nothing to tie me to the three deaths, and my past will stay hidden right where it is—in the past."

"But aren't you worried that someone else may find that same information like Barbara did?" Vanessa asked, panic rising in her voice. "You don't even know how or where she found what's in that folder."

Kathryn gazed at Vanessa for a long moment, and then with a tilt of her head, smiled. "No, not really. I know how hidden my past really is because I paid good money to bury it where no one would find it or connect it to me. Ever." She put up a finger. "Now, is it concerning that Barbara found what she did? Maybe just a bit. But the only thing that connects what's in that folder to me is an old, grainy photograph from over a decade ago taken from thirty or forty feet away." She turned to Lydie. "And very few people would recognize me from that photo."

Lydie glanced at Vanessa, thinking back to the library and how her partner hadn't recognized Kathryn until Lydie herself had told her who she was looking at. Kathryn was right about that.

She felt her own panic rise.

Kathryn heaved a breath, and then looked between them with satisfaction. "Well, I'd say that wraps everything up neatly. Or should I say, everything but the two of you. Now what am I going to do with you?"

"No, not quite everything, Kathryn," Lydie spoke up, trying to ignore the barrel of the gun pointed directly at her.

"Oh? And what have I missed?"

"The brownies? That had to have been you as well, right?"

Kathryn frowned. "I'll say it again. You are a sharp cookie, Lydie. A bit too smart for your own good, though."

"You tried to kill me, Kathryn."

"Oh, don't be stupid. I knew the brownies wouldn't kill you if you ate them. I didn't put enough holly berries in the batter to do more than make you ill. I wasn't trying to kill you."

Lydie cleared her throat. "So, Nick was right. It was a deterrent."

"Not really even that." Kathryn actually looked a little sheepish. "I truly didn't expect you to eat the damn things, considering that I'd left them on the front step at the shop. Really, why would you eat something that's been left on your doorstep without knowing who left it there? Especially with everything that had already happened." She pinned Lydie with a confused look. "But then you did. Why?"

"Yeah, well, my aunt is staying with me, and she's using Enchanted Affairs' industrial kitchen for some recipe testing," Lydie explained. "I'd been gone all morning running an errand up the coast, and Aunt Wilma found the basket and set it on my work table. I came home while she was out and about, and I thought she'd left a new recipe for me to try."

"Ah, that makes more sense now." Kathryn nodded. "I'd called earlier and got no answer, so I thought I might be in the clear to swing by with the basket. I saw the car in the lot when I pulled in, which gave me pause, not wanting to be seen and all. But then when I tried the shop door, it was locked and had a BE BACK IN AN HOUR sign in the window. I figured I was golden. I left the basket on the doorstep and got the hell out of there."

Kathryn smirked. "The brownies were just supposed to muddy the waters when I turned up at the ER after supposedly being poisoned myself. They were just meant to throw off suspicion. I thought you'd call your detective and tell him what you'd found. If I'd been poisoned but you'd received the brownies as well, then hopefully, it would shift the focus away from me. Somebody else would have had to have been responsible, right?"

"Wait... what?" Vanessa gawked at the woman. "So, you're saying that you poisoned yourself just to throw off suspicion?"

Kathryn chuckled. "I think that was a touch of genius, don't you? I mean, who would've thought that I would poison myself?"

Vanessa looked appalled. "But that's crazy."

Kathryn's face turned a mottled shade of red, her mood changing so abruptly that both Lydie and Vanessa were taken by surprise. "I am not *crazy!*" she screamed, waving the gun back and forth between them. "Don't say that. Don't ever say that."

"Okay, okay, take it easy," Vanessa blurted, putting up her hands. "I only meant that it was a dangerous thing to do."

Taking several calming breaths, Kathryn made an obvious effort to get herself under control, and Lydie watched her aura change slowly back from angry red to orange. Kathryn was unraveling, and Lydie knew they were almost out of time.

"Like I said, I didn't put enough berries in the batter to do any serious harm," Kathryn muttered after a moment. "And I only ate half of a brownie, so it wasn't that dangerous." She shot Lydie a resigned glance. "Look, the police were getting nowhere. It was almost finished. I'd done what I'd needed to do. Barbara Drake was dead, and I was free again. End game."

"But then we kept asking questions," Vanessa pointed out quietly.

"Yes," Kathryn replied, a pleading look on her face. "The two of you wouldn't stop poking around. I just wanted you to stop. I *needed* you to stop. Unfortunately, now I've got a couple of loose ends to tie off. I like you both, I really do, but don't you see? I have to protect myself and my family."

"Kathryn, this isn't going to help you to do that. It's over.

Please don't make it worse for yourself or your family," Vanessa murmured.

"Funny, the last time I checked, I'm the one holding the gun. Once the two of you disappear, it will truly be over, and this time for good."

"No, Kathryn." Vanessa shook her head and pulled her cell phone out of her pocket, holding it up for both Lydie and Kathryn to see. "As you can clearly tell, my cell is on and connected. It has been this whole time. And my cousin, the detective, is on the other end."

Kathryn took one step forward, and then another, disbelief registering on her face. "No. You're lying to try to save yourself."

Lydie's mouth dropped open and shock stole her breath. Nick had been on the phone and listening all along? She prayed it was true and that it wasn't just a ruse to buy more time.

Vanessa shook her head. "It's true. He's heard every word."

"I don't believe you. That can't be. I watched you hang up," Kathryn all but shouted.

"You watched me *pretend* to hang up," Vanessa replied. She pressed the speaker button on the phone, and her gaze connected with Lydie's. "Nick, can you hear me?"

Lydie held her breath. Please let him be there, she thought. And her breath came out in a *whoosh*, when he answered.

"Loud and clear, Van," Nick said on the other end of the line. "We're almost there."

They could hear the sirens on Nick's end, but Lydie suddenly realized she could hear them outside the house as well. They were muffled but getting louder.

Kathryn turned, distracted. The sirens blared as they were coming up the long driveway. She had taken several steps toward Vanessa during their conversation, and Lydie used Kathryn's lack of focus to rush her, going for the gun.

"Lydie, no!" Vanessa screamed.

Everything went into slow motion as Lydie grappled with Kathryn for the gun. They spun around, and then around again, and the gun went off. There was the sound of breaking glass as the first shot went through the dining nook window. There was another crack as gunfire erupted again, but Lydie had no idea where that shot went. She hoped Vanessa had taken cover, because Kathryn was strong, and Lydie was holding on for dear life in a desperate attempt to wrench the gun away from her. There was a crashing sound as they rammed into the buffet, knocking a vase to the floor where it shattered.

The sirens were screaming now, obviously right out in front of the house, but Lydie struggled not to think about that, to concentrate on Kathryn and the fight for the weapon. She couldn't let go, couldn't let Kathryn win. There was no telling what the woman would do in her state of mind, but Lydie was sure that she and Vanessa wouldn't be alive to find out. They whirled again, and then suddenly there was a solid thud. Kathryn's eyes rolled back in her head, and she let go of the gun, crumpling slowly to the floor.

Vanessa had made good use of a cast iron frying pan.

In the next instant, the room was flooded with police officers, guns drawn, led by Nick and Andy. As Andy and two uniformed officers reached a semi-conscious Kathryn and called for an EMS medic waiting outside, Nick made a beeline to Lydie.

"Are you okay? Are you hurt?" he asked, looking for any obvious wounds.

"Boy, am I glad to see you," was all Lydie could say as her head spun, and she collapsed into his arms.

"Well, I'm just glad the whole thing is over. I'd hate to leave for home and have to worry that you might still be in danger,"

Aunt Wilma was saying as Lydie was unpacking yet another supply shipment. Hopefully, the last one for a couple of months.

Three days had passed since the ordeal in Kathryn Wilks-Raymond's kitchen, and Aunt Wilma had finished testing all of her new recipes for this year's season. She'd debated heading home just yet, wanting to make certain that Lydie and Vanessa were safe before doing so. But this afternoon, she was packed up and ready to hit the road, and while Lydie had enjoyed having her aunt stay, she was ready to get back to her life. Just her, Circe, and Vanessa during the day. She wanted that sense of normal again. Some peace and quiet.

"I'm telling you, that woman is a loon."

Lydie straightened and smiled at her aunt. "Now, Aunt Wilma, Kathryn had some serious issues, which she came by quite legitimately, but—"

Wilma pointed her finger at Lydie. "Don't you dare make excuses for that one. She was a homicidal maniac. She killed three women."

Lydie sighed. "I'm not making excuses. I'm just saying that there were underlying factors." She put up a hand when Wilma would've argued. "And, while taking a human life is abhorrent, for whatever reason, Kathryn had escaped with her life from a terrible situation before. She'd found love and remade herself, only to have it all jeopardized again with a similar terror and the prospect of the old terror resurfacing."

"As I understand it, nobody really knows her real name. Is that true?"

Lydie emptied another box and nodded. "But I expect the authorities will find out in short order, now that they have the article from the Las Vegas paper to start their search. They can get in touch with Vegas law enforcement and go from there. Of course, Kathryn may just tell them. Who knows? It's been well over a decade since she ran for her life. A lot can change with the passage of that much time."

"But to kill two innocent women just to get to the one causing the problem?" Wilma clucked her tongue. "Terrible business."

Lydie stacked several canisters of crushed herbs on the work table. "Well, at least one was fairly innocent. Henrietta Stone definitely wasn't guiltless but didn't deserve what she got, for sure. And Kathryn explained her reasoning for killing Henrietta and Doris."

"Evil, selfish reasoning," Wilma muttered.

"I suppose." Lydie stopped and lifted Circe—who'd been weaving between her legs—into her arms. The feline purred and gave a soft meow, her bright, green eyes wide.

"Yes, my sweet girl. I was just thinking exactly that. I wish to get back to peace and quiet, too." Lydie was pensive for a moment. "Look, I'm not condoning what Kathryn did by any means, trust me, but I do understand the kind of fear she must have felt, that drove her. I've experienced it in my visions, and though it's not quite the same thing, it's insidious and can easily make even the best of us come apart at the seams."

"I guess I can see that," Wilma grumbled. "But I don't have to like it. She nearly killed you. Twice."

"You are not wrong." Lydie set Circe on the work table and leaned down next to her. "The person I feel sorriest for is Dr. Raymond."

"Kathryn's husband?"

"Yes. He was out of town at a conference during this whole thing. Vanessa said that, over Kathryn's objections, Nick had contacted him at his conference. He evidently told Dr. Raymond the basics of what had happened, and the doctor rushed back yesterday. Sounds like he was devastated and in shock over what had transpired."

"I would think so. To find out that your wife has made you a party to bigamy and is also a murderer, to boot? That would be quite the shock."

"And to have to explain something like this to the children, as well. As I understand it, they've been with their grandparents in San Francisco for the summer. I can't even imagine how terrible that will be for him."

Wilma shook her head. "So many lives damaged or destroyed outright. We humans are very peculiar beings."

Lydie laughed, and it felt good after so many weeks of stress and ugliness. "You can say that again."

Wilma stood and stretched. "Well, I guess I'll hit the road, get myself home at a decent hour. I'm sorry I won't be able to say goodbye to Vanessa."

"She'll be sad she missed you, too. She had a business meeting with the director of the Seal Point Country Club about Enchanted Affairs handling a party for their spring tennis tournament. It's a big deal, and we've been trying to get a foot in the door there for a while."

"Give her my love when she gets back."

"Will do," Lydie replied just as the workroom buzzer went off as someone pulled into parking lot. A few minutes later, they heard the tinkle of the bell over the shop's front door, and she and her aunt headed out to the storefront to see who'd arrived. They found Nick Sutton standing at the counter.

Lydie hadn't seen Nick since coming home on Monday after giving her statement at the station, and her pulse sped up at the sight of him. Don't be an idiot, she chided herself. It's just Nick. But then their eyes met, and the butterflies started in her stomach.

"Lydie," he murmured with a nod.

"Hey, Nick," she replied, and felt the tension in the room increase.

"Good afternoon, Detective Sutton," Aunt Wilma greeted him, grinning while looking back and forth between the two of them.

"Hello, Aunt Wilma." Nick glanced back at the duffle bag sitting next to the door. "All packed up and heading home?"

"Yep. Was just about to hit the road. So, let me just say that it was lovely to see you again, Nick. Take care of our girls, please, so that I don't have to worry."

Nick's deep chuckle seemed to fill the room, and Lydie swallowed back her nerves.

"Will do," he promised.

Wilma turned then and pulled Lydie into a bear hug. "Take care, baby girl. And stay out of trouble... if that's possible."

"Doubtful," Nick murmured, earning a glare from Lydie.

Turning back to her aunt, she smiled. "I love you, Aunt Wilma. Come back soon."

Wilma started for the door with Circe on her heels. The feline gave a fierce meow followed by a couple of shorter, clipped ones. Turning, Wilma scooped Circe up and held her close. "Now, you know that I always drive carefully, but I can't make any promises about keeping it under the speed limit."

Circe put a paw on each side of Wilma's face and meowed softly.

"Yes, dear one. I love you, too. Now, you go back to the casting room and take a nap." Setting the feline on her feet, Wilma smiled as Circe headed for the workroom... and the casting room beyond.

Nick shook his head at the exchange, but didn't say a word. His expression said it all.

"Alright then," Wilma began, picking up her duffle bag at the door. "I'm off, kids. Thanks for letting me use the kitchen, sweetie. Come and see me. Ciao." And then she was out the door, crossing the parking lot, and driving away with a toot of her horn. Aunt Wilma had never been one for long, drawn out goodbyes.

The silence in the shop then was deafening, as Lydie and Nick stood staring out the windows where Wilma's car had been only moments ago. Lydie glanced over and studied him for a moment. He was so dang handsome, just looking at him made her heart pound and her mouth water.

Then he turned and their eyes met, and every thought flew out of her head. She finally cleared her throat and let out the breath she hadn't been aware of holding.

"Is this an official visit?"

A smile tugged at the corner of his mouth. "Not exactly."

"You want to come back to the office? Have a cup of tea?"

The smile spread. "I would."

She was hyper-aware of his proximity as he followed her down the hallway and back to the workroom. When she stopped and turned to ask him what kind of tea he wanted, she found him closer than she'd anticipated, and her pulse jumped. "W-what kind of tea would you like? Or would you prefer coffee, instead?"

Her pulse jumped again when his gaze dropped to her lips, and he licked his own. "Surprise me," he replied in a quiet tone that had her blood heating up.

As she turned back toward the kitchen, she heard him say, "On second thought..." Then he grabbed her by the arm, spinning her around and into his embrace. Her heart nearly skipped a beat at the intensity in his eyes.

"Don't you *ever* do that to me again," he said.

"Don't do what?" she all but whispered.

"Scare the crap out of me like that." His voice was low and full of anxiety, sending shivers down her spine. "I'd just taken you to the ER a couple days before, and you promised to stay out of my investigation. Then you scare a decade off my life when you almost get yourself killed by waltzing into a murderer's kitchen with nothing more than an old photo and a newspaper article."

She gave him a patient look. "It wasn't quite that dramatic, Nick."

"Really? Because when we finally got there—and none too soon, I might add—you literally collapsed into my arms. And from Vanessa's terrifying description about what happened before we got there, and from what I heard over the cell phone connection on the way, you actually fought with Kathryn over the gun."

She felt the blush sweep up her face. "Okay, when you put it like that, it may have been a bit more dramatic than I'd planned."

"Geez, Lydie." He slipped a strand of hair behind her ear. "I was terrified for you. I never want to feel that way again. So, no more sleuthing, do you hear?"

"You bet. The last couple of weeks were enough for me. And with Barbara and Henrietta crossing over, that's behind me as well."

Nick frowned. "I beg your pardon?"

"Oh, yeah. They both popped by one more time just to say goodbye, which I could've done without, by the way."

The look on his face was comical, and she giggled. "You should see your face right now."

He sighed and shook his head. "Just promise me you'll never put yourself in that kind of danger again. I don't think I could take it."

She smiled up at him. "I promise. Now go sit down in the office, and I'll bring in a pot of tea. Then you can tell me how you've tied up the investigation."

"How did you know—"

"Please. I can read you like a book. Now go."

He chuckled but turned and disappeared into the office.

Lydie went into the small kitchenette to pour a pot to steep when she found Circe at her feet. The cat meowed several times, and Lydie lifted her up for a quick squeeze.

"Yes, he is very handsome, and I do like him quite a bit. But let's not get ahead of ourselves, okay? Let's just wait and see where it goes." Setting Circe down again, she gave the feline's chin a scratch. "Okay, now you do as Aunt Wilma said and go take a nap. I have very important business in the form of a handsome detective to take care of.

Placing the steeping pot on a tray with two cups and a plate of lavender cookies, she headed for her office.

ABOUT THE AUTHOR

A native of Oregon, Joni Sauer-Folger spent twenty-two years with an airline traveling and moving around the country before settling down near the beautiful Pacific Ocean with her three very spoiled cats. She writes Urban Fantasy and Paranormal Romance under the name J.G. Sauer, and Cozy Mysteries and Romantic Suspense under Joni Folger. When she's not spending quality time with the characters she creates, she enjoys gardening, crafting, and working in local theater.

For more information, visit:
www.jonisauerfolger.com

 X

ALSO BY JONI FOLGER

Hidden Treasures